THE TWO NUNS

THE
TWO NUNS

ANNE HURÉ

Translated from the French by Emma Craufurd

SHEED AND WARD : NEW YORK

First published in the French language in 1962 under the title *Les Deux Moniales* by René Julliard, 30 and 34 rue de l'Université, Paris 7e.
© René Julliard, 1962
This translation © Macdonald & Co. (Publishers) Ltd., 1964.

Library of Congress Catalog Card Number: 64-16123

Manufactured in the United States of America

"Your error lies in thinking man has something
to do in this life."

Mgr. Darboy to Father Hyacinth Loyson
(quoted by Unamuno in *L'Agonie du Christianisme*).

I

Nuns were passing up and down under the Romanesque arches of the cloisters, whose heavy rectangular pillars alternated with fine columns, surmounted by richly decorated capitals.

It was nearly time for Vespers. Summer was at its height, and as the great abbey lay exposed to the dazzling rays of the sun it was suddenly wakened by a volley of bells.

Beyond the arches, gardens full of roses were visible; beds of white phlox, marigolds, evening primroses, gladioli and lilies.

The novices, distinguished by their veils of stiff white linen, were hurrying in the direction of the atrium, where the community assembled, ten minutes before the great bell announced their solemn entry into the choir.

On one side of the hall a door opened onto an avenue of limes, on another side the door led to the Abbess's garden. The third door led into the cloisters. The sun shone through the stained-glass windows, splashing them with a hem of mauve. Its light was transfused with a fine shimmering dust.

Already a hundred nuns had taken their places in the atrium. They had come to the middle of the hall where the holy water stoup of black marble stood. It was supported by twelve bronze oxen in memory of the biblical sea of brass,[1] and ornamented with carvings of famous baptisms. There the nuns waited in order of their rank. They crossed themselves

[1] Reference to vessel in Solomon's Temple, *II Chronicles, IV, 15.*

with a furtive hand, half hidden in the black woollen sleeve of their habit. Then, with eyes lowered, each went to her appointed place in the procession.

Through an immense doorway, the vast choir was visible, with its five long rows of Gothic stalls, carved with scriptural characters, saintly and diabolical. Beyond the black grille, the orange flame of the sanctuary lamp shone above the high altar. Still the nuns kept arriving by one or other of the doors, slipping in on silent feet, calm and recollected. But the Abbess's place remained empty. The crosier of sycamore, inlaid with gold and precious stones, stood upright in its steel socket beside the one and only stall in the whole atrium, the Abbess's seat, where the black *coulle*[1] was laid ready, with its sleeves hanging down on either side like a great night bird. Four novices stood around the seat. One of them carried a velvet cushion on which lay the breviary with its bookmarkers of liturgically coloured ribbons; another held the silver bowl; a third, the amphora filled with pure water; while the last gently manipulated the long enamelled chain of the censer from which fumes were already rising.

At last the great bell rang out to mark the third hour after noon. At the same instant the organ sounded its opening chord, while the Prioress went up the three steps leading into the choir. There was a rustling of skirts and the sound of moving feet and swinging rosaries. At that very moment the Abbess crossed the cloister. There was nothing to suggest that she intended to be present at the Office. She was accompanied by a nun with whom she was in deep conversation. The animation of her manner was punctuated by gestures which, though controlled, were implacably stern. Tall and majestic, she appeared to be about fifty, but alert and vigorous for her age.

The last nuns in the procession had reached their stalls. The sacristans closed the doors.

[1] The *coulle* is a long, full gown with large, flowing sleeves, worn over the ordinary habit by nuns in choir, at Chapter, and at certain other ceremonial times.

"So your Grace dispenses me from the Office—for today?"

"And I am dispensing myself, too—solely in order to listen to your complaints, Mother Stanislaus," said the Abbess. "Let us go out. A walk in the fresh air, the gardens, the flowers: all these things are helpful in conversation and make for calm."

"I don't know why you always try to humiliate me, Madame. My complaints? Have I made such a habit of complaining?"

"No, I must agree with you there. Rather than make complaints, you prefer to act on your own initiative and do as you please. That fits in better with the organization of your life."

"There is nothing arbitrary in the organization of my life, Madame. I follow the Rule of Saint Benedict, like all the nuns of this abbey. The only thing which distinguishes me from the others is the hatred you bear me."

The Abbess made a conciliatory gesture.

"There is no other word for it, Madame: hatred. And it has been going on for twenty years. Besides," she continued, "you need not defend yourself. There is nothing base about hatred as such. If we remember that it concentrates our energies in a single direction, and for that very reason makes us capable of admirable disinterestedness in other fields."

Mother Stanislaus, tall, thin and full of vitality, must have been about forty. There was sweetness in her clear eyes, and there was irony; there was also a hint of discreet impertinence. Her most distinctive feature was incontestably her intelligence. For a moment the two nuns walked in silence. It was the time of the first peaches and the last raspberries. The blackberry bushes were heavy with fruit. In a little wood near the Calvary there were some wicker seats and a table. They sat down. The Abbess seemed to be thinking. She was not finding it easy and, as though searching for the best line to adopt, she kept automatically slipping her ring with its large jewel up and down the finger of her right hand.

"Would you like to draw up the balance-sheet of our life, Mother Stanislaus?" she said at last. "If so, I will leave it to you, and I am ready to listen. You will, I am sure, know how to introduce into it facilities and indulgences in your favour, which I should certainly omit; for the sake of your character."

From the top of a nearby cedar, the strident cry of a bird sounded.

"Would you find it inconvenient today, just for once, to admit that you have never ceased to detest me, Madame? Ever since the end of our novitiate? Come now—there is no question of precedence here. Our souls are laid bare. We are face to face. There is no mystery, no protocol. And it is you who invited me to embark on this painful and hazardous journey into our past. What do you say?"

"It pains me to notice that you always deliberately avoid addressing me as your Mother," said the Abbess.

Mother Stanislaus made a gesture of disillusionment. "Madame—do not let us wander from the point," she said.

The Abbess placed both her hands flat on her knees, where they rested on her long black scapular. Below her white linen gimp, the pectoral cross flashed scarlet. A weariness, made up of too heavy and too vibrant memories, settled down upon her features.

"Mother Stanislaus," she said at last, "you have always refused to recognize that I hold my office in order to uphold the Rule; it was with this in view, and this alone, that the community elected me. And I have solemnly promised on oath to lead it to God by this means. Benedictine life as you conceive it is not a religious life in the strict sense of the word. It is the studious life of a humanist. A life full of charm, I agree, but a purely human life. The intellect, after it has reached a certain point in its development, is bound to turn back upon itself, if it is deprived of the support which comes from union with day-to-day realities. It creates for itself a hot-house atmosphere—an unhealthy climate of inadaptability and dissatisfaction. I cannot follow you along this path."

She paused for a moment. "But I will come back to that a little later. We have plenty of time, and it is I who am listening to you."

Mother Stanislaus was fingering the long strap of black leather which serves as a belt in the Benedictine habit. Her glance was tinged with melancholy. She made a gesture as though to accept what appeared to be unavoidable.

"It was in the Abbey of K—— that we were clothed with the Benedictine habit," she said, after a long moment of silence. "Do you remember it, Madame? There were only a few days between our clothings. It will soon be twenty-one years ago. At that time you loved me. Do not deny it. You loved me, Madame, and with a very human love, as deeply as God could permit. And for my part, I thought I had found in you a beloved sister. I was twenty-two years old and you were thirty."

The Abbess made a gesture of assent. Her expression had softened. A kind of secret anguish could be read in it.

"A year passed. Our novitiate was ardent, full of tenderness. Our religious profession was mentioned as exemplary in zeal and fidelity. At the end of that year of formation, we were sent to Louvain. You, Madame, were to learn Hebrew and I to prepare for my degree in philosophy. Do you remember the days just before our vows of obedience? Our fears at being separated. Our submission to whatever was in store. You really did love me, Madame. And, indeed, in a completely human way."

The Abbess's face was very pale; but Mother Stanislaus went on with her story.

"Three years passed. It was in the course of those years that you began to hate me. And yet. . . . By the end of the first year I had become the faithful disciple of a Dominican Father who taught metaphysics at the university. He persuaded me to obtain permission from our superiors to prepare a thesis later on. I was already beginning to publish articles in such reviews as *Etudes* and *La Vie intellectuelle*. Our life was a good one: rich, leisurely and happy. The community at Louvain had adopted us. But you were already drawing away from me."

"I did not become a religious either to learn Hebrew or to study philosophy, Mother Stanislaus. I did so in order to serve God."

"Your pride at that time was already immense, Madame. And since then, responsibilities and honours have marked you with an incurable sclerosis."

The Abbess made a movement.

"Wait, Mother Hildegard, let me go on. No one can hear us in this place. We have reached the hour of truth, and you yourself invited me."

There was a certain surprise, mingled with arrogance, in the Abbess's expression. It was such a very long time since anyone had called her by her name.

"When the three years of our temporary profession came to an end, we returned to K—— to make our final vows," Mother Stanislaus continued. "During the months that followed you seemed to come closer to me. The Abbey encompassed us both with the love of the same faithful heart. Old Mother Cyprian of P——, our Abbess, was a soul of supernatural serenity. You were thirty-four years old, Madame; I was twenty-six. The peace continued all through a marvellous summer—like the one we are having now, if you come to think of it. It was a summer full of carefree sweetness. At night, on our way to Matins, we could hear the sea beating against the rocks, and some of us saw daybreak in the leafy avenues of that great and beloved Abbey of Notre-Dame. Do you remember, Madame?"

"I remember that you were already dispensing yourself from reciting the psalms of Compline in choir in order to enjoy the last of the daylight. I remember that you absented yourself in this way frequently and without permission, and that you did so even on the very day after taking your solemn vow of obedience. Is this not true?"

"In cases of uncertainty you always choose to believe there is sin, Madame. In reality, I had always obtained the necessary authorizations to do this, but you knew nothing about it. And instead of clearing up the matter and freeing yourself from your suspicions, you preserved your virtue and kept me at a distance. Already our intimacy was compromised; but I will go on with my story. Every moment it is going to become more thrilling. You will judge for yourself, Madame. And I am sure that your Grace will appreciate fittingly and in detail certain things which have remained unspoken between us for fifteen years, things which I would willingly have confided to you if only you had given me the slightest encouragement."

The Abbess turned her head, but Mother Stanislaus's clear eyes were calm, and a suggestion of irony was scarcely perceptible in the tone of her voice.

"I entered religion in order to unite myself with Christ Crucified, Mother Stanislaus, not to form friendships. I became vividly aware of the implications of my choice on the morning of my perpetual vows. This fact led you to the conclusion that I was detaching myself from you."

Mother Stanislaus deliberately kept silence for a moment.

"As I was saying," she continued a little later, "we finished the summer at K——. From that time on we wore the *coulle* with wide sleeves and the gold ring. We were eligible for great responsibilities. We were also eligible for important studies and for the most unexpected undertakings. And now, listen carefully; listen, Madame, to the thing for which you have never forgiven me.

"It was early in October, a day of thick mist and bitter cold. During the night at Matins one of our sisters in the novitiate had fainted. I am giving you these details to show how clear my memory is. In the course of the morning, our Reverend Mother Cyprian sent for me. This need not have surprised anyone who happened to notice. We were waiting to have offices assigned to us. I spent two hours with her Grace. Then, at the Obedience which follows the dinner Recreation, I was officially nominated to the Biblical College at Jerusalem. I was to write my philosophy thesis there and at the same time embark on patristic studies and research under the direction of the Dominican Fathers. It would be difficult to describe the look you gave me when, after Obedience, we met by chance in the hall of studies. It was a look of hatred, Madame."

"No, Mother Stanislaus, no. It was certainly a look of fear and affectionate anxiety—anxiety for the dangers which would beset your vocation far from our usual monastic surroundings. It was only that. The liberalism of your doctrines was already germinating. In due course my fears have been justified."

Mother Stanislaus's expression was vague.

"Let me go on, Madame," she said. "For your part, you were nominated Bursar of the Abbey, in place of our poor dear Mother Mark, whose health was failing. It was an important office which admitted you to the Abbey Council. The appointment was a sign of consideration and confidence rarely accorded to a young nun, and it established you firmly in the saddle and opened the way for ambitions which until this very day have always been satisfied. No, your Grace, no. Let me go on. As a matter of fact, I have been waiting ten years for this moment. My life in the Middle East does not matter much. When, after three years, I came back, you were here at this Abbey of D—— and under the rule of our Mother Gertrude X—— you were the Prioress. I heard about it when I returned to K—— and I was pleased for your sake. I had known for a long time that you needed responsibilities. But I did not know yet that it was the first place of all that you coveted. I was soon to find this out.

"I remained at K—— for a year, having a kind of studious rest, but without any very special task. It was about this time that my book on Dionysius was published. This was the subject of my thesis. My work on articles for reviews took all

14

the time left me by conventual life. Then there came that day in September. I was thirty: you, Madame, were thirty-eight, and your hour was about to strike. Well then, on this September day, Mother Cyprian joined me in the cloisters, after the Office. You know how simple and familiar she used to be. I remember it was a clear day at the season of the grape harvest. We walked for a long time, her Grace and I, among the vines of the convent estate. We were rather melancholy. She was always so maternal and kind, and I was heavy-hearted, with tears in my eyes. The next day—the very next— I left for this Abbey of D—— where we are now."

She paused. She was visibly moved.

"The Very Reverend Mother Gertrude was dying. I did not know the abbey. When I arrived all eyes were on me. I was only thirty years of age, but I must have been the only one among all the professed nuns who had not reflected that Rome has instituted indults in order that they may be granted, and that, in point of fact, age has nothing to do with abbey elections. A month later Mother Gertrude died. And now a more serious chapter in our story is beginning. No, Madame, no, you cannot stop me. Four days later, on the day after the funeral, the nuns of the Chapter went into conclave. You were the Prioress and you presided. You and I were both candidates. I, almost without knowing it, and you, with all your hopes concentrated on success. The conclave lasted for the usual ten days. The abbey was as full as it is today. In any case, the Chapter numbered a good two hundred nuns. There were a hundred or more lay Sisters and about twenty-five novices. But that is beside the point: the novices and lay Sisters had nothing to do with the election. At the first round, I had eighty votes. You needed two to be elected. At the second I had eighty-seven, and you lost several to Mother Jerome. At the third, I had eighty-nine votes, but you were elected."

She paused for a moment. Victor Hugo's line from Hernani flashed into her mind: "I only needed three more votes,

Ricardo, yet I have lost everything. . . . I might have been Emperor. Oh, how infuriating that I am not. . . ."

Her lips betrayed a fleeting smile, but it left no trace. A warm breeze enveloped them. The Abbess had not moved.

"After ten years," Mother Stanislaus continued, "there is no need to keep our votes secret. I can therefore tell you without infringing our constitutions that I did not vote for you on any of the three rounds. This was not out of hatred, I assure you. I have no hatred for you. It was only because I thought you unsuitable for government. And so you are. . . . As far as that goes, you are as unsuitable as I should be myself. With your Grace's permission, let us now speak of the last ten years. They have been trying years, Madame, very trying for me, I assure you. I will not mention the daily difficulties and wounds which are due to our characters and to your arrogance. No, such things are not important. But there is something more serious. Five years ago you refused your permission for me to go to our abbey in Rome when the Fathers there invited me to come and work under their direction. They wanted me to help with a critical edition of Tertullian. They had reserved for me all the works dealing specially with the discipline of consecrated virgins in the early Church. I was hoping at last to be set free from you. . . . I was hoping. . . ."

The Abbess made a gesture.

"Mother Stanislaus," she said, "I have always considered my nuns to be, before all else, daughters of Saint Benedict. To be a writer in the Order is to have an employment, comparable to that of cellarer, bursar, organist or sacristan . . . it is that and no more than that. You can carry out your task so long as our Rule is safeguarded, and you can do so here, in the abbey which is henceforth your home and from which you will not move until your death—or, at all events, until mine, if such is God's will."

"Oh, please do not bring God into all this, Madame."

"In addition to the three ordinary canonical vows, our Holy

Rule requires another vow of stability in the same abbey,"
the Abbess continued. "For reasons of personal convenience
this is sometimes lightly set aside. And the abbesses who
countenance such things incur serious responsibilities. It
sometimes happens that God and virtue may require such
changes, but——"

"Do not keep involving God in all this, Madame."

"But when it is only a question of studies and mere intellectual curiosity, I would never encourage such undertakings."

"So you consider Tertullian as a subject for mere intellectual curiosity?"

"It is possible to live without Tertullian, Mother Stanislaus.
It is not possible to live as a true Benedictine without obedience
and submission of spirit. Moreover it is very remarkable that
you always want to leave the beaten track—to separate yourself from the group. I know that your contacts with the outside world are only too likely to encourage you in this. But
a healthy organism protects itself against disintegrating agents.
To separate oneself from the group—the group which one had
freely chosen—is always a sign of weakness; I should say of
moral weakness. The word religious should be taken in the
etymological sense of something which unites and binds men
together."

There was a long silence. Mist was rising from the fields.
Mother Stanislaus remained thoughtful.

"The Fathers of our Order never ceased to encourage me,"
she said.

"Apart from the fact that monks do not run the same risks,
they do not take the vow of enclosure, and they have a very
great liberty in the practice of dispensations. Actually that
might be deplored. But I am not called upon to pronounce
judgment in the matter."

The sun was setting, yet the heat persisted. Insects were
humming in the golden haze. A far-off bell sounded; a single
note, pure, clear, isolated.

The Two Nuns

"I think they are ringing for your Grace to go to the parlour," Mother Stanislaus said in an even tone.

The Abbess rose. "Yes, but it is of no importance," she said. "It will not take more than a few minutes for us to go back to the portress's lodge, and this conversation was necessary. As a matter of fact we have only made a beginning. I still have to hear the most important part—I mean that which deals with the actual situation."

"The things that count are never expressed, Madame. And perhaps that is just as well?"

They were now walking along the path bordered with currant bushes. They kept silence—a silence full of memories. As they approached the cloisters a nun came towards them—she was young and full of life—her face was beautiful and expressive.

"I beg your Grace's pardon for ringing," she said, "but we could not find you anywhere, and it is his Excellency. He is in the parlour."

"But there is nothing to apologise for, Mother Paul of Verona," said the Abbess kindly. "We have Our name written on the list of bells like any other sister. We will meet again soon," she added, extending her ring to the lips of the kneeling Mother Stanislaus.

Novices were passing, carrying baskets full of verbena and lavender. Mother Stanislaus returned to her cell.

2

It was the Novice Mistress—the superior of the whole novitiate. She was seated in her high-backed chair at a table piled with books, reviews, letters and papers. A large vase of peonies towered among them. A flat watch lay immediately in front of her, and beside it an ebony crucifix with the figure of Christ in silver. She must have been about sixty-five. Kindness radiated from her gentle brown eyes. She was slightly bent and, despite the unbearable heat, entirely enveloped in shawls. Surely she was one with a taste for long murmured recitations of the rosary, for contemplation and colloquies of love in dimly lit sanctuaries, for meditative walks. Her name in religion was Mother Cecilia, but in the course of the twenty-five years that she had been the Mother of the novices, her official name had been almost forgotten. She had trained a whole generation of Sisters. She was spoken of with affection and respect. All her life she had been a faithful and exemplary nun.

Golden rays of sunshine penetrating into the room illuminated an engraving of Saint Teresa on the wall, then bathed a statue of Saint Benedict with their glowing light.

Mother Cecilia turned towards the young Sister kneeling beside her. A novice of twenty, her complexion had the flawless delicacy of fruit sheltered from the wind. She was radiant, full of ardour and spontaneity. Her eyes were grey-blue like flashing steel, but the keenness was tempered by innate good manners.

The conversation seemed to be animated. Then suddenly silence fell, and it was as though a stone had been thrown, shattering a delicate crystal.

"You have nothing else to tell me, Sister John of the Cross?" asked the Novice Mistress. "At times it seems as though you were hiding yourself from me. You must not be afraid. I am your mother. If there is anything troubling you, I am here to help."

There was a silence charged with hesitation.

"Mother . . . there are certain problems which one cannot discuss without embarrassment. I know that I should have faced this one long ago. Each day I have kept putting off what has now become inevitable."

She paused for a few seconds. The Novice Mistress's expression showed that she was listening attentively.

"You see, Mother," the novice said at last, "I am quite out of harmony with Mother Abbess. I really believe that I do not like her. That, after all, is rather hard to endure."

The utter simplicity and calm with which we speak of extraordinarily serious matters was discernible in her voice. The old nun made no gesture, but her expression registered stupefaction—something approximating terror. Unable to formulate the thoughts at the back of her mind in a sentence, she remained speechless, her eyes wide open.

"Mother . . . I am perfectly aware of how unprecedented such an avowal must be. I beg you to see it only as a reply to your question."

"But, my dear child, I never condemn frankness. This room of mine is like a confessional. I am here to help you. You have nothing to fear."

They remained silent for a moment—plunged in thought.

"I only want to understand," the Novice Mistress continued. "I want to know what gave rise to this feeling in you."

"Mother, such things cannot be put into words. They are impressions. When I go to see Mother Abbess, she always receives me graciously. I do not know how to explain what I mean. I feel it. That is all."

"Sister John of the Cross. . . . It is already quite clear to me that you have received a call to enter the Benedictine Order —that you have what is known as a vocation. You are at the end of your canonical novitiate. In less than two months you will be asking *misericordia* from the Chapter for your profession. This step must be taken in an atmosphere of serenity and with great liberty of spirit."

The young Sister remained silent.

"Until today, I have been unwilling to intervene in a matter which nevertheless is within my province," the Mother continued. "But," she hesitated, "have you not felt certain

influences?" (Sister John of the Cross made a gesture.) . . .
"My child, it is no secret, either in the novitiate or in the
community, that you are very intimate with Mother de
Neuville. The Rule and Canon Law are very wise in forbidd-
ing close contacts between professed nuns and Sisters in the
novitiate. For a variety of reasons I have shut my eyes to this.
I hope that by so doing I have not encouraged anything
undesirable."

"Madame, Mother Stanislaus is my tutor in Greek."

"My dear child, you must be well aware that by rights the
canonical year of the novitiate should not be disturbed by any
classical studies. I am tolerant of a great many things because
the programmes of the degree students are very overloaded.
But it would never do if such tolerance proved detrimental to
the one thing necessary. Already because of this relationship
with Mother Stanislaus and for reasons which, it is true, may
not be purely supernatural but which exist nevertheless, you
have alienated some of the community and forfeited a certain
amount of good will. Your admission to the profession is
not endangered, thank God! We can collect enough votes
and more than enough. But there are . . . consequences. Do
not keep on kneeling," she added, changing her tone. "Sit
down."

"Nothing prevents me from confiding in you, Mother. I
have told you all that I consider essential about my difficulties."

The Novice Mistress seemed to be considering. In an
adjoining hall someone was practising the organ.

"Is it Mother Stanislaus who is leading you along the road
you have chosen?" she said at last. "It is imperative that I
should know this. Not with regard to her own life, which
does not concern me—and I may add that you can rest assured
that whatever you tell me will go no further. But I ought to
know whether this drawing away from Mother Abbess is
spontaneous and due to you yourself, or whether it has been
more or less implicitly suggested to you."

"I know that relations between Mother Stanislaus and

Mother Abbess are somewhat strained, Mother. Actually we never speak about her Grace."

Through the half-opened window there was a glimpse of trees. Parallel with the hall of the novitiate there was a veranda where the young Sisters had a nursery for delicate plants.

"You see, my dear child, you tend to underestimate the *sacramental* blessings, and I use the word sacramental advisedly, inherent in the hierarchically constituted body—in short you tend to underestimate the Church as a means of grace. Of course you do not do so in theory, of that I am sure, but you do so in your inner reactions and in the orientation of your inclinations. Our abbey is, as it were, the Church in miniature. It is informed by the same preponderant reality as the Church and, like her, is an institution of truth and grace. The blessings found therein are not the result but the cause of such an institution. I implore you not to separate yourself from it. Our abbey is not a group of faithful souls organized for purposes of practical convenience. It is a mystical reality. It is, as it were, a flock, of which our Very Reverend Mother is the Shepherd or Pastor. Her will, and indeed her slightest counsels, are, as it were, the deposit of revealed doctrine and form a harmonious whole which affords an objective and clearly defined guide for the attainment of salvation."

The novice's impulsive gesture of impatience was checked almost at once, but her expression registered an intense and deep-seated rejection. The superior raised her hand pacifically.

"Please allow me to finish, my child. It has been the error of Protestantism to insist upon the unilateral transcendence of the Church divorced from the body and thus free of her discipline. The Church gives us birth and forms us. She is, as it were, the mother and the matrix of Christ's members. We exist for Christ, only by her and through her. Through her ministry and her sacramental nature, for she is the one all-embracing sacrament of Christ. Such are the essential realities of the Church as an institution of salvation."

"A religion without transcendence, Mother, is a political

entity. You know that I am always outspoken. I am in complete agreement with you concerning the Church. But our abbey is not the Church. That would involve attributing infallibility to the Mother Abbess. I cannot bring myself to do such a thing."

"The abbey is the reflection of the Church, my dear child. It is an assembly of faithful souls—a gathering together for all eternity of those who hold the faith in a very perfect and sublime life. Just as of old the Israelites under Moses left Egypt and crossed the Red Sea in order to attain the Promised Land. Mother Abbess has been canonically elected and set apart. She is the head of this church which is a symbol of the other —the great Church of Christ. You cannot alter that. It is a reality."

Sister John of the Cross's face remained unmoved.

"And if Mother Abbess made a mistake—in a serious matter? We should, I imagine, be obliged to pay for it? Mother, I don't think you could dare to tell me that she cannot make a mistake."

Her tone was calm and respectful but implacable. The expression of the Novice Mistress became fixed in amazement. There was a long pause.

"Let us come back to Mother Stanislaus," the old nun continued, while a hint of irony was discernible in the eyes of the younger sister. "It is natural that you should be mutually attracted. By her every feature and characteristic Mother de Neuville represents a certain human brilliance which exercises considerable charm." (The young novice made a gesture of protest.) "I use the word charm advisedly. But dilettantism is something inferior—it is something to beware of. Be on your guard against it for the future." (The novice was silent.) "Have you read her latest work?" the Mother added abruptly. "This *Tertullian* which has just been published? Have you read it?"

Her voice registered a kind of dry disapproval in which, in spite of all her efforts, fear predominated.

The Two Nuns

"I have read it, Mother; I read it in manuscript."
"And what do you think of it? A great deal of good, no doubt."
"I think it a very fine piece of work. But I cannot agree with Mother Stanislaus in the line she has taken. What is wrongly termed the heresy of Montanism involves a wrong interpretation of the notion of heresy. Montanus did not concern himself with dogma. It was the discipline of the early Church which interested him. Mother Stanislaus maintains that Faith, Discipline and Liturgy are inextricably united. I do not agree. Thus when she thunders against Tertullian I remain unmoved because the essentials of the thesis do not touch me. What may be true with regard to ideology should not for that reason give rise to arbitrary anathemas. The internal and disciplinary structure of the Church has nothing to do with theological tradition. I have discussed all this at great length with Mother Stanislaus. She sticks to her position and I to mine. All the same I do not like Tertullian any more than Mother de Neuville likes him. But for different reasons. It is equally certain that you, Mother, would like him and that Mother Abbess would give him the very first place. I only say this to show that I remain completely independent in spite of the great warmth of my affection for Mother Stanislaus. It is possible, indeed it is certain, that dilettantism and charm are to be feared—in different degrees, as it happens. It is none the less true that an excess in one direction does not justify the opposite extreme, even though this second might be less harmful than the first—and that is not certain. You wanted to know how I felt, Mother. I have told you."

A considerable time passed. A cloud of sadness seemed to envelop the Novice Mistress. Her face was suffused with a deep red.

"I am going to think all this out," she said as soon as she had recovered a little. "I will send for you in a few days. You must pray, my child. Pray very earnestly."

She rose. She seemed to be more bent than before. Her

features betrayed the deep distress which she could no longer hide. At the door, she traced the sign of the Cross on the forehead of the young novice. She did so with a timid finger, as though feeling her own powerlessness. From the organ next door rose the heart-rending strains of César Franck's *Choral*.

3

Some days had passed. The Novice Mistress was making her way to the choir; her tread was heavy, and dragged like that of one in pain from an incurable illness. In the dim light of the great staircase she leaned on the banisters. She drew her shawls even more closely around her shoulders and over her long black veil. "Lord, you have entrusted me with the care of this soul, this soul which you have chosen for yourself—set apart. Is the evening of my life to bring so great a failure? Lord. . . ."

It was the end of summer, and evening was drawing in. Under the cloisters the light was still clear and soft, gently relaxing. From the darkening choir the sanctuary lamp was visible as it glowed in immutable stillness beyond the grille.

Here and there a nun was seated. Near one of the side gratings a novice, whose identity the Novice Mistress guessed, was kneeling, her eyes riveted to the tabernacle. "Seeking the consolations of sensible devotion," she thought to herself.

With the same painful step, she reached her choir-stall. In passing, her habit brushed against the body of a Sister prostrated face downwards on the polished floor. Another, who was following the Way of the Cross, moved like a ghost from station to station, kneeling for a while in front of each.

The darkness was soothing. The air was fragrant with an indefinable perfume in which the smell of fresh wax and carpet blended with the scent of flowers, and particularly the rather heady scent of lilies from the altar of Our Lady.

The Novice Mistress's limbs were aching as she genuflected painfully, and then sank into the security of her high stall, in the row reserved for the most eminent nuns—the Mothers in office and the senior members of the community.

Suddenly a rapid step made her start. She saw the outline of a slender figure wearing the white veil of the novices. This figure was crossing the whole width of the Choir and coming in her direction. "Sister John of the Cross," she said to herself. "Lord, I commit her to your care, as I do every day. But today, more fervently than ever. Save her from pride. Save her from human attachments. Save her, O Lord, I implore you."

The novice was crossing the lower rows of choir-stalls. Without a word she held out a folded note to her mistress. The latter touched the switch of her light. Each stall had an independent lamp which enabled the nuns to read or use their prayer-books as they wished in the hours of darkness or dusk.

In the immense body of the Choir, a little spot of bright light shone for a moment. It was like a cry. Then all fell back into shadow. Soon afterwards the bell for Compline announced the end of the day. It rang out solemnly, like an agonised call for help.

4

The last days of October spread a curtain of mist on the garden. Great heaps of dead leaves were burning in the paths. It was mild. The main staircase was deserted. It was about ten o'clock in the morning. Some Sisters were at work in the library. They were all young. One of them, on a ladder, appeared to be engaged in meticulous research. Through the window the trees were shedding the last of their leaves. Mother Stanislaus came into the hall; she glanced all around and finally went up to a novice who was bent over an octavo, writing. She put her hand on the novice's shoulder. It was a shapely hand, with firm muscles.

"Come," she said. "Come to our room."

Sister John of the Cross raised her head, smiled, shut the book and stood up. They went together down the long corridor of the cells. It was paved with black-and-white marble. They did not speak. They were on the first floor, belonging to the Mothers of the Council and the old nuns. One of them, who was leaning on a stick, smiled a greeting to them. Sister John of the Cross was much liked by the elderly members of the community on account of her gaiety, her deference and her good manners.

A door was pushed open and they were in a spacious room full of light. It contained a bed, which showed it to be a room for rest, but it was also a room which gave every sign of great intellectual activity. Piles of books, a table loaded with papers, a small typewriter and a heap of carbon copies and galley-proofs, a lectern on which a dictionary in Hebrew characters stood open and a house telephone with its multiplicity of dials —all proclaimed it to be a retreat for concentrated, arduous study often lasting well into the night.

And there, on a corner table beside an empty page, a pen which could write with discernment and sarcasm lay as though abandoned.

"Tomorrow the Chapter is going to vote for you," said Mother Stanislaus with simplicity. "For your profession. It is an important day!"

"Yes, and I am worried about it. I am specially worried because those who like me have been looking at me lately in a questioning, affectionate way—as though they feared for me."

The Two Nuns

The two of them were seated. The air was mild and caressing.

"There are two hundred and four of us with votes," replied the Mother. "You will need at least a hundred and three ivory balls. Anyhow, Mother Abbess could decide in your favour if you only needed one vote."

"I know all that. But, Mother ... the very fact that you talk in this way makes me wonder. Is there so much to fear? You all seem so frightened. As a rule such an admission goes of itself. No one talks about it. It is a mere formality—from the moment the Novice Mistress presents us. Unsuitable candidates leave before this stage. . . ."

Mother Stanislaus's face grew more serious. She was fingering a little angel carved in scented pear-wood.

"Yes, Sister ... as you say, Mother Cecilia *presents* a candidate, but it is we, the whole body of nuns in the Chapter, who admit her. Mother Cecilia only has one vote like the rest of us. To admit a subject to profession is to admit her to our close intimacy for the duration of her life. It is an important step and needs careful consideration. I am speaking now, of course, in a purely theoretical manner, but I insist upon it. The reception of a subject to profession is no mere formality."

"How solemn you are this morning, Mother."

"Solemn, no; but serious. Perhaps it is because I am anxious too? Do you remember what our Father Saint Benedict says in the Rule when he directs the Master of Novices to familiarize the aspirant with all that is calculated to repel and discourage him, in order to test his vocation? You are a very remarkable aspirant, my child. Very brilliant; original. You are what the unthinking multitude would term *advanced*. I know this house very, very well, and I know that the community, taken as a whole, are frightened by such qualities."

Sister John of the Cross had slipped on to her knees and was leaning against Mother Stanislaus, who put her arm round her.

"That is how you have alienated Mother Irenæus," the

Mother continued, "and Mother Irenæus counts for at least twenty votes. Do not be shocked at such free speaking," she added, noticing the mute astonishment of the young Sister. "Yes, it is twenty or twenty-five votes that we shall lose in losing hers. These are not things one talks about, but they are none the less true."

"I have never understood the distance at which Mother Bursar keeps me. Her Reverence and I have not so much as spoken together."

"This coldness had its origin in your affection for me, Sister. You need look no further. Mother Irenæus would willingly have taken you under her patronage, even to the extent of entrusting you with important tasks, if only you had given her the opportunity. And she has great influence. Since you never did give her such an opportunity, however. . . . Besides, Mother Irenæus has a very keen sense of pragmatism in her philosophy. She is probably quite unconscious of it, but I do not think a single one of her gestures could be termed spontaneous. Her every action for better or worse is taken with a view to what promises to be the eventual outcome. To this day she has managed to steer the most delicate of courses. You see how difficult it would have been for you to come to an understanding with her."

They were silent for a moment. Sister John of the Cross was considering. "But, Mother. . . . Such calculations are unthinkable! We are nuns. We have left all to gain the one thing necessary; that better part promised to Mary. I came to you spontaneously in complete liberty of heart. It never occurred to me to make use of anyone's influence with a view to acquiring responsibilities."

The novice's voice was resignedly sad, but, all the same, she was thinking that next day, if, as was very probable, the Chapter gave her a favourable vote, she would not fail to thank Mother Bursar very specially during the kiss of peace at the conclusion of the ceremony of reception—Goodness! It would take at least half an hour to kiss all those nuns!

"Of course, Sister," Mother Stanislaus continued. "And your own intentions have nothing to do with it. What does count is the view the Chapter takes—the decision it will reach tomorrow. Believe me, there are novices who will present no problem. That is because they pass almost unnoticed. They will be absorbed into the community and their presence will not change the spirit of the house in the slightest degree. Religious profession in an abbey is a social engagement. It is necessary to please the majority in order to be accepted. If you come to think of it, that is quite normal. You must always bear in mind that when a member of the Chapter is required to give her vote to a novice, and the novice in question represents a certain value, or, if you prefer, carries a certain weight, she will say to herself: 'That one might quite possibly become my abbess one day. I must beware!' And that is only human. Voting by the Chapter is an ancient custom which already existed in the sixth century—at the dawn of our Order. Our Father Founder had a special predilection for the rite."

Sister John of the Cross placed her hands on Mother Stanislaus's knees. Her expression was confident, full of youthful enthusiasm and hope.

"Do you think, Mother, that we can count on Mother Francis de Sales?" she said after some thought.

"There is no doubt of it. You have won the heart of Mother Organist from the very first days. Your love of Bach was enough in itself. And then you were clever enough to ask her advice. Everybody closely, or remotely, connected with music in this house is on your side. With the Mothers who sing and those in charge of ceremonies you will have nineteen votes."

In the eyes of Sister John of the Cross there was a gleam of reproach, suggestive of a kitten of three or four months, whose saucer of milk is drawn away.

"Mother, I would rather keep my illusions about Mother Francis de Sales, who, from our very first meeting, must have known my affection for Bach was entirely disinterested."

"Naturally, Sister. But at any rate, we can make the most of our advantage."

Her clear eyes were smiling maliciously. Perhaps she was deliberately accentuating this expression. Perhaps it was on purpose that she made no comment on the subject of illusions; and the young nun's face grew sad again—with hesitations and unspoken fears.

"I have counted them up," said Mother Stanislaus. "We are sure to have ninety-two votes. After that, there are probabilities, possibilities, uncertain votes. Several of our Mothers are very secretive."

"And the Prioress?"

"Mother Anselm? You have won her over by your bearing and your manners; but she may never give you any sign of this. She is a great lady, Mother Anselm, you know. The greatest lady among us all: and she is a person of real spiritual distinction. Later on, when you are one of us, you will appreciate her."

"It is because of her bearing that I, also, liked her from the very start. But I thought her very haughty. She never speaks to us. She seldom even smiles."

"But the Prioress is not supposed to speak to the novices. Surely you realise that; it is forbidden for all of us, and goodness knows how the fact is dinned into us at a time like this."

There were inflections of irony in her voice—a kind of audacity.

"Oh, Mother. I really do not know how you can say such a thing seriously."

"It does not look as though I were too serious, does it? And besides, it is unseemly to joke on such an occasion."

The first stroke of the bell for Sext chimed. They rose. Doors were silently opening and shutting. The corridors were full of nuns, moving to and fro. At the copper basin with eagle-headed taps, a Mother was washing her hands. They waited on the landing at the top of the stairs.

"Can we count on Mother Teresa of Avila?" said the young sister.

Mother Stanislaus was putting on her *coulle*, with its immense sleeves and long folds reaching to the floor.

"Perhaps. But her vote is very uncertain. I have always deplored (though admittedly for other reasons) that you do not seem to be particularly interested in German philosophy. To admire the great Germans of the scholastic period is a sure way of gaining the good will of Mother Teresa. One can't foresee everything, though, can one, my little angel?" she added, placing her hand against the cheek of the young sister. But there was still perplexity mingled with reproach and sadness in the eyes of Sister John of the Cross.

"And Mother Vicar?" she asked. "I should say she is remarkable for her supreme indifference. I suspect her of neutrality with regard to most things—a kind of general neutrality. Am I right?"

Mother Stanislaus's expression had become attentive.

"Mother Mechtild? We will talk about her quietly, one day when we have more leisure," she said.

Some nuns were passing. They stopped for a moment in the cloakroom to put on their *coulles*, then they made their way to the choir by the lesser staircase.

All at once there was a strange silence. A silence not only due to the cessation of speech, but emphasised by a controlled quietness of action, gesture and movement. The black-veiled heads bent, the outlined figures passed furtively, bowing as they went. Sister John of the Cross suddenly felt shy in this part of the house reserved for the professed religious. She did not know the reason for her shyness, but the experience was vivid and painful.

It lasted only an instant. Then she turned, as though to go downstairs. Her eyes were lowered. She saw beneath her the iron spiral which led to the ground floor. Suddenly, without knowing how it happened, she found herself gazing into the eyes of the Abbess. She was overcome with giddiness. The Abbess was standing immediately in front of her. No word was spoken, but an aura of majesty surrounded her. They were close—so close—within touching distance.

She gave a start. Her eyes widened. For an instant she was unable to move. At last she knelt down, but the Abbess did not hold out her ring to be kissed. Her eyes were cold like steel. The nuns drew aside and made their way downstairs like shadows.

"Neutrality is not inspired by indifference, nor by egotism, but by an over-ruling regard for the community as a whole," the Abbess said at last. "Furthermore it would be better to recognise as an irrefutable fact the providential intervention of the Holy Spirit in deliberations of this nature. I may add that this is neither the time nor the place for conversation."

Her voice was icy and distant, and contained an unusual note. It was not the custom for the Abbess to rebuke or criticise anyone, directly and in public, outside the Chapter. It was clear that her reprobation was something quite out of the ordinary.

No one spoke. Indeed no one else was left. The Abbess then fixed her eyes on those of Mother Stanislaus, who was still standing upright and impassive like an officer on guard—a protective bulwark. For a moment it seemed as though the two Mothers were measuring each other's strength.

The silence was prolonged. It seemed interminable.

The second stroke of the bell for Sext sounded.

At last, Mother Stanislaus turned away.

In one of the Abbey parlours, with its sculptured wood-work, an oblate was laying two places with silver and delicate glasses at the round table. The window looked out on to a little garden planted with gold-coloured tulips, forget-me-nots and pansies. A log fire was crackling on the hearth. It

33

was noon. The pale October sunshine fell upon the walls, illuminating a set of engravings of scenes from the life of Saint Benedict. Luxuriant green plants had been arranged in copper flower-stands.

Presently two priests entered. One of them wore the black habit of a Benedictine monk. He was about thirty-five to forty years old. He had a lean, bony face, and the eyes behind his glasses were keen and lively.

"Here we are, Father!" he said. "This is where we shall have our meals. It is in the house of the oblate Sisters. There are not many of them; only ten. As you know, they live a regular life which makes them truly religious. Their time-table varies according to the convent, but basically it is always the same. They are bound to say the day Office, but are dispensed from Matins at night. They go into the enclosure for meals and recreation. They come from good families, but they are not strong enough in health for the strict observance."

"I know. They are of great value to the abbeys. I am familiar with their way of life. We have them now almost everywhere. It is a pity that vocations to this somewhat easier religious life should be so rare."

The speaker was a tall friar of about fifty, clothed in the white Dominican habit. His comfortable plumpness suggested a peaceful temperament, and his clear, very blue eyes, which were rather startling at first, finished by exercising a peculiar charm. Great calmness flowed from him, and his deep voice had a range of inflections which could be persuasive and compelling. Full of kindness, he yet preserved a certain distance, though without arrogance. He had arrived at the Abbey that morning to conduct the annual retreat, which took place during the last ten days of October and ended with the solemnity of All Saints.

The two priests took their places at table. For a while they ate in silence. A kind of secret peace surrounded them. It settled down upon the whole room, isolating them from everything outside. The Sister had placed the dishes on the table.

She brought in a trolley with cheese, fruit and pastries. Then, silently, she withdrew.

"It is an important abbey, not only on account of the numbers of its subjects, but of their quality—also, I think, because of the perfection of its liturgy?" said the visiting monk.

"Yes, it is a very interesting community from every point of view," said the Father Confessor with a smile. "A little tainted with philosophism, perhaps, especially among the younger nuns, but the novitiate is fervent. There are remarkable qualities at all levels."

"But what a task you have each week with the regular confessions. There must be quite three hundred nuns in all?"

"Three hundred and eleven. Oh, I spend my life in the confessional."

The Dominican grew suddenly thoughtful. His blue eyes became peculiarly insistent.

"Mother Stanislaus de Neuville belongs to this abbey, does she not?"

A keen light shone in the Father Confessor's eyes.

"She has been here for the last ten years. Yes, she is a very remarkable person. Nurtured on the Fathers of the Church and the original texts of the Bible, she reads Hebrew and Greek better than we do Latin."

"She is said to have great liberty of thought on a great diversity of subjects. Is she not at work just now on a book about the Council of Nicaea? Some Fathers were talking about it the other day at our priory."

"Yes, but she is a metaphysician first of all. Sometimes rather disconcerting. She comes to my confessional each week, as the Rule prescribes, but I am not her director. She has frequent visits from specialist Fathers of our Order. Our Very Reverend Father often goes to see her. She is the only nun in France who is an authority on questions of ecclesiology, and of philosophy for that matter. She has written a treatise on the pseudo-Dionysius which is very ingenious and full of discoveries. The Early Fathers count for a great deal with her."

"I believe she is quite young?"

"She is forty."

The Dominican calmly went on with his meal. His eyes indicated a sustained interest. Neither spoke for a while. The sunlight played on the glasses, the china, the fine white linen of the tablecloth. In the fireplace the flames were subsiding over the glowing logs.

"And the Abbess?" the visitor suddenly asked.

The silence of the Benedictine grew oppressive—difficult. It suggested fears, and a sort of withdrawal which he was at pains to hide.

"The Mother Abbess is an austere soul," he murmured.

"But lacking in serenity? Is she not?"

"Oh, I should not go so far as to say that. She is rather rigid about everything which concerns the observance of the Rule. But she can unbend. Yes, I think it is only fair to say that she knows how to unbend."

The Dominican was crumbling some bread on the table-cloth. He was perplexed and seemed to be thinking.

"It is whispered in our priory that each year her government of this abbey becomes more and more high-handed. Not only is she an imperious and unyielding autocrat, but she shows signs of self-sufficiency in her relations with God, setting up and exercising a certain spiritual domination which was once illustrated in a manner still sadly remembered. Reprehensible as such an exercise of power always is when it transcends the ordinary ethical level, it is still more to be condemned for the very quality of the thought on which it is based."

The Father Confessor was silent for a space.

"You see . . . it is rather difficult to say so, but the whole of our Benedictine way of life is at stake here in its very structure. The Abbess *is* an autocrat. Fundamentally, that is what she is required to be."

The Dominican was not convinced.

"So long as the spirit of the Rule is safeguarded—yes! I will grant you that; although it is very debatable. But constitutionally, and by the very essence of religion, without accepting any formulae, the superior is not, and never will be, anything but the servant of the Rule. Immediately he, or she, goes beyond the limits of his office (and those limits are very clearly defined) he departs from its spirit. With you this very essential point is quite often forgotten in practice. Am I not right?" he added, his eyes suddenly alight with a charming friendliness.

"I think, Father, that it is a question which must always remain one of autonomy. Each abbot or abbess sets the seal of his own life on his government. Here, her Grace seems to have a very high sense of her duties."

"Perhaps I have not made myself clear? It is notorious and is already known throughout most of the monastic world of the west, that this abbey is somewhat tinged with Jansenism. You see that I do not mince matters."

The Confessor raised his hand in a pacific gesture.

"Oh! That is very much exaggerated. Although all religious life draws a certain glory from renunciation, our life here is not exactly penitential. You, yourself, know this. It is far more centred on praise. Great austerities are not in keeping with it. I have never thought that we went beyond a normal and very moderate level in the practice of mortification, which, in fact, is very wisely controlled here."

The Dominican passed his hand over his face. It was a broad hand, suggestive of energy.

"Look, Father, I am afraid we are wandering from the point. One can be a Jansenist and practise relatively little mortification, and one can be very orthodox and do a great deal of penance. Jansenism is, before all else, a direction or tendency of the mind. This tendency consists in putting too great a value on works, and an exaggerated emphasis on their excellence as a means of salvation. That is all it is. Just as Molinism is the reverse. I am afraid that this abbey lacks what

Saint Paul termed the holy 'liberty of the children of God'. Do you understand me?"

They were silent. The Sister came in and cleared away their lunch. Then she put a silver coffee pot on the table. She was young, and her features had a refined beauty. She was by no means an ordinary servant girl. There was a gentle modesty in her bearing. One might have seen her as one of the great Roman ladies offering the Agape of brotherly love to early Christians.

"Although I can't judge of all this on my own, since I have only just arrived," continued the Dominican, "I am telling you of the rumour which is beginning to spread. That is all. We can talk about it with greater certainty . . . and better arguments," he added, "in the course of a few days."

The Dominican had lit his pipe, and a cloud of grey-blue smoke enveloped him. For a long time they sat there in sunlit peace. They were talking now of familiar things, concerning their preaching and their ministry. When they left the room, the bell was sounding for the end of Recreation.

5

"It was a delicate mission, but you have handled it well, Father Mareuil, and the information you have brought is of the greatest interest."

"These ten days were scarcely necessary to acquaint me with the situation, Your Eminence. From my very first interview with Abbess Rouart, I knew that our fears were well-founded. After that I only had to discover the depth and scope of the disaster."

The November sun still glowed with an autumnal radiance

which illuminated the Cardinal's spacious office. From the high windows, the Tiber, which could be seen beyond the gardens of the Sacred Congregation of the Holy Office, seemed almost motionless in its course.

The Cardinal Prefect was sitting in the full light, at a table on which were heaped files, documents and letters. He wore the black cassock with red buttons and the wide scarlet sash of his office. His rather full face was remarkable for its kindliness, in spite of the jet-black eyes which sometimes shone with an inner flame. He was over sixty. His gestures betokened resolution, and his whole bearing was indicative of a balanced and healthy mind. A picture of Saint Francis de Sales, framed in bronze, stood on the table. Shelves of books in a variety of handsome bindings covered one wall. On another there was a very beautiful Renaissance tapestry depicting the story of David and Bathsheba. The Cardinal's folded hands rested on a blotter of purple morocco leather.

"And, from what you say, I imagine great damage has been done?" he asked.

I think that the damage has crept into the very heart of the community. And it has been happening almost without the Fathers of the neighbouring abbey being aware of it, despite the fact that many of them are frequently in touch with the most representative of the nuns. The harm would be difficult to estimate. The prestige of the Abbess is immense."

"Have there been any definite manifestations of this restrictive tendency?"

"There have—and they have been stupendous and excessive. Even the most open-minded and orderly seem to be losing their way."

The Cardinal thought for a moment.

"Did you see Mother de Neuville?"

"I saw her many times. In spite of a few idiosyncrasies of a purely disciplinary order, she seems to me to be blameless. She has a clear mind, nurtured by the Greek writers. I had no previous acquaintance with her, but immediately we began

to talk I was conscious of the solid foundations which safeguard her thought. She is very much influenced by Saint
Thomas, and his vigour enters into her intellectual formation.
At the same time she had the precision of Cartesian scepticism,
which relates her to the great English philosophers of the
eighteenth century; but this last influence is more a matter of
form than of substance. With it all, she has great charm. Her
books are a complete expression of herself. She is one of the
rare spirits who have understood the danger and combat it.
Her *Tertullian* is the clear expression of her thought with regard
to the question before us. A few less supernatural elements are
involved in her ardour. But fundamentally her rectitude
is unimpeachable. She criticizes Mother Rouart without
making a mystery of it; sometimes with great freedom and
humour. It seems that the conflict between them is very
acute."

"I am glad that Mother de Neuville has preserved that sure
judgment which led me to form an excellent opinion of her
some years ago. If the situation becomes embittered, we
should think about finding a shelter for her. She belongs not
only to the Order but to the Church."

"The serious thing is, Your Eminence, that now nothing
but a pontifical decree can free her to choose another abbey.
Mother Rouart refuses to release her from her vow of stability
—even temporarily. As for any permanent change, it is quite
out of the question. The situation is inconceivable. Our
Fathers have been asking for her for months, I was going to
say for years, without success! The Mother Abbess remains
unassailable in her authority."

"The whole situation seems rather dramatic."

For a few seconds the Cardinal rested his gaze on the black
marble crucifix on which the suffering figure was outlined in
the shadow.

"What do you propose, Father Mareuil?" he said at last.
"Obviously your visit must remain a secret; it cannot lead to
any immediate measures."

"The date for the usual canonical visitation should be fixed as soon as possible."

"Yes. . . ."

The Cardinal seemed to be thinking. A perplexity in which moderation and kindliness blended came over his face.

"Did you see the monks?" he asked at last. "And the Father Abbot? He is Dom Germain Delors, I think."

"Dom Germain received me when I arrived and when I left. I told him my fears and tried to get him to share them, but he openly takes the side of the Mother Abbess. As far as that goes, he is in perfectly good faith. He has a great respect and admiration for Mother de Neuville. I must admit that he is quite enthusiastic about her. He tolerates from her things he would not accept from another nun, because he considers that a certain consideration is due to her great intelligence, but none of this affects his point of view with regard to the Abbess. At least that is how I see it. Besides, he is a man who responds to a certain kind of poetry—like all men of action. He is aware of what I described just now as charm. For him, Mother Stanislaus is exceptional, and for that very reason he makes allowances in her case."

"But, for heaven's sake! She *is* exceptional. But that is not the question. What is important is Dom Germain's position with regard to the Abbess and her community—her community as a whole—quite apart from whatever an influence as powerful as Mother de Neuville's might be."

"Well then, your Eminence, let us say that he is like Bossuet giving his support to Louis the Fourteenth in his differences of opinion with Innocent the Eleventh." (The Cardinal smiled.) ". . . I also saw Father Anthony du Colombel, their confessor," continued Father Mareuil. "His is a soul of classical austerity, although tolerant by conviction. The exact opposite of what is required. He personally remains very orthodox, but his eyes are closed to the risks the community is running."

41

"Did you see all the nuns?" the Cardinal asked, after a silence charged with thought.

"In the confessional, yes. In the parlour about a hundred—those who came to me of their own free will. There is, in the novitiate, a young Sister whose spirituality seems of a very high quality. I talked with her for a full hour. She is called Sister John of the Cross. She is one of the Paléologue family and must be related to the former Ambassador of France at St. Petersburg. She had already formed her opinion of the Abbess and the convent, and I think it was correct. Her precision and objectivity surprised me. She is not yet fully formed in the religious spirit, but her good will is excellent. She could be a great nun."

"Unless she is spoiled on the way, during the years of scholastic formation. For this first impression is never effaced. Under a deformative influence natural spontaneity can be perverted. The constraint in her present surroundings must be considerable. . . . And the Novice Mistress?"

"Mother Reyer? She is a fine and heroic soul with a very healthy approach to the subject we are discussing: at least, that is what I believe. But her inner formation is rigid and dominated by asceticism; and this, in the present case, deprives her of all clear-sightedness with regard to the Abbess. For her, the superior is incapable of error."

The eyes of the Cardinal Prefect were tinged with sorrow—and also with weariness.

"I wonder whether the nuns in conclave for the election of an abbess are not in a more dangerous and alarming position than we are when we come together to elect a pope," he said a little later. "Yes, I wonder!" he repeated with deep feeling.

The Dominican smiled.

"What a terrible excess, Father Mareuil! This life . . . this daily life—stretching on for each and every day. And these three hundred nuns. And this authority which envelops them and which has no limits! For, in fact, it has none. It encircles the individual with dogma and discipline, and there is no way of escape! And this notion of the infallibility of the superior which is taught in the novitiate with iron rigidity. It is quite astounding. . . ."

The Cardinal became more and more excited. Several times he thumped the table, and his ring of office made a clear, tapping noise.

"It is past question," he went on; "for them, the Abbess *cannot* make a mistake. For them, even in matters of sin—open sin, she cannot. And the more ardent they are the more joyously do they follow this road. They would obediently plant leeks upside down—and expect them to grow! This might still pass in small communities where there is no philosophical formation. But good heavens! The case in which we are interested is not like that."

"Out of two hundred choir nuns, more than fifty are doctors in some subject," said the Dominican. "More than a hundred have a university degree. They all have their baccalaureates! Even the lay Sisters."

"And just think what that represents! It seems like a dream."

The sunlight now completely filled the spacious office. Noon was striking.

"Father Mareuil. . . . I am going to think about this conversation. Is it not Dom Hilary Lemaître who usually makes the canonical visitation? Will you write and ask him to come and see me? Give him a full account of the situation. Get him to come, if he can, within the next fortnight. I leave it all to you. Inform him of everything."

The Cardinal stood up. "Goodbye, Father. We must meet again soon. Your advice is always of value to me in these cases which are so difficult—and painful."

"Goodbye, your Eminence."

The Cardinal knelt before the great black crucifix.

The Angelus was sounding from Saint John Lateran.

43

6

It was nearly a month since Sister John of the Cross had received a favourable vote from the Chapter, allowing her to make her profession. In a few weeks she would offer the Abbess her promise of obedience and stability. She would change her linen veil for a longer one of a white woollen material. For the ceremonies in choir she would now be wearing the little *coulle*—without sleeves—over her habit. Although she had not entirely finished her novitiate, the door of the community would be open to her and she would begin the cycle of scholastic philosophy.

December had now clothed the Abbey in wintry garb. There had already been a fall of snow, and this morning a thick mist shrouded the gardens.

Sister John of the Cross was walking quickly through the cloisters. She drew her thick white shawl tightly around her shoulders. It was the middle of the morning. High Mass had finished an hour ago, and the nuns were back at their work or their studies. The cloisters were empty and the whole house seemed deserted.

The Abbess lived on the first floor of the southern wing. Her apartments consisted of a cell like all the others, a room where she received her daughters and another fairly large one which served as her secretary's office and her private library. Everything was on the same level of personal poverty as the rest of the convent, but the furniture was in the severe style of Louis XIV, and there were rich tapestries and velvety Savonnerie carpets.

Sister John of the Cross hung her shawl on a clothes-peg at the entrance, then she resolutely knocked on the door. It was opened by a nun who smiled a welcome to her. She was very young, perhaps scarcely thirty, but she already wore the gold ring of her first vows. Her rather sad smile was well known to all in the convent.

"Her Grace is expecting you," she said.

The Abbess was seated at a vast polished table whose bareness was rather surprising and, just at first, a little disconcerting. On it was a telephone, a black morocco writing-set, and, lying flat where she could see and touch it, a plain mahogany cross without the figure of Christ. On the far corner of the table stood an alabaster statue of Our Lady of Sorrows, very pure in style. On the wall hung an engraving by Jacques Callot of the Temptation of Saint Anthony. There were a few prints by Jean Morin, a portrait of Pascal and, in a well-lighted corner which brought out all its beauty, there was the austere face of Le Grand Arnault[1] engraved by the burin of Gérard Edelinck.

Sister John of the Cross bowed. Then she went and knelt before the Abbess and kissed the ground.

"I asked you to come this morning, dear child, so that we might see that all the formalities for your profession are in order. Your mother telephoned to me from Paris yesterday evening. All the invitations have been sent out by your family. If you can think of anything more personal that has to be done, you must tell me today. The sixth of January will soon be here and the feasts of Christmas will hold up the final arrangements."

"Yes, Mother, I believe we have thought of everything. My mother's last letter was reassuring on that head. My family and friends will be arriving the day before. My uncle the Bishop on the fourth, I think. I hope that your Grace will allow me to see Father Hilary in the parlour in spite of my retreat. He will be coming with my uncle from Solesmes. Your Grace will remember that he used to be my director."

"Yes, I know. Father Hilary is our canonical visitor, and there is nothing to prevent your seeing him. All the same, I

[1] Antoine Arnault, a celebrated theologian who defended the Jansenists of Port-Royal against the Jesuits (1612–1674).

must ask you not to have too many visits from priests, bishops
or even monks during this retreat. In principle the Rule does
not forbid it. But silence is far more important and profitable
for the soul than the holiest of conversations. You will, of
course, see Father Hilary and your uncle, but on the
other hand I do not think it will be necessary for you to
receive any of the teaching Fathers from the Abbey of Saint
Benedict. If you did, my poor child, there would be no end
to it."

Sister John of the Cross was silent.

"I suppose you are thinking of Dom Gregory," the Abbess
continued. "Well, I may as well give my answer at once:
it is No. And I hope that even after the retreat you will have
fewer of these visits. They seem to me unnecessary. Father
Gregory is a specialist in ecclesiastical history and you are
going to begin your philosophy. For the future your vows
will establish you in a stricter way of life as regards your
relations with the outside world."

"But Mother, Father Gregory is a wonderful monk. He
has an extraordinary understanding of souls. I am sure that
God enlightens him in a very special way."

The Abbess let a significant silence elapse.

"Sister John of the Cross. . . . You bear the name of a saint
who followed the way of absolute spiritual negation to the
degree of a daily martyrdom—a martyrdom of every moment,
perhaps. Saint John of the Cross means the *Nulla*. The *Nulla*
on earth and the *Nulla* even in heaven. The *Nulla* with
regard to consolations and to joy. If you have not understood
that, you are not on the road which leads to the essential
perfection God requires of each one of us."

Sister John of the Cross was silent. A shade of sadness came
over her face, giving it a kind of maturity.

"Mother," she said at last, "I entreat your Grace to allow me
to see Dom Gregory during my retreat. At least once. What
he has been for me all through these months is only known
to God and to me."

"My dear child. I never thought you were very mortified. Your virtues are by no means outstanding, and everyone here knows it. But I did hope that you had passed the elementary stage of self-will; if not, no religious life is possible for you. Not only do I forbid you to see Father Gregory during your retreat, but I must ask you from this moment to put an end to your meetings with him. If you are so bent on them, your inclinations cannot come from God."

Still kneeling with her hands crossed beneath her scapular, the young nun blushed deeply. Her expression was withdrawn, but she said nothing.

The silence became oppressive and was made more so by the Abbess, who was slowly arranging letters and pages of typescript on the table in front of her. Then her telephone rang and she listened for a long time to her invisible caller, replying with short, unhurried phrases.

Sister John of the Cross wanted to leave, but the Abbess motioned her to remain. At last she put the receiver down.

"And I want to take this opportunity," she said eventually, "of advising you not to indulge in natural friendships in this house. You are only too much given to them. Your relations with Mother Stanislaus have scandalised the Abbey during the whole time of your novitiate. From next month they will become permissible. None the less, in religion there is no place for human affection, and it is the A B C of virtue to understand this."

"Mother," the young nun protested spiritedly, "I am neither a Trappist nor a Carthusian. I entered the Order of Saint Benedict because it is the Order of praise and joy. Penance carried to such a degree is out of keeping with my line of spirituality."

The Abbess had raised her head, and her eyes flashed with a steely light. Her astonishment was mixed with compassion. For a moment she waited.

"You have no more to add?" she said at last in an icy tone.

"Yes, Mother, I have. I want to say this: I believe that God is Love and Charity—in the beautiful Latin meaning of the word. I do not believe in the excellence of works. I believe that if Faith without works is dead, works without Love are no more than temerity and spiritual pride. I think that it is good and necessary to be mortified, but I also think that one should preserve, in the depths of one's soul, that holy freedom which is one of the forms of humility. For Isaias said: 'Before Thee, O Lord, all our righteousness is as filthy rags.'"

Her voice vibrated, and there was in its depths that note of childlike innocence which increased its passion. Her clear eyes were glistening with tears, but she did not look away. "Please forgive me, Mother," she added, as soon as she had recovered a little. "I could not help myself."

A little later she rose from her knees, bowed low and went out of the room.

Through the window the gardens could be seen freed from the mist. A brilliant, unclouded sun was already high in the heavens. On a low table a bunch of amber-coloured chrysanthemums gleamed like fire.

7

Christmas was drawing near. Soon the chanting of the Greater Antiphons,[1] majestic, instinct with hope, and each day more compelling in their urgency, would fill the Choir, echoing with persistent confidence, solemnity and eager longing.

[1] The Greater Antiphons known as the Seven Great O's precede and follow the Magnificat at Vespers. There is one for each day from December 17th to the 23rd.

"O Key of David. . . . O Orient. . . . O Emmanuel. . . ."

There was neither snow nor sun, but the cold was so bitter that all doors were kept tightly shut. It was dark very early. Sometimes the lights had to be switched on by four o'clock, and from the inner cloister the Abbey looked as though it were fixed to the surrounding darkness by innumerable golden nails.

On this particular morning the temperature had dropped still further and registered minus nineteen degrees centigrade. Outside the cold cut like a knife, but as soon as one came into the inhabited part of the Abbey, a gentle warmth brought one's limbs back to life, and faces relaxed.

It was a Friday—the day of the Conventual Chapter. It was ten o'clock and the lesser bell was already sounding the required five hundred strokes to summon the nuns. It went on tirelessly, with a slow rhythm. Like a cry of agony.

Under its magnificently fluted roof, which radiated from a huge rectangular pillar symbolical of the abiding and immutable Rule, the Chapter-house was still nearly empty and gave an impression of vast immensity. Ten stained-glass windows looked down upon three rows of stalls. They were unornamented, hewn out of massive oak, utterly bare. There was a life-sized crucifix with the figure of Christ carved in ivory, expressive of infinite suffering. The statue of Saint Benedict was probably of the twelfth century. It was carved in citrus-wood and showed him with the finger of silence held to his closed lips. The Abbess's chair was a Gothic cathedral raised on three steps, in front of which a cushion of violet velvet had been placed.

One after another the nuns were coming in, some singly and some with all due decorum in little groups of three or four. They wore their cloaks, and paused to bless themselves with holy water from the marble stoups at each of the four entrances. Then they went to their places.

The bell continued to tinkle—mercilessly, interminably. It brought to mind the drop of water falling continually on a man's bare head which is one of the worst tortures of China.

The two novices whose turn it was that week were already seated on the steps of the Abbess's throne, which was still empty. The first, who was to the right of the top step, held in her hand a copy of the holy Rule, bound in black morocco with gilt-edged pages. The second sat to the left of the lowest step. A copy of the Constitutions in an austere sheepskin binding, with rough-edged pages, lay on her knee.

The hall was filling. There was a sound of sweeping skirts and quiet steps. One of the Sacristan Mothers was lighting the great candles of yellow wax to the right of the Abbess's chair. According to the rite, the Abbess would put it out before listening to the confession of faults. After the *culpa* it would be lighted again and would go on burning during her exhortation.

At last the bell stopped and the Very Reverend Mother entered. The four doors closed immediately and, as soon as the Abbess had mounted the steps to her throne, the cantor intoned the *Veni Creator*. The hymn continued slowly, with a solemn and compelling majesty.

> "Per te sciamus ad Patrem
> Noscamus atque Filium."

The nuns were now seated with their hands hidden in their enormous sleeves, and their eyes lowered. Only the two novices at the throne were left standing, and they remained so until the end, representative of Justice and Mercy entrenched within the Rule.

The novices rose and came forward in an orderly procession, beginning with the most junior. Two by two they bowed low, then knelt and finally prostrated themselves with their foreheads touching the ground. In this position they confessed their guilt: "Most Reverend Mother, I very humbly accuse myself of having failed in the observance of the Holy Rule and Conventions, by talking unnecessarily during the time of silence."

". . . I accuse myself most humbly of having spoken complacently about myself at Recreation."

". . . Of having failed in quietness of movement by banging my stall in choir."

". . . Of failing in charity by criticising one of our Sisters."

The Abbess raised her head, and with a little hammer of polished wood she tapped lightly on the front of her stall.

"Kindly say something else, Sister. That is not a matter for self-accusation in Chapter but for sacramental confession."

The young Sister grew agitated, kissed the ground, and continued: "I accuse myself of missing Matins last night without permission," she said at last, "through laziness."

Her clear young voice trembled with emotion. The Abbess nodded, and then slowly and with great solemnity, she raised her head.

"To make satisfaction, Sister, you will kindly recite the seven penitential psalms, at the foot of the cross, in the garden after Matins tonight," she said.

For an instant there was silence. Then there was a strange reaction in the upper stalls like the backwash of water in the wake of a steamer. Yet it was scarcely perceptible in the sound of rosaries, of feet moving slightly on the polished floor, of creaking wood.

The next novice whose turn it was to make her confession was still mute. The cause of her silence could have been inattention, or it could equally have been stupefaction.

"Sister John of the Cross, I am waiting for you," the Abbess said at last.

And the slow repetition of self-accusations continued. Interminably—like an incantation of mysterious secrets, with hesitations and pauses; interrupted from time to time by the remarks of the Abbess; by the advice she gave with the utmost calm, and the penances which she inflicted.

This lasted for a full hour.

Finally the Abbess came down from her seat, turned towards the crucifix and knelt in her turn. But, in accordance with the usual custom, she did not bow her head.

"I very humbly accuse myself of frequently lacking patience with you, my Sisters, and of having scandalised you by my unmortified indolence," she said.

All the nuns were on their knees, prostrated.

There was a short silence for meditation. Then the Abbess rose to her feet. She stood still for an instant, and then made a movement with her right hand demanding attention.

"Since we are in the season of immediate preparation for Christmas," she said, "I invite those of you who are willing, not to go back to bed after Matins, but to spend the rest of the night in prayer. This authorisation is general. There is no need for any of you to ask for special advice or permission. This is all I have to say," she added with a gesture of dismissal.

The eyes of Sister John of the Cross met those of Mother Stanislaus. A passion, or even a criminal aberration, sometimes attains such a degree of intensity that, far from becoming harmful, it succeeds in producing a momentary purification.

It effects that purging of the emotions or *catharsis* extolled by the Greeks.

One by one the nuns left the Chapter-house.

8

It had been snowing all the previous night and all that day, and it was still snowing as darkness came on. The gardens lay buried, soft and smooth under their deep covering. Silence reigned everywhere. In the house the nuns trod more quietly than ever, and on their faces—though their eyes were, for the most part, lowered—there was a kind of agonized depression. All was dominated by shocked amazement mingled with a nascent reproach, still restrained through fear but almost palpable in the atmosphere. In the event, it would express itself with sadness or vehemence according to the age, character and spirit of each nun—and the bearing of her heart.

It was five o'clock in the evening and night was falling. Behind the green pot-plants and statues, the subdued lights of the cloisters cast mysterious shadows.

The most striking thing was the quality of the silence, which in fact was practically total—a quiet not of this world. Sister John of the Cross was on her way to the parlour. She was walking quickly. Her springy steps were noiseless under the folds of her black habit. She opened a low door which grated like a stiff window. The parlour was small and warm, hung all around with tapestry and with a carpet which swallowed up the sound of steps. She pulled back the black curtain, and Father Gregory became visible on the other side of the grille.

"I came as soon as I received your call," he said. "You see! The young priest who sang Mass at the convent gave me your note. I guessed it to be something important. Was I right? Come on, sit down," he added. "I am listening."

His tone was collected and frank. It was clear that they understood each other perfectly; that he was entirely at her disposal. For a moment the novice remained silent, her hands hidden under her scapular, pensive, with imperceptible hesitations as to how to begin.

Father Gregory was fifty years old. His grey eyes were acute, but they could be very kind. He was tall, and had just that degree of stoutness which proclaims an abundance of good health. His personality seemed to find expression in an uninterrupted series of effective gestures. He had without any doubt worked out a philosophy which was harmonious and satisfying. He was in all probability a man of aesthetic taste.

"I suppose you know what has happened?" said Sister John of the Cross.

"I know that little Sister Andrew is very seriously ill," the Father replied, after a moment. "She has pneumonia, I think? That is all I know."

The young sister lowered her eyes. "Father, please do not be evasive with me," she said, with a touch of hastiness in her voice. "For two days now Sister Andrew has been in bed with a temperature of one hundred and four. I think that at Saint Benedict's the Fathers must be talking about it."

Her tone was imperious, but without the detachment which might have made it acceptable. There was a marked silence on the part of Father Gregory. It was not that he thought the tone unseemly. He was too well-bred and too distinguished in the Order to be upset by any liberties in the way of free speaking. But he made a point of preserving the greatest possible reserve in matters which struck him as important, and he tried to persuade those whom he considered worthy that such an attitude is the only suitable one. He looked into the eyes of the young Sister with that possessive calm which was part of his charm.

"I seldom leave my study," he said. "My work and the preparation of my lectures and classes keep me too busy. Besides that, I have never considered Sister Andrew to be worthy of special interest. So then?" he added with a vague gesture. "It is a sad business, but without any further information, that is all I can say."

"And you are waiting to hear what really happened—from me, or from one of our community, I suppose? Well, Father, you shall hear. Two days ago in Chapter, Mother Abbess gave Sister Andrew as penance to recite the seven penitential psalms at the foot of the crucifix in the garden after Matins."

"She is obviously quite mad," said the monk in a very ordinary voice.

"Wait. . . . Let me finish telling you. It snowed all that night, and it has not stopped ever since. At five o'clock in the morning one of our lay Sisters found Sister Andrew lying in the snow. She had fainted. In the course of the morning she was found to have pneumonia. The Turks must certainly be very near Byzantium[1] for such outrages to pass unnoticed."

The Father was silent.

"Like you," she continued, "I have no special interest in Sister Andrew—only the most ordinary sisterly affection. As far as she is concerned, I deplore this accident because no one deserves to be the victim of such intemperate commands, but that is all. Indeed, Father, you surely realise that when I called you it was to study the question from a much wider point of view."

Her blue eyes had the steely light of bitter experience, but only as she was telling her tale. Her youthful expression returned with the silence, and the slight pouting of her lower lip indicated a kind of regret—almost fear—lest she should have offended this priest whom she regarded as an oracle, and whom she loved and trusted. The Father was still silent. He folded his hands on the oak frame of the grille. They were firm, well-shaped hands and the square nails were hard. A multitude of thoughts were discernible in his eyes as they passed through his mind and were swallowed up in silence.

"Is the little novice worse?" he asked at last.

"Father, please!" She was almost crying. "Father, answer my question, the question which is tormenting me. Please do not evade it. What the Mother Abbess did was infamous!" she added vehemently.

A very long moment passed.

"Not infamous, no; infamous has a moral implication, Sister," he said quietly. "Something audacious and rash

---

[1] Reference to the occupation of Constantinople by Turkish troops while the monks there were engaged in futile discussions on a point of interior discipline.

would be a better term, and that is in keeping with her usual behaviour. But I have asked you a question, too. I want to know whether Sister Andrew is worse. I have a reason for asking this, but you never reply to questions. You go off at a tangent. . . ."

She became calmer. "At three o'clock the doctor gave up all hope that she would pull through."

"Does the doctor know the truth?"

"Not all of it. I do not think so. The Mothers in the infirmary have their orders—Oh! not expressed in so many words, but tacitly understood. It is well known that mystery and terror are the arcana of certain governments. I do not know what they think in the community, but in the novitiate, our Mistress has given us to understand that we had better hold our tongues and wait."

"I have no particular affinity for Mother Cecilia," he said, "but it must be admitted that she represents a valuable element in your rather special community."

"Oh! of course. There we have another influence to be taken into account. But that you should admit it? You, Father? That is what surprises me," she added.

There was a hint of kindly amusement in the monk's eyes, but it quickly vanished.

"There is a time for everything, my dear child. Mother Rouart has been adding to her imprudences and follies for many months already. This particular example is worse than usual. Other superiors have lost their cross and ring for far less."

"You do not know her, Father. She will manage to come through. She will triumph this time, as she always does."

"Even this time," he said thoughtfully. "Marking the peak of her folly!"

In the distance bells were ringing. They gave a solemn, stifled sound under their covering of snow.

"That must be the first bell for supper at Saint Benedict's, Father," she said, suddenly practical, with the prompt obedience to time-tables and orders which marked her un-mistakably as still belonging to the novitiate. "It is time to go."

They rose to their feet.

"I beg you to keep calm," he said. "I shall be singing the High Mass here in three days. I will spend the end of that morning with you. Good evening, my daughter."

The door of the outer parlour slammed to. The clock in the portress's lodge was striking half-past six. She wrapped her shawl tightly around her shoulders. The snow was falling again over the gardens under a dark, starless sky.

9

Two days passed. On December 20th Sister Andrew died. It happened quite quietly at about ten o'clock in the morning. The sun was already beginning to warm the earth. The sky was a beautiful transparent blue. The white-curtained in-firmary was flooded with light, when, instantaneously, with a little shudder, the decision came for death. Then the shutters were closed. There followed a murmur of lowered voices. Doors were left ajar. There were candles. There were flowers. And in death, for the first time, the young nun wore the black veil of her monastic profession. The face which it framed was very white and very beautiful. On her head was a crown of roses, and her hands were crossed over a rosary of box-wood. For the first time, her finger was encircled by the gold ring—the symbol of the final vows which were to endure for all eternity.

Mother Cecilia's face was marked with weeping. Her eyes were haggard. Novices were kneeling by the bed. They came in relays, hour by hour. The recitation of psalms never ceased. The professed nuns came in from time to time. They sprinkled the body with holy water. The light of the candles threw shadows over it.

The second day, the little Sister lay in state in the choir, under a catafalque of white starred with black. She lay in front of the grille and the slow procession of nuns began again. The sun brought to life the flashing gold and amethyst of the stained-glass windows. It scattered emeralds across the funereal hangings, the light oak of the stalls and the bowed veils. The snow had vanished from the garden except for a few hard, compacted patches here and there.

The body was placed in the coffin on the third day with due Benedictine rites, sweet and lovely in their majesty. There were no tears, but tender affection. The choir brought to mind a catacomb of the Early Church where the faithful were burying the martyr of the day.

Almost without a break, the Abbess was in the parlour receiving the family and friends of the young nun. She did so with her usual majesty. The dignity of her bearing on abnormal and painful occasions always surprised those whose knowledge of her went below the surface, but it was a subject of admiration and respect for the visitors. Priests came, former teachers of the young sister. Then a group of Girl Guides in uniform. She had been their leader.

The Archbishop presided at the ceremony. He was surrounded by the whole of his Chapter and a large number of monks and religious. Everything gave an impression of gentle sweetness, of confidence and peace, with that emotional reserve which so fittingly brings out the insignificance of anything excessive. The calm was untroubled. Father Gregory knew that there is always a point of view from which it is permissible to disregard individuals; he knew this to be something which can be acquired, at which it ill becomes us to be surprised. Moreover, it was apparent in his whole demeanour that he had long ago ceased to let anything surprise him. While he was officiating at the altar beside the Archbishop, his expression was one of complete serenity. Mother Stanislaus and Sister John of the Cross were wrapped in thought, collecting their memories, of which they would soon be making effective use. There was no doubt of that. Mother Cecilia had aged ten years in three days. Perhaps some of the novices were unconsciously going right back to their childhood, in order to regain some sense of an overruling protection.

Christmas Matins was sung on the night following the funeral; and after the days of mourning the whole abbey seemed to be filled with that solemn and austere jubilation which is experienced on coming away from a sacrament. Then everything fell back into silence.

Sister John of the Cross began her retreat on the evening of December 28th, the day of the Holy Innocents and the feast day of the Novitiate.

The cold weather had returned. The frost was very sharp again, after easing with the snow. It held the earth, the gardens and buildings in an iron grip. The novice entrenched herself in close solitude, only leaving her cell to go to the choir or one of the chapels.

She moved about the house or through the cloisters with her veil over her face, and she faithfully restrained herself from seeking Father Gregory in the parlour. The latter, on his side, made no attempt to see her. They knew that the acceptance of a discipline can sometimes cause feelings to develop to their maximum intensity.

Mother Stanislaus scarcely put in an appearance with the rest of the community. Her essay on the Pontificate of Clement XI was to be published in January, and she was very busy correcting the final proofs. A young girl entered the novitiate as a postulant. Life went on as usual. Then, at last, Epiphany dawned, and with it the day of the Profession. The guest-houses of the two abbeys were invaded by a crowd of visitors. There was much coming and going. The drive was crowded with parked cars which had not been able to find a place for the night in the village garages.

The cold was more severe. It was biting and harsh, like a burn. The sun came out, gilding the red roofs and white stone walls. The countryside lay motionless. It seemed as though even the usual sounds were stunned into silence by the cold.

In the great entrance-hall groups were forming. Old friends were recognizing each other with emotion and pleasure. Fathers from the Abbey of Saint Benedict were arriving on bicycles. They came one after another, silently, their hoods pulled over their heads, their faces red with the cold. The oblate Sisters were receiving the guests with deferent courtesy, and with an eye to everything. The dining-rooms were ready—decorated with flowers—the tables loaded with refreshments, fruit and cakes. Presents and delicacies were streaming in on all sides.

The ceremony was to take place at ten o'clock. Since eight the Abbess had been in her parlour. She was indefatigable, seeming like an affable and protective sovereign of this other-worldly kingdom.

The bells of the abbeys were answering each other. They rang out triumphantly, sweeping the cloudless sky with their calm and almost uninterrupted rhythm.

The clock in the courtyard struck the three-quarters after nine, and thereupon a silent movement began towards the church. At first it was scarcely perceptible, shy and hesitant; then it became more clearly defined. Isolated groups still lingered under the porches, then gradually they thinned out and finally broke up to join the stream.

The drama of the rite unfolded in all its pure nobility. It began with the singing of Terce and the Pontifical Mass. The naves, the ambulatories, the narthex and even the parvis were a medley of bright colours; furs, scarves, gay hats. The sunshine was everywhere. The ceremony lasted till past twelve. And as Sister John of the Cross, now wearing the white woollen veil and the sleeveless *coulle*, was saying goodbye to the last visitors from behind the grille of the big parlour, the solitary little stroke of one o'clock sounded its punctual note. It was almost lost, however, in the clamour of bells from both abbeys which ceaselessly vied with each other, filling the countryside with their triumphant chimes.

10

Dom Hilary Lemaître of the Abbey of Solesmes was back from Rome, where he had only spent a brief forty-eight hours. A long interview with the Cardinal Prefect had brought him up to date with all that Father Mareuil had not yet told him.

He was an adroit man who for many long years had been conducting canonical visitations of women's convents. He did this as a sort of semi-official job of which he spoke only in veiled terms, even with his brothers. In fact, he visited not only Benedictine Abbeys but numerous convents of the great orders, and he combined real holiness with remarkable insight and unerring judgment.

He must have been about sixty years old. He was tall and thin. So thin that he attracted attention and held it. His quick, piercing eyes were without softness. He was a good listener and never spoke beside the point. The effectiveness of his diplomacy lay in his apparent lack of any skill in this "virtue", which in reality he cultivated to a pre-eminent degree. He could recognize a face of which he had had no more than a passing glimpse twenty years ago. And he did so as easily as if he had seen it the day before. He read Greek and Latin with no more than average ability, and only admired these two ancient languages in so far as they served to train the mind and confer upon it a certain discreet elegance. He had no special favourites among the saints or pontiffs, unless it was Saint Francis de Sales, who was very dear to him and whom he resembled, not so much with regard to his noble birth and bearing as to his moderation, common sense and a particular kind of tolerance in his judgments.

He arrived at D—— on January 25th, for the Conversion of Saint Paul, having given no notice of his visit except by a telegram on the 24th.

The same day, the Archbishop had telephoned to the Abbess asking her to arrange for the annual canonical visitation to be put forward a few weeks, on the pretext of Father Hilary's coming departure for the Middle East, which, in fact, was being planned.

It was a grey day. The clouds were low. It had been raining, or it was going to rain. Half-past nine was striking when Dom Hilary arrived at the door of the abbey. He was accompanied by Father Anthony, who had gone to the town very early to meet him at the station.

Dom Hilary knelt in the choir for a brief visit of adoration. Then he had a short interview of courtesy with the Abbess. Finally he went up to the room prepared for him, where he shut himself in until lunch time.

While they were at table, he told Father Anthony that he would start seeing the Sisters immediately after Vespers, and that he would send for the lay Sisters first in the usual manner. This settled, he spoke of ordinary matters, carefully avoiding anything connected either closely or remotely with the Abbey. All was done in the polite and precise manner which characterized him. His conversation was smooth and easy. There was nothing studied, no beating about the bush, no trace of subtlety. He never forgot that from the time of his arrival in the Abbey he ranked as a bishop, by virtue of his office. Though this may not have been apparent in a formal outward manner, it was nonetheless implicit, and held good for all that counted in his eyes: the efficient ordering of the visitation and the satisfactory outcome of his interviews. He tacitly demanded the deference due to his office. And, for him, this deference meant no more nor less than the recognition from the very first day that he had the right to order his own personal life and the lives of all the others for the duration of his stay.

He may not yet have realized that his stay would last two months. But perhaps, after all, he was not quite ignorant of the fact. Father Anthony took it for granted, but said nothing.

Sister John of the Cross, who had formerly been the spiritual daughter of Father Hilary, was the subject of conversation for a moment, but only with regard to her personal concerns: her studies, her family, the brilliant future which seemed to be in store for her.

Then they talked about Rome and the Ecumenical Council which would soon be summoning the bishops. They spoke of the Sacred College of Cardinals and the life of the Church in general.

Father Anthony, who had been Chaplain to the nuns for less than a year and who did not know the monk from Solesmes, came away from their meeting full of admiration and quite won over.

II

On February 2nd, which is the Feast of the Purification of Our Lady, Dom Hilary sang the High Mass in the nuns' abbey. The sky was white. The cold continued to be intense.

The canonical visitation seemed as though it would last for ever. It was whispered that it could not come to an end before the beginning of Holy Week, given the long-drawn-out and detailed enquiries which the Visitor made during his interviews with the Sisters.

In twelve days he had just finished seeing the lay Sisters,

who numbered seventy. He had scarcely begun to interview the first postulants of the choir. And there were forty or more Sisters in the novitiate. As for the professed nuns, they numbered two hundred. And there were still the oblate Sisters to be examined. Then there was the visit to the abbey itself and all its offices and departments. There were the Bursar's accounts to be checked. There would be the meeting of the Abbess's private council, and finally the closing Chapter.

Easter fell at the beginning of April that year. Never had a canonical visitation lasted so long even in the largest of communities! But time did not count. Dom Hilary seemed to be settling down. At six o'clock every morning he said Mass at one of the side altars. Then he made his thanksgiving and his hour of mental prayer. At half-past seven he breakfasted. At eight he went into the parlour, which served him as an office and was outside the enclosure. The canonical visitor is not, in fact, allowed to go inside the abbey except for the visitation of the buildings between dawn and sunset, which has to be continued next day if necessary, and for as many days as he thinks fit.

At noon, Dom Hilary went to the dining-room where he lunched with Father Anthony. Then they took a walk in the grounds outside the enclosure. Father Hilary seemed grave, even solemn. But it was his habitual manner. During all the years that he had visited the abbey, he had never had any other expression, and the oblate Sisters who saw him close up each day had no cause to be uneasy on account of this.

Some time in February Mother Stanislaus received a letter from Rome. It was from the Dominican Fathers of Santa Sabina, who begged her to see if she could not come at last to work for a few months in the university of their Order.

It had to do with certain studies to be undertaken in common with a view to a possible reunion of the Western Churches. The matter was urgent. The Catholic world seemed to be more interested than ever in this enterprise and its possible outcome. Those who were closest to the Holy Father said that he made no secret of the immense value he attached to an eventual understanding. A great deal of research had to be done. Study groups were being planned. Articles would be published to keep the whole of Christendom informed of future developments.

Actually, this was not the speciality of Mother Stanislaus, and she had long ago passed the stage of being unduly influenced by an honour which did not promise any useful results. But, on the other hand, she reflected that this research would without any doubt be concerned with the Early Fathers, in whose writings convincing reasons for reconciliation might perhaps be found. That would be in her department and she could not refuse so tempting an offer.

She put the matter to the Abbess, who refused her permission. The interview took place without a storm. It only lasted a few moments.

"I have always thought that for a Benedictine the vow of stability outweighs in excellence every other consideration," her Grace said, to wind up. "You know this. Do not let us return to these questions."

The vow of stability was indeed for her an insuperable barrier in spite of the open door of dispensations. Mother Stanislaus, who reserved her own judgment, did not insist.

The canonical visitation proceeded slowly. At the end of February Father Hilary began to receive the fully professed nuns. His face showed nothing. Only at the end of the day he looked rather tired, but the signs of this quickly disappeared.

At seven o'clock he installed himself in the sitting-room, where he dined alone in front of a huge log fire. Then, in the dim light which is so helpful for meditation, he finished saying his office.

On several occasions Fathers who came to stay at the abbey kept him company. They were relations of the nuns, or friends of the house. Dominicans or Jesuits. That was all. He carefully avoided contact with the outside world. He did not go to the village and only very seldom to the Fathers' abbey. On

Sundays, after High Mass, the Abbess received him for a few moments in order to make sure that he had everything he wanted. It was purely an act of courtesy. Neither he nor the Abbess touched upon burning questions, or even debatable ones. Such questions could have been present in his mind only —since the Abbess had not the slightest premonition that her government might be subjected to any special investigation.

For that matter, there was no outward sign of such an investigation.

Meanwhile Lent was unfolding with its sober liturgy, calm and subdued. March brought but little sunshine. Then, on the twenty-first of the month, came the Solemnity of Saint Benedict and a ceremony of Solemn Vows. The abbey was gay once more with the gaiety of a feast. There was a breath of the bustling activity which characterises the reunions in which the world bears a part, but it was only momentary.

Father Hilary's face still showed nothing. Dom Anthony still had the same special smile which must surely have come from a sense of duty conscientiously accomplished and of a confidence which nothing could ever shake.

Now, as the days grew milder and the cold wind was less biting, the big Alsatian dog from the portress's lodge followed the two Fathers as they walked in the woods.

In the evening tar was still burned to protect the vines and fruit trees. But the spring was coming to birth. There were buds everywhere.

On the Monday of Passion Week, Dom Hilary went to the village.

There was a pale sun in the sky and its soft light had a certain melancholy charm. The well-tarred road stretched smooth and glossy. The poplars moved gently in the wind. Smoke was rising from some of the cottages. It was morning, and the housewives were on their way to market.

The monk directed his steps without hesitation to a prosperous-looking white house, surrounded by a well-kept garden

of trees and flower-beds. A black Dauphine was parked at the
door. It was the doctor's house. Dom Hilary remained there
nearly an hour. When he came out, the square was animated
with groups of people. He took the same road back to the
Abbey. The sunshine glowed with beautiful golden tints.
The wind carried the sound of the monastery's great bell
summoning the monks to Choir.

At half-past twelve he rejoined Father Anthony for luncheon.

12

"The Fathers of Santa Sabina certainly have no luck with
regard to Mother de Neuville!"

The Cardinal Prefect spoke with a good-humoured smile.
In the depth of his eyes there was a glint of mischief.

"Come," he added. "Do relax, Father Mareuil, and tell me
what you really think, apart from the particular question which
is on your mind and which, though unfortunate, does not constitute an irremediable injury."

"I think, your Eminence, that during the last few weeks
there have been a great many new developments in the whole
affair," said Father Mareuil in an icy tone. "Facts which can
no longer be set aside. I think that a decision is imperative,
and that it should be made without delay."

The Cardinal passed his hand over his face, which suddenly
looked weary.

"Yes, the death of that little novice. I know! Obviously
. . ." he made a gesture of uncertainty, in which his habitual
moderation and his longing for conciliation were expressed.
"I am awaiting Dom Hilary Lemaître's report, and the end
of his canonical visitation. . . . After which we shall see what
has to be done. But never has a visitation lasted so long!"

The Tiber flowed on peacefully. The morning air was full of sunshine. The light must have been playing on the clumps of fuchsia in the courtyard. The great gilded gates were already opened to visitors. Through the window the white stonework of the Basilica of Santa Maria Maggiore was visible, shining as though touched with hoar frost.

The Cardinal and the Dominican were silent for a moment. Someone knocked. Priests and secretaries of the Sacred Congregation came in one after another: for advice; for a signature; to remind the Cardinal of the day's audiences. The face of Christ on the big crucifix of black marble was as sorrowful as ever. After the visits, calm descended once more. The Cardinal was plunged in thought. He would surely have preferred that for that day at least they should call a truce over this affair.

However, Father Mareuil did not seem inclined to bring the interview to a close, unless he were explicitly ordered to do so. He had folded his hands over his scapular—his hands, which he kept clasping and unclasping in rhythm with his thought.

"You are thinking about Mother Stanislaus, Father Mareuil, and the work of your colleagues. I can see that, plainly enough," the Cardinal said suddenly. "Intellectuals must surely be allowed to write. Is that not so?"

"It is quite obvious, your Eminence. A man's equilibrium consists in exercising the powers which have been bestowed upon him. And I am strongly opposed to this obstinacy which forbids it. Yet, to tell the truth, it is rather from the general point of view that I envisage the problem."

"The whole business is most annoying," the Cardinal said in French. (When he was tired or his nerves were on edge, he always spoke the language of his interlocutor.) "It is most annoying, and I can quite understand that the monks of Santa Sabina are put out by these continual refusals—and also by the ill-will with which their requests are met. But I can do nothing about it. And, indeed, I cannot decide anything about the

68

affair as a whole before receiving Dom Lemaître's report. Tell your Prior that I sympathize with him. I am not surprised that you make common cause with your brother religious," he added with a smile. "I can only deplore that Mother Rouart is not more liberal. But, after all, I cannot anathematise her for difficulties of a private order. I repeat that I am waiting for the result of this visitation. Tomorrow is Palm Sunday. Everything should certainly be finished before the first singing of Tenebrae; that is to say, by Tuesday evening at the latest."

Father Mareuil was silent.

"Will you come and see me again after Low Sunday?" the Cardinal went on, kindly. "By then we shall be able to see what line to take."

The old man's voice was truly courteous, with a touch of melancholy which gave it a special charm. It could calm the heat of passion, bearing witness to a sure knowledge (born of age and experience) that scarcely anything is good or bad except by comparison. But this was a temporary leave-taking. Father Mareuil stood up.

"I can only hope that Abbess Rouart will understand what is in her own interest, your Eminence, and that the conversations which she must have had with Dom Hilary will eventually succeed in enlightening her," he said in a tone as frigid as ever. "But I doubt it."

The Cardinal smiled. "Come, come!" he said. "We shall be meeting again soon, Father. Till then goodbye."

In the courtyard the shadow of a flight of wild pigeons cut through the air and fell upon the grey flag-stones like a great silken mantle.

13

Mother Anselm Denoix, Prioress of the Abbey, had a well-defined task. She needed a balanced judgment, prudence, and that rather special diplomatic skill which is indispensable for those who hold high office in the government of a constituted body while still remaining under the control of a superior authority.

The Prioress was chosen by the Abbess, who could remove her from office at a moment's notice without explanation. On the other hand, there was no limit to the time of her appointment, which could last for the rest of her life. The temporal government of the abbey was in her hands; but the Abbess always had the right to intervene, to control her initiatives, and to veto her decisions. In fact, although she was second-in-command of the abbey, she was much nearer to the Mother Vicar, who came after her, than to the Abbess, who preceded her. For it was inherent in the character of the Abbess, as such, to be isolated in her office—alone and, as it were, of a species apart. Moreover, her election, which was for life, gave her character a certain distant kinship with that of a priest, set apart, by virtue of his ordination, from other men. Of course, this was purely symbolical, but nonetheless it gave the more fervent nuns a constantly renewed sense of security and satisfaction.

In the daily life of the community the Prioress takes the place of the Abbess at all times and places when the latter is prevented from being present, but she cannot sing the *Pater Noster* at Vespers or Matins. That is the prerogative of the Abbess. At Compline she can only give a general blessing, and the nuns do not kneel and kiss her ring.

The Two Nuns

Mother Anselm was fifty-five years old. Her most marked characteristic was her reserve. She belonged to the upper-middle-class of clerics and lawyers. She had a brother who was a bishop, and nephews and nieces belonging to various Orders. She was well-liked throughout the abbey for her good manners, and respected for her virtue. She was tall and thin, with long pale hands and soft brown eyes, calm and beautiful. She never raised her voice and never said a word more than was necessary. She was a pious and faithful nun, but no shade of excess had ever troubled the serenity of her life and she would have judged as unseemly any display of zeal or fervour.

Her cell on the first floor was just like any other. On the ground floor she had a large office, with a little room adjoining it for her secretary. She had very special control over everything concerning the outward ordering of the house. Thus, whenever a professed nun, or even a Sister from the novitiate, was dispensed from one of the Offices in Choir or any other communal exercise, she was obliged to let the Prioress know. It was enough for the novices to be excused from Matins by their Mistress without applying to the Abbess, but in every case they were obliged to notify the Prioress.

On this particular morning the weather was fine. Easter week was nearly over. The gardens were jewelled with spring flowers. The woods were full of birds' nests. Over the pond beyond the novitiate there was still a little mist, but it was barely ten o'clock and the sun would soon clear it. Sheep were grazing in the meadows. High Mass was over. Here and there the Sisters and nuns were going to their various tasks. Mother Anselm was walking along the cloisters in the direction of her office. It was at the extreme east of the southern wing and would certainly be full of sunlight by now.

On the heavy oak door there was a wooden board on which were carved in black letters the parts of the abbey to which she might have to go: *Choir, Library, Mother Abbess's Office, Infirmary, Garden, Parlour,* etc. An ivory stud marked her whereabouts for the benefit of visitors, who were thus spared from wasting an unnecessary time waiting for her. All the cells and each of the offices of the Mothers-in-Charge had a board like this, only the form varied according to the seniority or importance of the occupant.

Mother Anselm hung her *coulle* and shawl at the entrance. Then she took off the ivory stud marking *Choir*, and entered her office. It was a vast, light room with oak wood-work. It had book-shelves and a large table overloaded with brightly coloured files. There was a telephone and a typewriter. A vase of narcissi had been placed there. The flowers had surely been chosen specially, for they suited her personality perfectly. In one corner there were some ferns.

The furniture was all of the Regency period, less imposing than that of the Abbess, but far more intimate and comfortable. The light parquet floor was uncarpeted and shone with a high polish.

She took a quick glance at her letters which were piling up on the maroon leather blotter. She did not sit down, but put off dealing with them till later. Then she went towards a glass-topped door which she opened without knocking. While the room was empty a light tap sounded from the entrance. It was followed by another, and almost immediately the outer door opened and Sister John of the Cross came in. The veil of ivory-coloured wool which she had been wearing for the last three months, and which fell in soft folds almost as low as the big black veil of her final vows would do, transformed her. Something about her had changed. It was not that she had acquired more self-assurance. She had not needed to do that. But a certain decision animated her features, and that tranquillity which showed that she knew herself to be from henceforth an integral part of the community. Through her first vows she had become more or less detached from the novitiate in the strict sense of the word, and was promised in the near future to the blessings belonging to the final stages of her profession.

She came a little way into the room and stood waiting by the window. Some minutes passed. At last Mother Anselm returned and smiled with her usual kindliness.

"You are very punctual, my child," she said. "It is I who am late. Do sit down," she added, with easy courtesy, "and let us have a talk. I think I can guess what has brought you. I will answer you as far as I am able to do so."

Through the big window facing her the sunlight flowed in waves, illuminating the face of the young nun. She blushed slightly, but there was confidence in her eyes, and her smile was full of grateful ardour.

"Mother. . . . The step I have taken frightens me rather, now that I am in your presence. I am not yet a full member of the community."

"But of course you are . . . the Mothers like you. You have understood the meaning of our life. For my own part, I have been watching your progress from a distance more than you realised. I have a real friendship for you."

A few seconds passed during which their eyes met, and Sister John of the Cross understood that she could pursue her way bravely.

"Mother, for you are really my *mother*," she went on, intentionally stressing the word; "what I have to say to you is delicate enough to make me feel embarrassed before I start. Nevertheless, I have to say it. Last month, during the canonical visitation, I had a very serious conversation with Dom Hilary. You realize that I have known him for a very long time. I would rather not have to put into words all that I feel and all that I have been thinking as a result of that conversation, unless your Reverence will open the way for me yourself."

For a moment she stopped. Then she continued in a clear, expressive voice: "I have very definite ideas about Benedictine life and the life of a religious in general. These ideas are clear and, I believe, very sound. And I am greatly alarmed about everything which is going on. Mother Cecilia, the Novice

Mistress, is no longer any help to me. She knows it. She herself has asked me to seek advice elsewhere . . . but I am purposely avoiding discussing these questions with Mother Stanislaus. So then . . . I have no one but you to turn to, Mother. It is legitimate that I should come to you, but my choice is also prompted by preference and affection. Will you allow me to explain myself more clearly?"

For an instant Mother Anselm's expression was clouded with melancholy. But already Sister John of the Cross's eyes were shining with a light from which all sweetness had disappeared. Gone also was that suggestion of childhood which at times contrasted so strangely with the general purpose of her words.

"Mother," she said, in a completely confident voice, "Mother, this is not a question of judging the characteristics of those set over us. It is not a question of personal attraction or antipathy. It is a question of very serious matters. Nothing was more irremediably condemned by Our Lord than the giving of scandal . . . nothing."

Mother Anselm made a calming gesture. "My dear child . . . we are sometimes required to live for years with a wound in our very heart. Saint Paul has already provided an answer to all our perplexities by saying that everything works together for good and to the sanctification of those who love God. You have told Dom Hilary about your fears. Others, no doubt, said very much the same thing, according to their character, the form of their spirituality, and also their age and experience."

"And also their overwhelming inertia, which surely cannot come from God, Mother. That is startlingly obvious to those of us whose spirit is still unfettered. Oh! I am well aware that inertia is sometimes the frustrated expression of despair. But——"

"I was speaking of their experience and the supernatural insight which is given them," the Prioress calmly continued, "which indeed come to the same thing in the end."

She was speaking with the tranquil courtesy of those who, by the choice of their words, by their intonations and their movements, let it be understood that they have been thoroughly examining, over a long period, a problem which, though serious, is none the less soluble. That everything will come right in the end, to the advantage of those who know how to wait and keep their serenity during the most unusual and trying circumstances.

The young nun had blushed deeply.

"Please forgive me, Mother," she said after a moment, her face still burning.

The filtered sunlight softened and mellowed her expression. An indulgent clarity was filtering through to her.

"I think that Dom Hilary will have known how to assess the whole situation," continued the Prioress. "A canonical visitation is a serious undertaking, full of significance. In an abbey with so many subjects as we have, the light is sure to triumph in the end: for the greater good of all concerned."

"Mother . . . oh! What can I say to you? If it was only a question of one act, or even of a number of isolated, unconnected acts. But it is a whole spirit. It is no longer possible to give way to such unreasonable claims, such exaggerated ideas. God cannot ratify what He does not inspire."

"God always sanctions the acts of a legitimate and canonical authority, my child. They will soon be teaching you in your theological studies that even if God's permissive will puzzles us, it is still holy."

There was a silence which Mother Anselm purposely did not break.

"What is to be done?" Sister John of the Cross said at last. Her hands were folded on her knees. Her childlike simplicity and charm had returned. Only a slight touch of sadness still remained.

"But there is nothing to be done! Wait, little Sister. Wait, and keep yourself interiorly at God's disposal. That is all He asks. From the confidences they have received, our superiors

will know how to reach conclusion which will make everything clear. You can rest assured of that."

They stood up. Mother Anselm was already accompanying
the young nun to the door. The smile on her habitually gentle
face was serene again. She radiated maternal charm.

There was no mention of the Mother Abbess. This silence
was more significant than speech.

14

Rain was falling over the town. It was four o'clock in the
afternoon. On one side of the Cathedral Square there was
a girls' High School and next to it an annex for the higher
examination classes. Groups of children were coming out.
They hurried off to the neighbouring streets, their heads bent
over armfuls of books or leather satchels which they were
hugging.

The lilac trees in the Archbishop's gardens filled the air with
fragrance, made more penetrating and heady by the rain.
It was a gentle spring rain, but it was setting in for the night,
enveloping the rose-coloured town in a mantle of grey.

Some of the large Gothic windows on the first floor of the
Archbishop's Palace were shutting one by one. There was a
grating of rusty gates and the clanking of chains and falling
padlocks. A long black car entered the precincts. Then, once
more, there was the sound of chains and padlocks as the gates
were locked. Someone was running in the courtyard. Then
all fell back into silence. The clock struck a quarter past four.

In front of the school, nurses were waiting for the younger
children to come out.

"Apart from these personal letters, I have been through all
the evening post, your Excellency. There is very little of

interest. There is this, however, which has to do with the Abbey of D——. Your Excellency will have to take a look at it."

"The copy of the report on Dom Hilary's canonical visitation? Yes, I know." The Archbishop sighed. "They have already telephoned to me from Rome about it. Last night. I have not spoken to you about it yet, Father, because I find these matters so irritating. I might say that they have been poisoning my existence for several weeks—that would be nearer the truth."

A single lamp lit the immense table with its tray of thick, dark-coloured wood, leaving the rest of the office in semi-darkness.

"There is also this, your Excellency."

The priest held out a square envelope, addressed in firm, vigorous characters. "This also comes from D——. I recognize the handwriting. I have not opened it."

Deliberately the Archbishop unsealed the letters. The topaz of his ring made a brilliant splash of colour on his veined hand.

"Mother de Neuville will always be a surprising woman," he said after reading it.

The priest stood silent. He was a man of forty. His face had a look of energy, and he had a strange expression which, though conciliatory, was full of a hidden forcefulness.

"Come on! Say something, Father. You surely have some interesting ideas about these questions. Each time that you have remained silent over serious problems, it has turned out afterwards that your silence was to be regretted."

"No, your Excellency, no. I have nothing to say, precisely. Still less, since this time I do not know anything about the grievances of Mother Stanislaus. As she had just seen the visitor, I imagine her letter concerns something quite recent."

The Archbishop held out the letter.

"Oh! There are no grievances. There are only two lines. She wants to leave for Rome, and naturally this clashes with the ideas Mother Hildegard has on the subject. But what can I do? She has studied Canon Law enough to know that in circumstances of this kind I am powerless."

The Archbishop was well over sixty. He might have been sixty-five, but was more probably sixty-seven or sixty-eight. He was handsome, with blue eyes and completely white hair. Gold spectacles with tinted lenses protected his short-sighted eyes. His absent-mindedness and his kindliness were legendary. A peculiar youthfulness in his old age gave him an aura of innocence.

"Well then?" he asked.

"Your Excellency, I do not think we share the same ideas about these questions," said the priest.

"Are you speaking of the problem as a whole? Or are you thinking of the journey to Rome?" asked the Archbishop with a sudden smile of good-humour.

"I am speaking of the problem as a whole. For that matter it all hangs together."

"I suppose, then, that your views fit in with those of the canonical visitor, Father. I am going to read the report. It is my duty to do so, although I can more or less guess the essentials. But it does not come under our jurisdiction. I shall therefore be fully in agreement with you in saying that these problems are beyond us."

"You are right, your Excellency. These problems are beyond us. They have passed beyond us *now*, in any case."

"They were always beyond us, my dear friend. When I was appointed to this archbishopric, Mother Rouart was already Abbess. Moreover, the canonical election of an abbess is independent of us and outside our control. You know that. And unless something serious occurs, we cannot intervene."

Five o'clock struck.

"What exactly does your Excellency mean by 'something serious'?" the priest asked with calm confidence.

"Scandals."

His tone suddenly became definite and sharp with a kind of hardness which was unusual in his voice.

The priest passed his well-shaped hand over his face.

"I know that one generally uses the word scandal in a rather special and precise sense," he said. "And yet. . . . You see, it bothers me when I find certain incoherencies raised to the dignity of a method."

The Archbishop turned abruptly. "My dear Father . . . the death of the little novice was an accident." He stressed the word heavily. "An accident of a disciplinary order. It was that, and not more than that. It is to be regretted, but we cannot do anything about it. It is not for us to enter into considerations which touch on the fundamental spirit of the Abbey. Mother Rouart is the sole judge of her government. When all is said and done, her only fault was that she was too fervent—too full of zeal."

"Your Excellency, the virtue of prudent discretion is one of those which Saint Benedict recommended most highly to his abbesses. Since you have asked me what I think, my opinion is that we have come to a very serious turning point. The paramount importance which is given in the Abbey of D—— to a harshly exaggerated tension of effort as opposed to the joyful accomplishment of God's will—that is what falsifies the whole perspective of the monastic state. Spiritual life has its classical disciplines, like all philosophies. As soon as one departs from them. . . . And I mistrust the exaltation of certain hidden forces of the instinct. The most well-reasoned pretexts do not succeed in disguising its romantic side. This gives grounds for uneasiness. Dom Hilary's report seems positive on this subject. He asks for a control. That speaks for itself."

The Archbishop was still silent. No doubt he was listening to the sound of rain falling on the leaves outside.

"And a control requested by a canonical vicar," continued the priest, "means no less than the nomination of a coadjutrix."

"You must be mad!"

"Once again, your Excellency, there are facts. And this time the facts are precise. And I am not speaking of the accident which happened; only of the canonical report and the telephone call from Rome. And of all that is to follow. All that this will bring in its train."

The priest's voice was calm and steady, in spite of the intense feeling behind it. One was conscious of all the detachment he was imposing upon himself. The Archbishop sighed.

"I know," he said at last. "I know."

"Personally, you see," the priest continued, "I should go so far as to think that moral irregularities which, unfortunately, occur from time to time in certain monasteries are of far less importance than the problem before us now."

"But, after all . . ." said the old man with some emotion. "After all. . . . How worked up you are, Father!"

"Yes, your Excellency, as a rule moral scandals in religious houses remain isolated events in our day. We are no longer living in the sixteenth century, nor the eighteenth, remember. In an abbey like the one of which we are talking, where the subjects are all well-bred, conventions are respected and things can be kept quiet. Generally the removal of one person settles the whole business to everybody's advantage. But you will not be able to prevent the matter we are now discussing from smelling of heresy—from coming dangerously close to the stake. That is something of a very different order! Do you realize, your Excellency, that there are souls who are being ravaged in some monasteries?" he added. "Souls who are being mortally wounded, hounded to death, destroyed. And might we not see such a place as one of the gates of that human hell, that hell which begins here on earth, of that kingdom which is, like the other, within ourselves? Moreover the facts do not matter much. That which holds the power always exceeds that which is in process of development."

The Archbishop crossed his hands over the blotter. There was a knock at the door. A footman was bringing in the tea.

"Sit down, Father. You are quite right to talk. I always value your views. The diocese keeps us very busy, and there are plenty of problems of quite a different nature. I am going to think this over. You see, they want me to go to the abbey. They want me to see Mother Rouart. To be very precise with her. To try. . . . But, gracious heavens! What am I to do? It is well known that my relations with her Grace are most affectionate. How difficult it all is. How difficult, Father."

The priest remained silent. In a corner of the room there was a fine portrait of Bossuet, and, on a table, a bunch of anemones.

15

"I received your letter last night, Mother. It was too late to come then. I had to wait till the morning. Dom Gregory will have brought you my brief message when he came to celebrate the first Mass."

"Thank you for coming so quickly, Most Reverend Father. It is true that I am very much disturbed. I had a visit from Monsignor[1] yesterday afternoon. But let us sit down."

The Abbess's parlour, with its red velvet hangings and polished furniture, and its full-length portraits of former patron cardinals, was bathed in cheerful sunshine. The light fell full on a sketch made by Titian for his portrait of the Farnese Pope (Paul III), so that it stood out—striking and strangely alive.

It was ten o'clock, and the morning was full of the song of birds.

The Father Abbot, Dom Germain Delors, who ruled over the neighbouring abbey, was a man of medium height. His

[1] Monsignor is the common title of bishops in France.

age was probably a little over forty. He was thick-set and vigorous almost to the point of roughness. His eyes were quick, his speech decisive. His somewhat abrupt manner was a little startling until it was recognized as the characteristic of a man of action.

"The canonical visitation is over, Father. . . ."

"I know. It seemed to me that it lasted longer than usual? I saw Dom Lemaître only twice, and very briefly. I had the impression that he did not wish to prolong our interviews. At any rate, just then. I am so excessively busy myself that . . . Well, Mother, what do you want to tell me? Are you worried about anything?"

"Father . . . I am still astounded by the interview I had with Monsignor. Have some of the Sisters been complaining? Has my government been taking too severe a line? Demanding too rigorous a stripping of self? It appears that Dom Hilary made a report to this effect? You know how kind and considerate his Excellency is. I imagine that there are a great many things still left for me to discover; that the most important have been kept from me."

The Abbot was silent for a while.

"Mother Hildegard," he said at last, "an ordinary canonical visitation does not produce results so quickly. Nor is it so meticulous and so long-drawn-out: even in an abbey as populous as yours. I therefore beg you to look back into the past and see if you can remember anything which could give grounds for uneasiness. Anything of a much earlier date. Dom Hilary appeared to me to have more than ordinary powers: to be already well-informed. Of course, he gave no explicit sign of this; but it was in the air. This visit had a dangerous resemblance to an Apostolic Investigation; and you must know that the powers of the Apostolic Visitor are immense—I might almost say unlimited."

The Abbess reflected. She said nothing.

"To tell the truth," the Abbott continued, "I was elected only three years ago, and I know very little about your abbey.

At least beneath the surface. There are elements with which I am perfectly well acquainted—the most representative. There are others about which I know scarcely anything. As for the community as a whole? The body of the Abbey? My impressions are very vague. I only know what you tell me, and what the Sisters who come to me for advice tell me. Your surprise today proves. . . ."

"I think that your Grace sees Mother Stanislaus very regularly?" the Abbess said with great calm.

Dom Germain gave a smile in which there was a certain amount of irony and reproach.

"Come, Mother. . . . Do not let us mix these serious matters —which are also important matters—with petty quarrels which are in great part baseless. I know that you have again refused to let her go. I have already told you that I disapprove of this attitude where there seems to be—where, indeed, there is—a system involved. The journey to Rome is neither good nor bad in itself. . . . For you must agree that this is an exceptional case. I have not advised you to allow her to go. Nor have I advised you to keep her here. I have merely advised you not to make yourself hated unnecessarily. Your relations are already strained enough; and this has been going on for a long time. There is urgent need for conciliations. You have confided the care of your soul to me. . . ."

"But not that of my government."

The Abbott raised his head. "Yes. These are obviously shades of meaning which have escaped me. I have no gift for such subtleties. Mother Stanislaus is also my daughter. I see her frequently, in fact. The least that can be said is that my task is not easy between you two."

"I shall not change my mind with regard to the journey to Rome, Father; nor with regard to any other change of abode. I have very fixed views about our vow of stability."

"You have very fixed views about everything, Mother Hildegard. I am afraid you are the only person not to admit it. But we have already been discussing that for a long time.

I have told you what I feel. I will not repeat it. What is important today seems to me to lie elsewhere. Does it? Yes or no?" the Abbot added, with a shade of harshness in his voice, while the Abbess remained silent.

In the distance a bell sounded. It rang out three times; then five. The sky was a beautiful satiny blue. Through the window the plum trees were a mass of white blossom.

"What do you want me to say to you, Father? Monsignor was very evasive." The Abbot made a gesture as though to say that he had guessed as much—that he knew it, without anyone taking the trouble to tell him. "His Excellency has put me on my guard. I did not imagine that I had enemies among the Sisters. . . . For that matter I make no difference between my daughters."

"And there you are wrong. There is nothing more stupid, and sometimes nothing more unjust, than to give equal treatment where there is no equality."

"I mean to say that I show myself kind and helpful to each one. I try to rouse some of my subjects from their torpor and to spur them on to virtue. That is all. I think that my intentions are pure."

The Abbot was listening. With his left hand he had taken hold of the golden cross which he wore on a chain of heavy square links. It was a flat cross, inlaid with ivory.

"Your intentions, yes. I think that among all the people who must by now be studying this problem, and, believe me, there are quite a few, not one doubts the purity of your intentions. That is not the question. The personal tendency of your spirit inclines you to narrowness and restriction. You know it. It is an affair between God and you. Until today I did not see anything in it to give cause for alarm, although such tendencies must always be kept under control. They need careful guidance. In a word, they are rather bad signs in the spiritual life . . . destructive . . . and for my part I should on the whole prefer the opposite tendency. But be that as it may. . . . Things become more serious, however, where your government is concerned. Apart from what is definitely laid down in our Holy Rule and Constitution, you should give your daughters full liberty, Mother Hildegard. And even where the Rule is involved, you should know how to offer them certain mitigations, certain facilities, certain latitudes. I insist upon this. The Rule was made for the Sisters, not the Sisters for the Rule. Suffering does not necessarily have a purifying effect. Psychological shocks can produce the very consequences which they are intended to prevent. You should do as I say, and this is all the more essential because you cannot trust yourself in a certain direction—and you know precisely what I mean."

The face of the Abbess was like a mask, except for a shade of something which might have been compassion.

"Oh! I am under no delusion," the monk continued. "You have an able mind, where everything is well arranged, with order and method. But you lack a certain unction . . . that unction which has nothing to do with outward forms, but with the counsel of souls. That unction which is so necessary for all who govern."

"Most Reverend Father. There is Christ our Lord and there is our holy Rule. I see nothing else."

There was an urgent insistence in the eyes of the Abbot, and a shade of hesitation before what he had to say.

"Yes, indeed," he said at last. "Monsieur de Saint-Cyran[1] said just that."

There was a long silence.

"Mother, we said very little at the time about little Sister Andrew's accident," the monk began again.

There passed across the face of the Abbess a cloud of overwhelming depression which settled into hardness.

"It was an accident, Father," she said. "A very sad and regrettable accident."

"An accident which could have been avoided," continued the Abbot.

[1] A Jansenist theologian, 1581–1643.

"Yes, if Sister Andrew had come in in time. That is obvious. As soon as the snow began to fall she should have come in. It is as clear as day, in fact. . . ."

"An accident which could have been avoided if you had chosen a penance better suited to the weather and the time of year. Don't you agree, Mother?"

The Abbess made a vague gesture. "I could not foresee that it would be snowing just then," she said. "Anyone else would have come in. Sister Andrew's judgment was very uncertain and unstable," she added. "She was below the average of our Sisters, in spite of her birth and education."

"I can understand that you prefer this explanation. Obviously it is simpler. But it might also be argued that it was in this house, this abbey which you have been ruling over for twelve years, Mother Hildegard, that this uncertain and unstable judgment had become so deformed. Am I not right?"

"Most Reverend Father. I repeat yet again that as soon as the snow began to fall, anybody else would have come in. And one can always endure the cold. I never ask the Sisters to do anything of which I have not had experience myself."

"The thermometer was at minus nineteen degrees centigrade that night; or perhaps lower. It was two o'clock in the morning: that is the time when the temperature is at its lowest."

There was a silence.

"Sister Andrew was a very undistinguished novice, very colourless. . . ." the Abbess said at last.

"But one who carried obedience to the point of death, Mother. That should touch you, surely."

"The reaction of the Sisters at the time of this unfortunate affair was unanimous. They thought her insignificant and foolish."

"How easy you are to deceive, Mother, when your interest is involved. I have five daughters here in your convent. I see them every week. I hear their confessions. I have long talks with them. There was not one of them whose opinion was not the reverse of what you suggest. And it was unhesitating and completely spontaneous. What you term 'this unfortunate affair' was the subject of a great many conversations, I assure you. A great many comments were made. And the gist of them all had a meaning which seems to have escaped you entirely."

"Thank God! I have my loyal subjects. They are numerous and they are among the most fervent."

"In any case they are among the most proud, Mother. That is beyond doubt."

The voice of the Father Abbot had a new solemnity which betrayed an unaccustomed sadness.

Behind the grille, seated in her high-backed armchair, the Abbess remained distant. And in her face was a look of indomitable assurance.

"I only returned to this subject," said the Abbot, "in order to bring its importance home to you. Now that difficulties have arisen, it goes without saying that I will help you as well as I can, if need be. But I am afraid that it will not be as easy as one might at first think. If Rome begins to move in the matter, it may go far. . . . What did his Excellency actually say to you?" he added in a different tone.

"Monsignor advised me to use prudence, or perhaps I could better describe it as a kind of diplomacy, which is rather an odious quality, I think you must agree. I am not broken in to such exercise."

"That is the least one can say," the Abbot remarked with a smile.

"Father, my government is open to the full light of day. It is what I think God wishes it to be. I make no mysteries about what I do. And it is not in my character to agree to things of which I disapprove simply for the sake of peace. That would be very much like complicity."

"Peace is a most excellent state. It is the motto of our Order. You must seek it. Think about that."

"If I listened to his Excellency, this abbey would soon cease to be a monastic house. Monsignor uses different words from you, Father, but in the end what you both say comes to very much the same thing," she added with a smile and tone which would have seemed candid to anyone but herself.

"His Excellency is not your director, and he and I are not the same in character—nor the same age. But since it has come about that we can find common ground in such a serious matter, there must be some reason for our agreement. I hope that you will be willing to profit by his advice. For the future you must show yourself to be flexible. And God grant that it will not be too late."

"Thank you for coming so soon, Most Reverend Father," said the Abbess in a tone which had once more become natural and gay. "Would you like to see any of the other nuns?"

"I will come back tomorrow. Today I have to go to the town with my cellarer. It is already past eleven. Goodbye for the present, Mother," he added bowing, "and I beg you to keep and guide your house with gentleness and pliancy. There is everything to be gained that way."

Already the Abbess was drawing the black gauze curtain across the grille.

The first bell sounded for the Office of Sext.

16

It was the day after the Abbot's visit. That last week of April was a miracle of mild loveliness. On an oak stand in the Abbess's office there was a large bouquet of Spanish lilac. Its dark violet clusters were close and heavy, hanging like bunches of grapes which scented the air. On the writing-table there was a bowl of short-stemmed roses. It was two o'clock.

The Two Nuns

The Abbess came in and went to shut the windows. Then she called her secretary by telephone.

"Mother Dominic," she said when the latter appeared. "Will you please take away this bowl of roses. Don't you really think the lilac is enough? For some time past the air in this office has been stifling. Anybody would think it was a florist's shop."

Her tone was short and ironical, and her eyes had none of that sweetness which, though rare, sometimes illuminated them, tempering everything.

"And will you please ask Mother Vicar to come here?" she continued. "She should be in one of the libraries or in the print room. If not, ask the portress to ring for her."

The young Mother had flushed. Her hand was trembling a little on the crystal rose-bowl.

"Yes, Mother," she said, bowing low.

For a fairly long time the Abbess went on writing. Then there was a light tap on the door and the Mother Vicar came in.

She was young—about thirty-five, perhaps—tall and slim, with grace in her bearing and movements. But her face was austere and sad and had the thin transparency which comes from watching and abstinence. She nearly always kept her slender hands hidden in the long sleeves of her habit, so that only her finger-tips showed.

The Abbess gave her a smile full of solicitude.

"Come, Mother Mechtild. Sit down, my dear daughter. We have a full hour before Vespers to discuss our business. Have you reflected about it?"

The Mother Vicar's gentle eyes lit up with the radiance of black diamonds.

"I do not need to reflect, Mother. I only have to obey. I am afraid, all the same, that I am very inexperienced for so heavy a task. And very young."

Her voice was low and moving. It was one of those voices which the ear follows in all its modulations, as though each

89

sentence were an arrangement of notes which could never be repeated.

"I considered the whole thing for a long time before I spoke to you about it, my daughter. Your health made me a little anxious, but since you tell me you are well, I think there is no reason to draw back. Mother Cecilia needs a rest which she certainly deserves, and she has been urging me for a very long time to relieve her of her charge. You would take over the novitiate after Pentecost. By then the indult papers will have had time to come from Rome authorising you to hold this office in spite of your youth. I will write off for them this very evening, and from today you can go to the novitiate when it suits you, and Mother Cecilia will explain everything to you. It goes without saying that afterwards you will organise your little community as you think best. You have my complete confidence. It is an office which demands tact and firmness, and entails all kinds of anxieties. I know that most of the novices like you. Everything will be all right. As for your being so young, that will not matter. Fervour and the religious spirit are all that count, and they will make up for every human insufficiency. Responsibilities develop us and enable us to grow in stature. If we are deprived of them, our personality dwindles."

The young Mother gave a charming smile.

"I will try to provide for everything," she said.

They talked together for a long time. Then the Abbess had to go to the parlour. Three o'clock was striking. She did not go to Vespers that day. The portress had announced the visit of a Dominican Father who could not wait.

The conversation lasted a long time. Then the Abbess went down to the large parlour on the ground floor. She looked very grave and her eyes seemed enlarged against the pallor of her face. The Prioress was summoned by two strokes of the bell which rang out sharp and precise as though isolated in the silence of the Abbey.

Then it was the Mother Vicar who was called by three

rapid strokes, as though things were suddenly being pre-cipitated.

In like manner each of the Mothers of the Council were summoned. There were whisperings. The Mother Portress and the novice who helped her carried rush-bottomed chairs to the parlour. For a moment while the nuns were taking their places, the door remained ajar. The black curtain had already been drawn. Beyond the grille a friar in a white habit was standing. He was wearing a black cape, as for preaching or a canonical act.

The friar's face was placid and calm. He said nothing. It was Father Mareuil. Someone closed the door after the nuns.

17

The week that followed was portentous. The Abbess scarcely left her apartments. She presided at the communal exercises in Choir, but did not appear either at meals or recreations. During the walks in the gardens a group of novices used to gather together. They were always the same and they talked together in lowered voices. Surprise and wondering expecta-tion were written on their faces; and also a certain subdued tranquillity, as though in the presence of things which from now on could not be stopped in their course.

Mother Cecilia seemed to notice nothing. She knew that these were her last days in the novitiate, and she surrounded her daughters with affectionate solicitude. Mother Anselm presided over the nuns' recreations with her usual calm. Her inherent precision and her faultless manners were marked with a very special gentleness. The Mothers of the Council generally kept together in their walks. That was the custom.

Mother Stanislaus had a dreamy light in her eyes. During the hours of relaxation she seldom left the side of Sister John of the Cross, but their conversations, which were shared by two recently professed young nuns whose studies the Mother was directing, were remarkable for their indifference and detachment with regard to the subject which seemed to be overwhelming the whole community.

The Mother Vicar walked through the cloisters with her usual grace. She had extraordinary eyes, which seemed to contain an interior light.

Father Anthony, who spent his days in the confessional, came out with his face a little paler, and mauve shadows under his eyes. The oblate Sisters held their tongues. Visitors, who were always numerous, were received with the customary hospitality. But the Abbess scarcely came down any more to the parlour. The Abbot had been back and had shut himself in with her for a long time. Behind his tortoise-shell glasses Father Gregory looked thoughtful, his face tinged with an habitual irony.

May spread as it were two symbolical white wings in a sky powdered with gold. On this particular day they would be singing the first Vespers of Saint Monica.

The Abbey seemed to be resting peacefully in the midst of woods and meadows. Recreation was over and had been followed as usual by the Office of None. Two o'clock sounded.

And, immediately after the two sonorous strokes, the little bell started its interminable tinkling to summon the nuns to Chapter: five hundred shrill little notes, coming separately as though through a filter, and continuing for a quarter of an hour. A single chime of the big bell had warned the novices that the Chapter today was an extraordinary one and that they were not invited. The doors of the Chapter-house were open—the four doors. Beyond the closed windows the light must have been intense. It was scarcely dimmed but, as it were, variegated by the richly coloured glasses. The nuns went to their places.

Then silence fell. The doors were closed. The Abbess's stall was still empty. There was a long pause, during which no one spoke, no one made a movement.

In front of the Abbess's throne the bronze urn had been placed. The urn with its contours worn with age, and its green and old-gold reflections. Finally the Prioress left her stall and came to stand erect at a distance of a few paces from the urn.

"Your Reverences know why we have all come together today," she said in a calm voice. "Our Mother Abbess feels seriously unwell, and has asked the Ordinary to grant her a coadjutrix. We are here to choose someone who, for a time, will relieve our Most Reverend Mother of some part of her burden. We will do this in the liberty of our hearts, not forgetting, however, that the common good and the general interest of the community must guide our every step."

The nuns, who had turned slightly towards her, returned her bow.

She went back to her stall in silence. The chanting of the *Veni Creator* rose with slow solemnity as though expressive of an austere enthusiasm. Then the nuns sat down. There was a barely audible movement while two Mothers from among the youngest passed with blank slips of paper along the rows of stalls.

Then there was a period of waiting, hardly disturbed by the sounds of nuns kneeling, of swinging rosaries, the creaking of wood, deep breathing and sighs.

A full quarter of an hour passed. Then the procession towards the urn began.

The first Cantor intoned *a capella* the canticle of ascent— its lovely phrases succeeding each other like an incantation.

"I was glad when they said unto me: We will go into the

house of the Lord. Jerusalem is my native land. Jerusalem is my Mother!"

Meanwhile the nuns slowly advanced in procession towards the urn; their eyes lowered and the squares of folded paper hidden beneath their sleeves.

At last the Chapter was reformed. The nuns were seated in silence. The Prioress opened the urn with its heavy pad-locks. She held out the unfolded papers one by one to the Mother Vicar, who was helping her. It was done very quickly. She scarcely paused to write from time to time, noting a name in a black notebook. Her face showed nothing. It seemed as though the two nuns were carrying out some ritual. And the face of the Mother Vicar was equally expressionless.

Finally the last paper had been placed in the wicker basket. The Mother Vicar went back to her place. The Prioress remained standing in front of the open urn. She was still silent. Her face was very pale now. A strange wave of emotion passed through the assembly. The faces, which up to this moment had been impassive, began to turn towards her.

She gave a slight cough. Perhaps it was to clear her throat?

"With the exception of thirty-nine votes given either to Mother Stanislaus de Neuville or myself," she said quietly, "your choice is unanimously in favour of the Most Reverend Mother Hildegard Rouart, already holding the office of Abbess in this community. As the majority is clear and the decision of the capitulary nuns, united in a canonical assembly, is irrevocable, there can obviously be no second ballet."

A moment drifted by—like the wing of a passing dove.

"We can therefore disperse," she added, with a kindly smile.

The Mothers came down from their stalls and began to take off their *coulles*. The doors were opened. Groups began to form on the landing and in the cloakrooms.

The bell was already ringing for Vespers.

18

"What did I tell you, Father Gregory? Wasn't I right? You must allow me the privilege of knowing this community better than you do."

Father Anthony had rather a dry smile, indicating his satisfaction, not at the result obtained, but at having foreseen it in advance. Two days had passed since the Chapter. It was the end of a lovely day—about six o'clock. The weather was glorious. The priests were returning to their abbey by the little forest paths. The river was winding its way beneath a shimmering haze. The stillness of night was descending when nothing but the rustling of the waving corn kept the dogs alert. The monks were walking through the luxuriant undergrowth, with regular steps which kept time with the rhythm of their conversation and their anxieties. Father Gregory seemed thoughtful.

"I should like to know how Mother Stanislaus feels after this decision of the Chapter," Don Anthony said.

A blackbird whistled. The drawn-out modulations of its song seemed full of irony.

"You see," Father Gregory said at last, not replying directly, "there is something a little disconcerting in this attitude of the nuns as they face so serious a measure as this request for a decision to be taken at a canonical assembly. I do not know whether any good will come of it. I don't want to be a Cassandra, but nevertheless I am afraid that we are again approaching a battle."

"Oh. I know that you were deprived of the votes of a certain group of novices whose ideas on this question are a matter of little doubt among their acquaintances," responded the Father Confessor. "All the same, you must agree that they would not have changed the result. The huge majority of votes for Mother Hildegard is surely the work of the Holy Spirit."

"My dear Father. Do not let us talk about the Holy Spirit, who has very little to do with it, and, I am afraid, remains far outside these disputes. Nor do I know why you should find it necessary to imply that I am involved in them."

His tone was calm, and not without dignity, but a certain discreet and smiling irony was to be felt beneath the surface.

"It is no mystery for anyone, Father Gregory, that you are the director of nearly all the subjects opposed to the Abbess. There is no reproach in this; it is a simple fact. Moreover they are, from certain points of view, the most interesting. That little Sister John of the Cross, for instance, is like a force of nature, with all the audacity, all the effrontery of such a force. She would tackle the Holy Father himself!"

There was a depth of affectionate pride in the smile which passed across Dom Gregory's face. Neither of them spoke; they went on walking slowly, crumpling between their fingers the sweet-smelling herbs which grew along their path.

Then Father Gregory broke the silence. "I should like to return to what I was saying just now," he resumed. "For my part, I see the vote of the Chapter as revolutionary, with a touch of something which, it must be admitted, comes very near to insolence. Now then, Father Anthony, don't you really agree with me in your heart?"

The Father Confessor hesitated. It was his nature never to get too deeply involved, but now his hesitation was due rather to his humility and lack of confidence in himself. He was too well aware of Father Gregory's dialectical powers, and knew what a formidable adversary he could be once he made up his mind to defend a point of view.

"Everything depends upon the way in which the matter was presented to the nuns," he said. "I do not yet know anything about that. I have seen only a few of them since the Chapter, and it is clear that they prefer to hold their tongues on these questions. The Abbey Council was fully informed about the reality of the steps which had been taken. There is no question of that. They knew that Rome was acting through Father Mareuil. The stupefaction of certain Mothers was at its height, I can assure you, when the Father announced himself to be a delegate of the Holy Office. But the body of the abbey knew nothing. I realize that news travels quickly, but there is a certain incredulity so deeply entrenched that it cannot be shaken. For the majority of the nuns the reality was an impossibility."

"I am afraid I cannot believe that, Father. Perhaps the community only spoke about it in whispers, but you may be sure they spoke about it."

"I do not think so. No! I tell you I do not think so. They spoke about it in a certain circle, perhaps. Indeed they must surely have done so. But the circle is closed, very exclusive. For the community as a whole, it was given out that Mother Hildegard was unwell and had asked the Archbishop to relieve her from her responsibilities for the time being. They were all delighted to accept this explanation, a little far-fetched, I grant you, as a way out of the difficulty."

"Yet this was something rather abnormal, if you come to think of it. It was surprising enough, given the nature of our constitution, but incredible for anyone who knows Mother Rouart in the slightest degree."

"Yes, I am quite ready to agree with you there. But, all the same, it is a fact."

They were coming to a clearing which was in full sunlight. They were already entering the grounds of Saint Benedict's. The grey stone of its majestic steeple would soon be visible beyond the trunks of chestnut trees. The birds and black-and-yellow striped insects were waking up after the heat of the day. A hymn of praise rose from them, which mingled with the sounds of the nearby farm.

Two lay brothers with long beards came into sight. They were wearing brown overalls and were in charge of the hutches.

They were pushing two large low wheelbarrows, filled with a moving mass of soft, delicate fur. It seemed as though all the rabbits of Australia had suddenly emigrated to the abbey.

"There are also people for whom humour is a pleasure," said Father Gregory in a dreamy tone. "It comes as a relaxation from the discipline of the day."

"I do not think there is any humour in this abbey," the Father Confessor replied firmly.

"There is, Father Anthony. There is humour all right. I am afraid you only judge by appearances. You will find it below the surface, I assure you. And I am not speaking of my daughters. With them it is the contrary. The Mothers and novices I direct give an important place to rationalism. Their minds are precise. They see things very clearly, anticipating their developments and possible conclusion. There are in the abbey elements accustomed to the exercise of subtlety in quite a different manner. They are generally silent souls."

Father Anthony was perplexed. He moved the tip of his finger across his forehead, which was a little furrowed like the rest of his face.

"It is not necessary to look very far," Father Gregory continued. "Mother Anselm provides us with living testimony."

"Mother Prioress is a perfect Benedictine nun," said Father Anthony. "She has judgment, virtue and gentle manners."

Dom Gregory settled into a sort of interior dream, from which all anxieties were banished.

"One never knows exactly what she is thinking," he said. "She is not easy to fathom. From what I hear she does not belong to any group or clique. It seems as though nothing is less final than her judgment of people and events. Nevertheless it seems to me that she is not very much in favour of Mother Hildegard. This is not the result of any personal investigations. It is just an impression."

"It is true she is quite detached from everybody, with no special intimacies, nor does she receive any of the Fathers in particular. As far as her own affairs are concerned, at any rate."

They were approaching the outbuildings of the farm. The cherry trees were blossoming.

"The interesting thing now," said Dom Gregory, "will be to see the reaction of Rome."

He suddenly sounded amused, and his tone contrasted with the seriousness of the subject.

The Father Confessor considered him with an interest mingled with reproach and anxiety.

"You mean to say?"

"Well, I mean to say . . . I do not think that Rome will accept the situation with all the detachment which seems to be expected. That is all. Oh, nothing else at all!"

Dom Anthony had a worried look; he seemed to withdraw completely.

They had reached the cloister with its garden, pink with apple-blossom. The golden light from across a field spangled with a thousand daisies dazzled them.

They stopped.

"I will be seeing you later, Brother," Dom Gregory said in friendly fashion, with the captivating smile which was so valuable a means of winning souls. "Goodbye till then. Don't be too disturbed by all this. Things always work out all right in the end!"

"God's will will be done, whatever happens, Father Gregory. I never have a doubt of that."

His tone was cold. His eyes without a smile. "I am not talking of God, Father, but of men."

Dom Gregory moved away. It was a heavenly evening. The sky was pale green, with trails of reddish gold which warmed the heart.

At Saint Benedict's the great bell was ringing the Angelus.

19

The suggestion that Rome would not accept the situation with detachment was certainly no overstatement.

It was Trinity Sunday. The sun was blazing down from a cloudless sky and the courtyard of the Holy Office was like a furnace. The closely-mown lawns looked dried up and without promise, as though all vegetable growth had been annihilated.

The Cardinal Prefect stood beside a half-open window. He was wearing his scarlet moiré cassock. He had slipped his fingers between the red buttons at the place where the gold chain was fastened to his mozetta. He held a sheet of type-script which he was reading with close attention. His face was very pale and showed the utmost annoyance. At the big table two black-coated priests were seated in deep armchairs; two priests who must have been bishops. They were young. That is to say, they were young for bishops—about forty-five to fifty years old. They seemed to be dreaming. Their hands were pale. One of them wore purple socks and buckle shoes. The other looked like an ordinary priest except for a huge ruby ring which glowed on his right hand, like a sombre, blood-coloured drop.

"Oh, so that is the way my envoys are received!" said the Cardinal, coming back to the table. "Well! These nuns had better not make a slip . . . not a single slip, do you understand, my Lords? Or I shall depose Mother Rouart? Purely and simply, I shall depose her. She will have to go to a Trappist convent where she can give herself over to all the eccentricities she likes. We have had enough of this! Never did I imagine things had reached such a point. Pride . . . pride incarnate . . . a Satanic leaven . . . that is what this woman is! God only knows what has been fermenting in silence . . . for months, for years perhaps."

He spoke with sharp gestures, walking about the office, striking the furniture as he passed. His anger was like a torrent. He was breathing hard as he restrained his fury. The bishops held their tongues. Suddenly he turned to one of them (the one with purple socks) and said point-blank, his voice still sharp and with an underlying sarcasm: "What does the Archbishop have to say about it? What does he think of this rebellion? Why are you smiling? Oh, I know well enough that the diocese is accustomed to little upsets. But all the same! This passes all limits."

"Monsignor de T. is an old man, your Eminence. A man of very ancient lineage. Distinguished for his courtliness and good breeding. He is a Montfort. You know that. He is more at home in drawing-rooms than abbeys. Besides, I think he is optimistic in his philosophy with regard to good intentions and believes in the virtue of all the people he meets. He has an extraordinary degree of hope and a romantic predisposition to take a sympathetic line wherever possible. I don't think he would make an exception of the Abbess of D—— in these respects. If my information is correct, his relations with the Abbey are paternal and cordial. He makes no secret of his admiration for the nuns. I think he has a relative among them. One of the senior Mothers."

The Cardinal had seated himself. Little by little his anger was abating.

"But, in a word, at this moment, what does he think of the situation? What does he propose to do?"

"He must be very worried, your Eminence. As for what he proposes to do, I am afraid it is not in his character to make decisions, especially if they are painful and touch his heart."

"Yes . . . true enough. I see that there is nothing to be expected from his side." The tone had become normal again —deliberate and grave. "Well! Let us wait," added the Cardinal, with the moderation characteristic of him, which he had now regained. "I hope we shall not hear anything too troublesome in the months to come. By the way, I suppose that feeling must be running rather high in some quarters?"

"No, your Eminence," said the bishop calmly. "It seems that since the famous business of the Chapter, a sort of peace reigns. . . . There is a truce."

"Oh! Then . . . it is surely a peace like that of Clement the Ninth," said the Cardinal with a smile. "It won't last. Under the surface, and especially in the novitiate, there must be subjects who are reserving their judgment."

"At any rate, things being as they are, such subjects must be self-controlled enough to let nothing show. There are un-imaginable springs of patience in these abbeys—that is to say of supernatural virtue. There is also a certain shy reserve."

The Cardinal made a gesture.

"Shy reserve about our feelings is more to be feared in life than any vice," he said. "Well then," he added after a few seconds, "I don't want to detain your Lordships any longer."

The Bishops stood up.

"Goodbye till tomorrow," the Cardinal said, giving a friendly handshake to the Bishop who had not spoken. "We shall be meeting at his Holiness's. More serious problems will be awaiting us there."

He had regained his usual good-natured smile; he would show a kind of intrepidity in action as soon as things became clear to him. On the threshold he kept the bishops for an instant.

"In five, or perhaps ten years' time, shall we remember this worry? This suffering?" he added in a lower voice, as though speaking to himself.

Then, with his right hand he gave a farewell gesture, and it was like a blessing.

20

Mother Mechtild took over the novitiate during the first days after Pentecost. The novices liked her. She was accepted then and there by the great majority, and many gave proof of their acceptance with an enthusiasm which bordered on devotion. The Sisters had the sure instinct which belongs to youth, and they made no mistake either about her virtues or her warm heart. She communicated to them all a kind of inward strength. The only thing that made them wonder was a constant hint of sadness in her expression; but a certain reserve prevented any reference to this except in whispers. During recreation in the woods and gardens, animated and eager conversations punctuated by gay laughter, surrounded her like a rampart, affording a kind of vigilant protection.

The Abbess visited the novitiate more than usual. This settling-in time gave a pretext for prolonged conversations between her and the young Mother. It was well known to everyone that Mother Hildegard had a warm affection, enhanced by an ardent respect, for the new Mistress. Never before had she shown such demonstrative solicitude. The novices called Mother Mechtild "Our Mother" spontaneously, whereas Mother Cecilia had always been spoken of as "Our Mistress" and the Abbess as "Madame" or "Our Very Reverend Mother". It was only very rarely that some of the oldest Mothers sometimes said "Madame Hildegard", and then they usually had to repeat the phrase because no one understood it.

The door of the novitiate was still open to Sister John of the Cross, in view of her temporary vows. She used to pay long visits there, and was very soon intimate with Mother Mechtild.

In the course of her training the new Novice Mistress had specialised in illuminating. After her perpetual vows she had been employed in the restoration of old manuscripts and evangelistaries. Later, when she became Mother Vicar, she had more leisure, and it was said that she was secretly preparing as a present for the Archbishop, whose niece she was, a copy of the Book of Hours of Charles V. Her miniatures were very like the originals: hieratic, linear: with austere, sad-faced Virgins.

Sister John of the Cross was sometimes employed in making holy pictures for missals. Together with the making of hosts and candles, which was reserved for the lay Sisters, this was one of the industries of the Abbey. She thus had numerous pretexts for going to the new Mistress's office for advice. These conferences often developed into discussions concerning personalities and typical cases which the daily life of the Abbey offered to such an alert mind. Joined to a disarmingly even temper, Mother Mechtild had a deep understanding of other people's problems. Gradually the two nuns reached the stage of confidences.

The result of the Canonical Chapter had not brought any notable change to the Abbey. Mother Rouart had returned to all her former occupations, of which the most important was to receive the nuns for spiritual direction. With the correspondence and visits which came to her from outside, this took most of her time. Her face had regained its usual placidity. At times there may well have lurked a sort of asperity and bravado beneath the sweetness of her smile; but it would have needed the acute eyes of Mother Stanislaus to detect it.

The latter went on with her work and seemed suddenly to have detached herself from those around her. She received numerous Dominican Fathers in the parlour, and was in constant correspondence with the Benedictines at Rome. Sister John of the Cross now saw Father Gregory three times a week. She no longer hid from herself the affectionate admiration she had for him, and this was one of her favourite topics of conversation with Mother Mechtild.

Mother Mechtild strove to regulate, sometimes with a word of reproach, an enthusiasm which she considered inordinate, but that did not affect the sweetness of their relations, which each day became closer. To tell the truth, the new Mistress talked very little; but she knew how to listen calmly and with a good grace. Her eyes constantly held in their depths the same sadness which, though almost imperceptible, was real, keen and unfathomable for those who noticed it. But she gave the impression of being strengthened in her inward person by her total abandonment to God. Nevertheless her pallor was becoming more marked.

It was after Matins one night. Two o'clock had already struck. Most of the nuns had returned to their cells. Only a few had remained in their stalls praying. Some were slowly making the Stations of the Cross in the Choir.

Mother Stanislaus came out of the atrium. Under the lime trees the air was soft. The sky was clear, with an infinite wealth of stars. She crossed the gardens. For a long time she walked through the woods till she came to the meadows. She returned by way of the novitiate. There was no one about. Yet at this season the Sisters frequently came into the gardens after Matins to finish the night in meditation. Perhaps tonight they had gone further, and were following the woodland paths?

It struck three; she decided to go in. She had only come out to breathe the fresh night air. She was obliged by her work to have regular sleep. One day the Prioress had told her that she ought to ask to be dispensed from Matins for two or three nights each week; but when she spoke of it to the Abbess, her Grace replied that the Divine Office surpassed in excellence all the written work in the world; that she would willingly give her permission to rest and even to sleep during the day, if she felt she needed to, but that in conscience she could not give her a regular dispensation from Matins without a serious reason of health. It had to be agreed that this was sheer wisdom. Wisdom that Mother Hildegard would never temper with mercy. Mother Stanislaus took that for granted.

It had just struck three, and she was about to go back by the cloister which led to the great staircase, when she remembered that she had left in the atrium her copy of Saint Jerome's Bible. She usually kept the volume in her choir-stall, but she would be needing it today for a reference. She accordingly went back along the lime avenue. She was meditating in preparation for the work she was going to do in a few hours' time. It concerned the difference which divided the Jewish from the Gentile converts in the Early Church. It is well known that the Council of Jerusalem brought this controversy to an end. She was trying to remember what Saint Paul said to Barnabas in his famous letter on this burning question. It was only for a moment.

Someone had shut the door of the atrium. She went in, crossed the whole length of it and was going to leave after taking the book, when Sister John of the Cross came up to her and silently made a sign for her to follow. The sign was imperious. The face of the young nun looked extraordinarily disturbed. Mother Stanislaus nodded and followed her into the choir. A few Mothers were still there, seated in their stalls. In front of one of the side grilles a young Sister was kneeling in prayer, her arms extended. Sister John of the Cross guided the Mother into the shadow which was lit only by the orange light of the sanctuary lamp. Beyond there was complete darkness. They came to another grille which gave on to one of the side chapels, just beside one of the little altars which encircle the Church of the faithful like a white crown. Just there, near the sacristies of the enclosure, there was a kind of recess where one could be hidden, crouching almost near enough to touch the steps of the high altar, if it were not for the grille which one finally lost sight of. The young Sisters often went to pray in this place, especially at night. It was like an oratory of love.

Sister John of the Cross went around the heavy Gothic

pillar with its very beautiful sculpture of Christ kneeling before Saint Peter. She was walking without a sound, followed by Mother Stanislaus. In the recess, flat on the floor, a nun was prostrated. The whole of her body was stretched out, her face to the ground and her arms in the form of a cross.

Mother Stanislaus was the first to break the majestic silence of the night.

"It is Mother Mechtild," she said.

"Yes, I am worried. She has been like that since the end of Matins. She has not moved."

Mother Stanislaus placed a friendly hand on the arm of the young nun.

"Don't be afraid, Sister," she said gently. "It often happens to her. These are things which the whole convent knows. Mother Vicar receives extraordinary graces."

She still said "Mother Vicar," from force of habit. They were only a step away from Mother Mechtild, whose body was, in effect, completely motionless; with a kind of stiffness and rigid parallel lines; and that terrible impression of a broken back. Other nuns often prostrated themselves, but their bodies remained supple, as though in self-abandonment. Whereas here . . .

For an instant they remained there, on the spot, not daring to take a step. Already conscious of the creaking of the floorboards under their feet. Half-past three struck. The silence returned like a funereal offering. Mother Stanislaus had sat down in a near by stall, slightly turned towards the altar. Sister John of the Cross knelt a little behind, almost near enough to touch her. They spoke in lowered voices.

"Does the Abbess know about this?" asked the young Sister.

"Madame Hildegard always welcomes such a situation. These things are regarded as quite ordinary in their group, you know."

Irony was creeping in already, in spite of the strangeness of the hour, the place and the subject. Sister John of the Cross raised her head. Instinctively she drew nearer and pressed herself against the Mother, who put an arm round her shoulders.

"In reality we ought to find it very natural: and very enviable in this cenacle of our abbey where spiritual tension is so great. . . ." She was silent for a few seconds. . . . "I understand now why she always hides her hands," she continued. "This state is most often accompanied by a still greater grace."

Mother Stanislaus relaxed her arm a little. With her free hand she caressed the young face which was so near to her own, and suddenly so sad.

"The marks of the stigmata are very faint on her hands," she said. "There are days when they are almost invisible. The wounds on her feet bleed more profusely and, above all, her side."

For a long time they remained silent. Then, all at once, a slight noise made them draw apart from each other. Mother Mechtild had risen. She had knelt for a moment and was now standing, bowing low before the altar. In her turn, she went around the pillar without appearing to notice the presence of the two nuns. Then, with her eyes lowered as though continuing a secret dream, she passed down the whole length of the choir and went out.

Sister John of the Cross had come nearer again and was resting her elbows on Mother Stanislaus's knees.

"I thought that Mother Mechtild told me everything," the young Sister said at last, with emotion.

Mother Stanislaus smiled. "It is you who tell her everything. That is not quite the same thing. Mother Mechtild does not tell anyone everything—not even the Abbess—not even her confessor. Only God exists for her. She knows how to listen, though. She has a genius for listening. That is how she gives the impression of taking one into her confidence."

"I am so sad, Mother," said Sister John of the Cross. "Sad, as though things which no one expects were going to happen. Things which will turn out to be very serious."

"Let us go," said Mother Stanislaus, as she rose to her feet.

"Come on. Don't you think that enough serious things have already been happening here lately?"

The Choir was empty. They crossed the atrium so much in harmony with each other that their every movement proclaimed it. The veil of Sister John of the Cross showed up in the darkness with a ghostly white. In the cloisters they parted, going their separate ways with the silent, springy stealth of wolves. The young Sister reached the second floor. There was a full moon, pale as a ghost, watching over the gardens. A silvery blue mist was rising from the lawn. A cock crowed . . . then another.

The angel of the first Sabbath must have been moving through the countryside.

Soon Sister John of the Cross had shut herself into her cell.

21

The next day the student Sisters had their class in Ecclesiastical History.

June was about to begin, bringing in its train ripe fruit and gay foliage. There were borders of snapdragons edged with dark pansies which alternated with campanulas and forget-me-nots. A miracle of coloured blooms!

The class was at ten o'clock, shortly after High Mass. Father Gregory arrived early, while the young nuns were still preparing their books and fair copies. There were ten of them, just sitting down or hurriedly putting on their black aprons and turning back the long sleeves of their habits.

When he entered the sun-lit classroom, cut across by the grille of the enclosure of which the large central panel was left open for the lesson, he saw through the window the pale leaves of the poplars and the deep blue of the pines. He inhaled the scent of heliotrope wafted from the flower-beds. This room was used for the classes taken by monks and professors who could not enter the enclosure. Half of it was, in effect, part of the Abbey, while the other part was accessible to visitors.

It is well known, of course, that only cardinals are allowed to penetrate into the enclosure of women's orders—cardinals, the doctor, and the priest who brings the Viaticum.

Dom Gregory seemed in good spirits. He bowed to all the nuns with the light-hearted, slightly mocking civility which was characteristic of him.

The face of Sister John of the Cross bore noticeable signs of insomnia. With a poor attempt at a smile, she handed him a folded note. She did not say anything. He looked at her with sudden attention, but he wasted no time over it, taking her in at a glance.

The lesson dealt with the first session of the Council of Vienne: the beginning of the affair of the Knights Templars; Clement the Fifth; in fact, that doubtful period of the installation of the papacy at Avignon. The Father went on lecturing for a long time. The Sisters were writing. There were not many questions. At eleven o'clock he rose to his feet. He made a sign of goodbye without waiting at his desk, as he was usually so ready to do, and made his way to the parlour. Without any haste, Sister John of the Cross arranged her papers, took off her black alpaca apron, pulled the sleeves of her habit down over her tunic and went to join him.

"I am still amazed at what I witnessed, Father," she said, "and ill at ease. One is not accustomed to seeing such things close up."

"Yes, I understand. Yet one must take account of special people and admit that in certain cases there is no doubt of divine intervention. I think the case in point is of that nature."

"But of course. I believe that with all my heart. Mother Mechtild is so highly developed spiritually, so delicately adjusted and so completely detached; so outgoing and full of humanity. I only mean that these supernatural phenomena add nothing to her."

"Absolutely nothing, I agree. She is sure of that herself. I do not know her very well, but I am convinced that she suffers on account of this state."

They were silent. The parlour faced south and their faces were in softly shaded light.

The Father sought some diversion to relieve the awkwardness which was making itself felt.

"I wonder if you were not a little hurt to have been kept in ignorance about this?" he said with a smile which rested on her, penetrating to the depths of her blue eyes.

"Oh! Father, not at all." She hesitated. "It is true that Mother Mechtild had become a friend for me. For some time now," she added sadly.

"But no doubt she still is?" he said.

Then he broke off, and his eyes were suddenly serious.

"These are not things one talks about, don't you see? Especially when one is personally involved. I advise you not even to allude to it. And besides . . . I do not think that Mother Mechtild has quite the same conception of friendship as you have."

Another silence fell, and this time it contained a hint of anguish.

"Has this been happening for a long time?" she asked.

"A long time? That is rather difficult to answer. Certainly for six years. That is to say, from the time of her final vows. But very likely well before that. Mother Mechtild entered the novitiate when she was over twenty-five. She was already a soul far advanced in the ways of God. Her director at that time was a Trappist who has since become a hermit in Switzerland. But perhaps you knew that?"

"I know that she had once thought of becoming a Trappist herself. Yes, she told me that. But I think that since then . . . She seems very much at home in our vocation."

"Very much at home? Yes. Perhaps, after all; although that seems a little too much to say. There are appreciable differences between the fundamental structures of La Trappe and our own. The austerities are only one of the aspects. Between the Constitutions of Saint Bernard and those of Saint Benedict—and when one thinks of what Abbot Rancé introduced at La Trappe—there is a world of difference."

They were silent. There was a childlike quality in the expression of Sister John of the Cross—a dawning pain and distress. She must have been crying. Something seemed to be on her mind, and it was something else. It was something which went deeper and was bigger than the discovery she had made.

"Father," she said at last, "do you think that Mother Mechtild has close relations with Mother Abbess. I mean, in short, do you think they have . . . affinities?"

The Father waited for her to finish, but she said no more, hesitating and fearful lest she had said too much; as though it were a kind of sacrilege.

"I think that Mother Mechtild takes what is good from Madame Rouart, without overstepping the proper limits. You see, I don't know whether you have quite understood, but Mother Mechtild has long ago passed the normal stage of human relations. I think she has realised that degree of experimental knowledge which Saint Thomas associates with the gifts of the Holy Spirit. The interior life is already the reality for her; she is completely concentrated in God. She only skims the surface of things. Her inward gaze is already far above them."

"Then what about the novices?" she said. "I don't quite see—— It seems strange that our Very Reverend Mother should have appointed her to this office."

"That is obviously one of the basic errors of Mother Abbess. But really, when one comes to think of it, she has her own inner logic. Her government is not without a certain intellectual coherence. The idea is to make of this abbey a rather inhuman sort of spiritual coterie. Where she made her mistake was in thinking that Mother Mechtild would follow her on this road."

"Mother Mechtild is the very soul of wisdom," the young sister said, with an ardour in her eyes which lit up her face. I am certain that she would react if . . ."

"She has already reacted, but without any noise. She is a person of the most superior judgment. The awkward thing is that sooner or later the novices will notice something which should remain mysterious, a little apart. And it is their judgment which may then be at fault."

Sister John of the Cross was considering. She seemed to hesitate for an instant; then she made a visible effort at self-control.

"Father, do you think that at the last Chapter Mother Mechtild voted for the Mother Abbess?"

The Father smiled.

"I know nothing about that. Even if I were her director, it is probable that I should not know."

"But after all . . . what do you think?"

"Very decidedly, no. And the best reason is that the Chapter was proposed to the nuns in order to choose a coadjutrix; and Mother Mechtild is very obedient to Rome. I wonder whether the nuns realise, even today, how revolutionary their reply was—how much it savoured of contempt."

"Things were done with so much mystery."

"So much mystery, no. It is not customary to use a trumpet in such serious debates. You are still outside these movements of internal politics. Those who should have known, knew. You can take it from me. Ten days passed between Father Mareuil's visit and the Chapter. It was more than was necessary to trim the sails of the community. The truth is that the Abbey lacks flexibility. And that is what Madame Rouart lacks. It is like a vicious circle."

Quite close to the parlour there was a bell which began to sound in quick strokes.

"What do you think will result from all this, Father? In the near future? Because, you see, there are some of us in the study groups who think that something very serious is going to happen quite soon. By dint of making a pretext of our Father Saint Benedict and our Holy Rule, I am afraid that Mother Abbess may end up by becoming separated from Christ."

The Father sighed. "Alas! May Saint Thomas protect us from the Thomists," he said with a sad smile. The unfortunate thing about certain ills is that they bring others in their train—more serious ones—which cannot be held in check. . . . Come, my child, we will meet again soon," he said as he rose to go. "We will talk again about all this. In any case, I don't want it to disturb the peaceful course of your life."

"Oh! Father . . . Let the thunderclouds burst, let the storm break! Something must happen soon. . . . There are several of us who long for something to happen."

The Father turned round to face her, and retraced the two steps he had taken towards the door.

"No. You see . . . experience will teach you that a storm always leaves destruction behind it. No, in the interest of the greater number it would be better to avoid it."

He made a vague gesture. "Goodbye, for the moment," he said.

22

June passed. There was a clothing ceremony. The Archbishop presided with his usual gentle grace. The novice was the daughter of a landowner of the neighbourhood. She was twenty years old. She had magnificent eyes like shining violet stars.

The Two Nuns

Three postulants were added to the novitiate. All seemed to be going peacefully. Then Mother Mechtild had her first attack. It was in the early morning when the community were singing Lauds, which is followed by the time of silent prayer. The cantor had just intoned the first phrase of the *Benedictus*. All at once there was the sound of crumpling skirts in the top row of stalls. Then the nuns were standing aside, while four of their number supported the Novice Mistress, and almost carried her towards the atrium.

The singing continued, pure and clear: "To perform mercy to our fathers, and to remember His holy testament."[1]

The face of Mother Mechtild was waxen. Her eyelids looked bruised, and her eyes, ringed with blue, expressed a kind of startled terror. She was pressing a white handkerchief to her lips; but gradually she must have lost consciousness and the handkerchief slipped down, stained with blood.

The Abbess had made a gesture, but without leaving her seat. Soon the Office was over. Dawn was already breaking, and the light of the sun took on a magnificent coppery colour towards the western sky.

After the final antiphon, while the nuns remained to pray, Mother Rouart rose and left the choir.

The new Novice Mistress lay facing the light in the cell which had recently been given her in the rose-coloured wing where the young Sisters lived. The window was half open. From this room on the first floor one could scarcely see even a strip of blue sky, and it was still more shut in by the heavy branches of the acacias which almost touched the walls of the building. The doctor had come and was already talking with the Abbess in a parlour on the ground floor. In the cell there were two novices and the Prioress. The door of the adjoining office was open. Mother Mechtild was stretched on her bed. Her face was still as white as before, but now her eyes had a gentle expression. The light of terror had disappeared. She was not smiling, however. On her hands, which she no

[1] *Luke I*, 72. Douai version.

longer remembered to hide, the marks of the stigmata showed as a red line. It was crimson-coloured but did not bleed. Her features and her whole frame expressed a kind of impassibility —a detachment which seemed static and fundamental, as though independent of her mind or will.

The Sisters did not speak. They bore living testimony to the fact that the field of human consciousness is narrow and can only tackle one problem at a time. Perhaps they had known for a long period—in spite of their youth—that life must, from the first, be recognized as something that can die. And, in addition, their eyes were expressive of that deep tenderness which is felt for all that is in danger of disappearing.

One of them was sitting at the foot of the bed. In the adjoining office the low, almost stifled, voice of Mother Anselm could be heard, speaking with other novices. The telephone rang several times. A voice replied briefly.

Then, without knocking, the door of the cell was pushed open, and the Abbess came in, followed by the Abbot of Saint Benedict's. The Sisters bowed and left the room in silence. The door was shut.

On the face of the Abbot there was that utter sincerity and gravity which is stripped of all but the essential. They sat down. For a long time they talked. The Novice Mistress had not moved. Sometimes she smiled. Her words were very simple, coming as though from far away. On the table the little alarm clock in its black leather case went on ticking. Its minute hand made a complete circle.

At last the Abbot traced a cross on the white forehead with his ringed hand. His touch was gentle, expressive of deep humility.

The Abbess rose. Her expression was sad but calm, suggesting the depths of that ardent will of hers which never disarmed.

They passed along the corridor in silence. The cloister was full of sunshine, with its garden of irises and its fountains playing on the mosaic pavement.

"So, in your view, love is only to be prized if it is surrounded with constraint, restriction, and difficulty?" he said.

Someone was practising the organ. She was playing, "Jesu, Joy of Love's Desiring," soothing in the power of its recurrent melody. On the threshold of the enclosure two Mothers were waiting with their black veils over their faces.

"Goodbye, Father," said the Abbess. "I shall let his Excellency know."

The monk made a gesture meaning that that was not the problem. Then he went away, into a morning full of scents and nesting birds.

As he passed the hedge of white roses and cut privet and disappeared into the wood, a graceless anguish was mounting in him. Not stimulating and fertile but arid and, as it were, frozen.

23

The Archbishop came next day. It was the time of confirmations, and it had been impossible to get into touch with him until very late in the evening.

"My niece is very ill," he said to his secretary. "Do you know her? She is Mother Mechtild. She was never strong. They put her in charge of the novitiate a short time ago. I am afraid that it must be a very heavy burden for such delicate shoulders."

The priest shook his head. "I do indeed know her, your Excellency. Actually I know her very well. I will come with you to the Abbey. Gladly."

They set out early next morning. It was a long way off—a good two hours' run, with curves, and deviations by secondary roads—through orchards of apricot and cherry trees, the latter laden with fruit.

The country was glorious. Meadows and cottages were bathed in a diffused light. The cocks were almost strangling themselves with joy as they crowed.

"Have you any precise details, your Excellency, about the Novice Mistress's illness?" said the priest gently.

"It seems that she has had a hæmoptysis. She always had a delicate chest. But, beyond that . . ."

The car slowed down. They went through a village where the people were still asleep. The cottages were built of grey stone, with nasturtiums climbing over the balconies and honeysuckle and wistaria.

"She is very hard on herself," the priest said in an undertone, and as though speaking with difficulty.

The face of the Archbishop coloured. He gave a slight cough, then another, and he turned his head away to gaze at the fair countryside, stretching away into the distance.

"She is a good member of the order," he said. "A little austere for my taste. But, after all, different people have different kinds of grace. She and I did not have the same vocation."

They were quiet. Vague memories were in the air, with confused sensations of fear and solitude. There was a kind of constraint between them for a while.

"You would do better to say what is in your mind, Father. I stop seeing very clearly as soon as we get on to the subject of the abbey."

"Your Excellency . . . my judgment corresponds with that of the people you have been receiving at the palace recently; people who are interested in this same question. What has just happened is probably quite independent of the rest. At least I hope so."

"Father?" the Archbishop said sharply. "Did the Abbot telephone you yesterday? In the afternoon? Did you speak to him?"

"Yes, I did speak to him, Your Excellency. Though it would be more accurate to say that his Grace spoke to me."

"There you are! I thought as much. Generalities! Considerations! Views on the subject as a whole! I know Dom Germain is a great dialectician, and so are you. You are the same age. You are old friends. I know all that."

"I never dreamt of hiding what I felt from you, Your Excellency. I only wanted to wait till this evening when we got back. But since . . . On reflection, we might as well broach the subject now."

"But what on earth do you mean? Broach the subject? This concerns my niece. It concerns the Abbey, of which I am the immediate ecclesiastical superior. And people make mysteries for me: I am informed at second hand. And it is as much as they can do not to lower their voices to a whisper if I am present. Upon my word! It is a little too much!"

His temper was rising. It was imperious and passionate, in spite of the kindly face so full of natural indulgence that it seemed to belie its depth. And the old man's hand was trembling on the grey velvet cushion of the car.

"Monsignor!" said the priest, in a voice full of moderation and that blending of deference and respect of which he was a master, "Monsignor, the doctor who was called yesterday to the sick bed of Mother Mechtild has stated that she wears round her waist an iron belt as wide as a hand, and that it is studded with sharp points. The wounds from it seem to be deep, and have been there a long time. Some of them have become infected. Only the place of the stigmata has remained intact. Besides this he speaks of acute phthisis. He has not hidden it from the Father Abbot nor from Mother Rouart that this state could have been kept in check with prudence and care. I may add that the doctor is the same one who attended the novice who died six months ago."

The priest said no more. While he was speaking, the Archbishop's face became increasingly pale. A kind of despairing sadness was gradually taking control of his features. The deep lines around his mouth were accentuated. There were tears in his eyes. He did not say another word. Until they reached the abbey he remained submerged in an absolute silence. He thought he was touching the uttermost depths of sorrow; but he had still further to go.

24

A few days passed. The abbey had accepted with affectionate and resigned sadness the news of Mother Mechtild's desperate condition.

From the very first notice at recreation the Abbess did not try to hide it. No direct allusion was made to the excessive mortifications which the Novice Mistress had practised. The novices whispered about them on their walks; but only in veiled terms, as though they were afraid. They had by now grown very fond of their Mother. They seemed to want to protect her from all outside influence, and indeed from any blame or hasty judgment. They kept on hoping against hope that everything would come right, and looked forward already to "the time when our Mother is convalescent". But each day it became more evident that such hopes were vain.

At times of relaxation among the hollyhocks and jasmine of the Abbess's garden, the Mothers of the Council fell into two separate groups. Mother Stanislaus was the centre of one, and Mother Teresa of Avila, the new Mother Vicar, led the other. She was a rigid German nun, trained in the austere discipline of Tauber and Meister Eckart. Each group followed the line of thought and judgment proper to it, and it was quite clear that not one member of either group would open the way of reconciliation to the others. But for the community as a whole and the lay Sisters, life took its usual course. It seemed as though nothing could disturb its peace.

The time was not far distant, however, when a tempest

was to sweep through the Abbey scouring its very depths, and Abbess Hildegard Rouart would soon be feeling its first onslaughts. Since the accident and the death of Sister Andrew, a deep hatred had been developing between Mother Stanislaus and the Abbess. It was slow, but violent and implacable. Its sole cause, though they were unconscious of the fact, was the memory of their former affection at the dawn of their monastic life, and the failure which had followed. It is only fair to say that Mother Stanislaus always took the first steps on this dark, unlit path, where they struck against each other so dangerously. The Abbess returned blow for blow, but in order to do so she never took advantage of her title or her power. Their conflict always preserved a certain dignity and remained private. It was none the less painful on that account.

June was coming to a magnificent close on this unclouded morning of early summer. At Matins the Abbess had sung the ninth lesson of the Office of the Apostles Peter and Paul. It was a feast of the first class, and throughout the ceremonies of the day the Most Reverend Mother officiated in the choir. Here the spread-eagle lectern would not be brought, since, when the Abbess officiates, she always does so from her throne surrounded by her abbey household, and the long nave as it sweeps up the choir between the rows of stalls remains empty.

Now High Mass was over. The Abbess was going back to her apartments. She had chosen to take a roundabout way by the gardens. She was walking with Mother Teresa of Avila, and they were doubtless discussing the affairs of the abbey. The new Mother Vicar had been Cellarer of the community for a long time.

It was on the hydrangea path, a little separated from the rest of the gardens and deeply shaded, that it happened. The path led past the Oratory of Saint Jerome—a little chapel cut out of the rock and almost hidden by dark shrubs: red-berried yew, cytisus, broom. The little chapel was also known as Bethlehem in honour of the great hermit's retreat. Up and down beside this chapel Mother Stanislaus was walking. She moved slowly, as though time did not count. She was obviously waiting.

All at once the Abbess understood that the appointed time had come. She did not know what to expect, but she was positive that something was going to happen.

"Please leave us, Mother Teresa," she said. "Go in by the novitiate; we will finish this conversation later."

Her tone suddenly sounded tired, but well-disposed, as though implying a kind of consent. Without a word, the Mother Vicar turned and departed. Mother Stanislaus was now standing in front of the door of the Oratory. She did not even trouble to come forward, leaving the Abbess free, during the time needed for the ten paces which separated them, to choose one of the paths which went off at right angles towards the fields, if she wished to avoid her.

Without a word they looked at each other. Mother Stanislaus's eyes were calm: without irony. The Abbess knew immediately that she would not say anything that was not essential. She knew that the crisis would come there where they stood: in the shade of that particular cedar: near those peach trees already heavy with a profusion of rose-coloured fruit: and that the shady paths full of golden insects, where the tall foxgloves of July were already coming into flower, would not see the print of their feet nor hear the sound of their voices, calmed and indifferent for the future, until all had been said.

The silence between them grew ominous. There was no beating about the bush, no searching for suitable words. The attack was sudden. Its absolute calm rested upon incalculable reserves of hatred.

"Did you know?" said Mother Stanislaus in her usual voice, with its warm, musical resonance. "Did you know, Madame?"

The Abbess was standing less than a yard in front of her. Her shadow fell on the ground mingling with that of the moving foliage. She sought no escape.

"I knew nothing of the state of her lungs," she replied
firmly. "Nothing. I can assure you."

Mother Stanislaus made a brief gesture. "That is beside the
point. The question does not concern your integrity but your
judgment. You should answer. Did you know?" she repeated
authoritatively.

"Mother Mechtild always wore a *cilice*[1]. There are a great
many nuns who do."

For a moment Mother Stanislaus's eyes flashed with fury.
Then they became calm again, almost gentle. Neither of the
Mothers had moved. A light breeze was still swaying the
branches of the trees.

"Madame, will you please use the right words. This has
nothing to do with an ordinary *cilice*, but with a large iron belt,
rather a horrible one. Such things were scarcely to be found
in the fifteenth century. Had you seen the belt in question?"

"Yes, I had seen it. Mother Mechtild had been wearing it
for many long months. She assured me she was able to do so."

Mother Stanislaus looked down at the wild plants and
flowers that grew around the Oratory. Near her in the
woods were scattered patches of purple heather, and the air
was charged with the scent of warm mint and thyme.

There was a long silence.

"Madame," she said at last. "I have already written to the
Cardinal Prefect. I was waiting to make sure of this last
point before sealing my letter. It will leave by the evening
post. I shall be leaving myself tomorrow. I am going to
Louvain, where I have something to do at the university.
That will give his Eminence the time to choose a place to
which I can retire."

The Abbess let a short moment of silence pass. Her expression did not seem to change. "Mother Stanislaus . . . no
matter what your grievances may be . . . however great the
hatred which separates us and which makes you always choose
to think I am guilty . . . you are under my jurisdiction

[1] *Penitential belt.*

canonically. If you leave, you will do so against my will. Your vow of obedience is involved. I beg of you to appreciate how serious it is."

Mother Stanislaus made a vague gesture. "There are other problems besides that one which are equally serious," she said.

With infinite calm the Abbess raised the hand on which she wore her ring. "No, Mother Stanislaus. No. Write to the highest authorities. Do whatever you please; but you must not leave. You must not leave, because my will is that you should stay here, and you can do nothing against it. My will is the channel by which God shows you His own."

In her whole bearing and in her slightest intonations there was a certain austere majesty which, in spite of everything, commanded obedience. Mother Stanislaus's eyes were ringed as though with a mauve pencil.

"I know. You are the symbol. And in order to preserve the exterior properties of the symbol, it does not much matter if the rest of the people die. Is that not true?"

Then, as though without her knowing it, a suggestion of tenderness gleamed furtively in the depths of her pupils.

"Ah! Madame . . ." she murmured.

But her arm fell back with a weary little gesture, indicating that nothing would be of any use, that things had reached a point which could no longer permit of any weakening.

"I may add," continued the Abbess flatly, "that even the Cardinal Prefect is powerless to assign to you any place of residence other than the abbey of your profession, without my consent. My daughters belong to me, Mother Stanislaus, until their death or mine. This is a plain fact of which you are making a tragedy."

There were cruel lights once more in the eyes of Mother Stanislaus. For an instant she was silent. Some swallows swerved down in their flight, almost level with the ground.

"Mother Hildegard! The first condition of high tragedy is not to have recourse to monsters." She was almost shouting.

". . . D—— is not the abbey of our profession," she went on; after a pause—she said *our* abbey as though, in effect, their destinies were bound together for ever. "The abbey of our profession is K——. You know that as well as I do."

"K—— is, indeed, the abbey where you made your profession; but under the government of the Most Reverend Mother Cyprian, you agreed to change it. Remember, D—— has become canonically and by your own wish *your* abbey. No one can do anything about it."

Mother Stanislaus blushed. Her anger was rising in great waves. It was almost choking her.

"Madame! One word from you and we should be delivered. Do you refuse to say it? In any case I shall leave. If need be, Rome would release me from my vows. But I cannot live here any longer. I can no longer live under this government which has already been the cause of so many calamities. I shall go, Madame, and for the rest of your life you will have to bear the whole weight of it pressing on your heart."

"Do not try to raise an insufficiency to the height of a philosophy, Mother Stanislaus. Anyhow, I do not despair of reducing you to obedience and bringing you back to me by other means." She reflected for an instant. ". . . And think, all the same, of the importance of a rash gesture," she added. "To leave the enclosure in rebellion against the vow of obedience is punishable by excommunication. Don't forget that! And you can talk of getting yourself released from your vows. It does not make sense."

The end of the morning was glorious. The sun was scattering its golden caresses everywhere. There were joyful twitterings from the birds, and among the lower leaves of the green thickets there were sounds of hidden tumultuous movements.

The Abbess gave an almost maternal smile. "I hope that you will go and think it over. I was only too pleased to answer your questions, because you are among my councillors and also because I owe this gesture to our past friendship. But

I deplore the fact that you do not recognise the grace of God which goes before me and supports me in my charge. Goodbye, Mother Stanislaus, till we meet again. I am not inviting you to accompany me. I think you prefer your solitude." She made a friendly sign of farewell. "Till we meet again, then. You know that I am always there if you want me."

Mother Stanislaus did not move. She was dumbfounded. Suddenly her vision was confused—now with those memories she tried in vain to brush aside, now with the precise image of a drama which she foresaw and which she knew to be imminent.

25

The weeks passed. July brought no new development except for the fact that, towards the end of the month, while they were singing the Office of Saint Ignatius, Mother Mechtild died.

For several days before, anyone might have thought she was dead already, except for the slight, painful movement of her throat as she breathed. For the last twenty-four hours she had been smitten with immobility and silence. Very white, with a face which had grown even more emaciated, she looked as though she were sleeping. She died in the evening, at the time of Compline.

We are by nature unequally endowed with the sense of what is essentially right and proper. Or rather, each one of us puts the accent on whatever seems most suitable in his particular case. At any rate it is fair to say that the Abbess gave evidence of a deep sorrow. Monsignor appeared to be quite overwhelmed. He stooped more than ever. His trembling hand rested on the arm of his secretary. The latter's incisive and decided glance seemed like a promise of things to come.

On the advice of the Father Abbot and Dom Gregory, Mother Stanislaus had not left the abbey. She withdrew into a silent retreat and worked without respite. She frequently dispensed herself from communal recreations and even from the night Office—without permission.

The Abbess had sharply reprimanded her about this in Chapter and before the novices, with such uncustomary insolence that the Mothers of the Council who shared the rank of Mother Stanislaus felt that they themselves had been attacked through her, and were dumbfounded.

Mother Stanislaus replied in the same tone and in the Chapter itself—a thing unheard of in Benedictine history.

After that, she went on living apart, and if by chance she met the community on any of their walks, she never failed to challenge the Abbess in a light, ironical tone whose emancipated arrogance was evident to all.

The Abbess replied with a quiet self-assurance—the smile of an Assyrian god and on her lips—calm, patient, strong in her rightful authority. And those immediately surrounding her were silent—pained and reproachful.

Mother Anselm viewed all this with a pacific eye. It was impossible to know what she was thinking. When some of those who were fond of her and whom she gladly gathered around her questioned her with a gesture or a smile, or even a discreet allusion, she seemed not to understand and, without anyone knowing how it happened, the conversation was always changed.

Sister John of the Cross had written to Rome. Very likely others among the young, newly professed nuns had done the same. It was holiday time, however, and Rome was silent.

There was another clothing ceremony for the fifteenth of August. The Abbess received bishops from abroad, and an American cardinal penetrated into the enclosure.

Then September came. It was one of the first days, before the Nativity of the Blessed Virgin. The night had been hot and oppressive. In the early hours of the morning a storm had broken, with stripes of lightning flashing over the garden. Now a lovely, tinted transparency was restored to a sky swept clear. Little hornets, half drowned by the torrential rain, were still shivering in the velvety clematis.

It was half-past eight. The first stroke of the bell for High Mass had not yet sounded. The Abbess was in her office, writing. The window was open. There were roses and a big Delft bowl of purple dahlias.

The secretary half-opened the door. It was still Mother Dominic with her timidly subdued manner.

"It is Mother Stanislaus, your Grace," she said.

The Abbess put down her pen, crossed her hands on the table and nodded her acquiescence.

A sense of anguish passed through the room like a wave. Then there was a long moment of silence. Mother Stanislaus had seated herself in one of the armchairs in front of the table. She had not uttered a word. She had not even bowed. Her whole person expressed, with passionate ferocity, the intention to be impertinent.

"I did not ask you to sit down," the Abbess said quietly.

Mother Stanislaus did not move. "The Council of Elvira enjoined a bishop never to allow one of his priests to remain standing when he himself was seated," she said in a studiedly casual tone.

A light shone in the eyes of the Abbess. "Very well," she said. "I called you in order to make it clear that I cannot tolerate any more of these visits you have been having from T. Such visits——"

"Your Grace is no doubt referring to his Excellency's secretary?"

"——such visits are in no way necessary for your work and——"

"I am the sole judge of that, Madame."

"——and I beg you to put a stop to them. If you do not, I shall be obliged to inform Father X. myself, and, if need be, Monsignor," she added, while Mother Stanislaus preserved her usual carefree detachment. "I can put up with your personal lapses—which are no longer lapses but a very obstinate determination to be insolent—but I cannot accept deliberate infringements of our Rule. Useless and prolonged conversations constitute such an infringement—a serious one. Therefore . . ."

Mother Stanislaus was silent. In the pettiness of the pretext, and in the very rhythm of the words, she assessed with relish all the dignity the Abbess had forfeited in her eyes by sending for her first, in order to deliver such an equivocal admonition.

"I need not keep you any longer," added her Grace.

"Madame," she said at last, "I beg of you to accept my resignation from the Abbey Council. For some time now I have found its meetings very tiring. I would like to be free of them."

Her tone was a miracle of calm insolence. After all! It rested entirely with her whether she would pay tribute to God, or to Caesar. The Abbess raised her eyes and looked at her long and seriously.

"I do not accept your resignation," she said.

She addressed an envelope, fastened it down and stamped it with her seal. Through the window the smell of beaten-down grass was wafted by a fresh breeze.

"I am waiting for your crisis to be over. When you have calmed down and are . . . lucid, you will probably thank me."

Mother Stanislaus rose to her feet. "I doubt that," she said. "If I am staying here, it is only in the hope of being able to leave soon with all the necessary approvals. It will not take long now."

"The first approval you need is mine."

"I can do without yours."

"And yet it is the only one that counts."

"Oh, Madame! Do not push me too far. I might have an outburst."

The bell had rung for High Mass. On the first stroke the door opened without anyone knocking, and now the four novices whose week it was to represent the abbey household were standing on the threshold, dressed for choir, with their eyes cast down.

The Abbess stood up.

"I have grown accustomed to your outbursts—for some time now," she said. "I do not attach more importance to them than is necessary. Compliance is a passive complicity. You ought to have understood by now that I will never give in to you."

"And you, Madame, ought to have understood by now that your time is limited; that you are living through your last months at D——; perhaps your last weeks."

The Abbess still had the same peaceful expression. "Come! kneel down," she whispered, as she held out her ring. "For the sake of the novices."

"Neither you nor I can ever forget these weeks, Madame," said Mother Stanislaus. "Never can we forget them!"

Her voice had dropped. Her face expressed a concentrated fury. For a long moment the Abbess's eyes, peaceful and penetrating, met hers. Then her Grace went towards the door where the novices were waiting.

26

September was drawing to a close. In the mornings, when the early mist was rising from the fields, the birds were already plundering the hedges for berries.

Sister John of the Cross no longer went to the novitiate, where an austere nun whom she did not like had just been put in charge.

She spent her time in communal exercises, in the library or

in her cell. She was patiently awaiting a letter from Rome.
A letter which did not come. Her face wore the serious expression in which the sadness of first disappointments is to be
detected. Sometimes she strolled down an aisle of vines
reddened with autumn foliage, book in her hand; always
silent and alone.

Every day after High Mass she went to Mother Stanislaus,
with whom she worked for the rest of the morning. Study
and life with the community kept her occupied.

It was after Vespers on one of the last days of the month.
She was just about to return to her cell and was in the cloister
of Our Lady, near the novitiate, when the novice from the
portress's lodge came rushing after her, to ask if she would go
immediately to the parlour.

"I could have rung for you," the messenger said, "but since
you are here. . . . I think it is a priest who is asking for you.
He did not tell me his name."

Sister John of the Cross gave her an affectionate smile.

"That is all right," she said. "I will go."

She went instinctively to the parlour she always chose in
preference to the others. It was the parlour of Saint Peter, a
large square room with a southerly aspect. It was decorated
on either side of the grille with pots of fern and majestic portraits which recalled the paintings of Rigaud. It had comfortable furniture, and the scent of cut flowers came across
from the nearby sacristies.

She drew the black curtain from the grille. The visitor was
a tall ecclesiastic. He might have been about sixty years old.
He wore gold-rimmed spectacles which shielded his penetrating eyes. He had extremely thin lips and wore a little goatee
whose tip was tinged with white, suggesting a cat that had had
its chin in the milk. He evidently believed in the efficacy of
ruse, intelligence and tenacity. He bowed to her with polite
simplicity, asked her to be seated and sat down himself.

"The Cardinal Prefect has received your letter," he said,
without any preamble. "In the main, this letter sums up what

you had already told the Canonical Visitor; though with less restraint and more impatience, perhaps," he added calmly.

The young nun bowed her head. "Yes," she said.

The newcomer's smile was full of kindness.

"You must forgive me, Sister. I should have introduced myself. I am Father F. of the Order of Saint Benedict. I have not been wearing the monastic habit for a long time. It is a garment which would not be suitable for some of my activities. They are, alas, very varied. The most important is indubitably the visitation of monasteries—of monks and nuns—with apostolic authority. I suppose that you understand me?"

He spoke as though he were reciting something. His manner was utterly detached. Here was a situation which had to be stated but would not be mentioned again.

"I understand you perfectly, Father," she said.

For a brief instant they were silent.

"I am familiar enough with the question we are considering —also with the history of this abbey since Mother Rouart has been in charge of it. I have come to see you. I shall also see Mother de Neuville. And then . . . the Mother Abbess. But I shall see no one else. I have all the evidence I need."

His voice was clear, composed, reassuring.

He was playing with his long white hands. Sister John of the Cross fixed her glance for a moment on those hands, then her eyes rose to the Father's face. She gave him a smile of child-like spontaneity. At that moment a little cat jumped through the half-open window beside the Father. It was an irresistible black kitten, four or five months old. The young nun's smile grew more pronounced. Then the Father turned his head a little and his eyes had a gleam of amusement in them, while he twisted a narrow gold ring round his finger.

"You seem to recognise the transient blessings of joy every-where, and to accept them with gladness," he said with a serene kindliness. "It is quite certain that I must get you away from this convent."

"But, Father . . . I love my abbey," she said seriously. "I only want to be saved from . . ."

"I understand. We will see what can be done, though the task will not be easy. How are you employed here?" he added, his tone once more serious.

"I am preparing for my examination in philosophy, Father. The rest of the time I have not any very definite employment. Sometimes I take the place of the Mother Organist, in order to share in principle in the life of the community. This participation is purely theoretical," she added, smiling. "In reality my studies are very absorbing. I have begun to learn Hebrew and I also work for Mother de Neuville."

The monk made a movement which indicated all the sympathy he had for Mother Stanislaus, but also his understanding of how little time the young Sister had at her disposal.

"Oh! in that case . . ." he said with a smile. "You made your profession less than a year ago," he added after a few seconds. "Therefore, you are not one of the Mothers, nor are you still a novice. Nevertheless, I am going to ask you two questions. You must reply to them, and I want you to do so spontaneously, without too much reflection. Here is the first one: To whom are you most drawn in this convent by your natural preferences? Come on! I particularly want a quick answer."

"To Mother de Neuville," said the young nun fervently.

"I thought so. Now here is the second question: If the Abbess's seat were suddenly to become vacant, and you were one of the Chapter, to whom would your vote go?"

"To the Prioress, Mother Anselm Denoix," she said without hesitation.

The monk crossed his legs and settled himself more comfortably into the depths of his Empire armchair.

"You realise that those are very indiscreet questions," he said. "My task unfortunately obliges me to ask questions of that kind. I beg you to excuse me."

"May I ask, Father, whether you approve of my choice?"

"I think it is fairly judicious. In any case it is perfectly acceptable. But I also think that there are a great many elements in your community of which you only have a superficial knowledge. Elements of weight. Among the nuns who are still very young—those who are little over thirty years old —there is a very outstanding nun. Probably no one has thought of her. Yet there . . . perhaps. . . . But this is out of place for the moment," he continued in a different voice. "The thing only interested me in so far as you are concerned. I wanted to sound your judgment."

In the Oblates garden wood-pigeons were tapping their beaks against the walnut trees. The first September nuts were falling. The sound of a gay laugh was wafted to them on the warm air.

The monk allowed a silence to fall. It was a silence charged with thought. Sister John of the Cross hesitated.

"You were going to say something?" he asked kindly.

"Father, we cannot go on living like this. A decision is imperative. It must be taken."

"I know, I know. But there are not so many ways out of the difficulty. You can take my word for it that I have studied the question. It would scarcely have arisen if Mother Rouart's mandate was coming to an end at a definite date, as in most Cenobitic convents. But according to our holy Rule and constitutions, you know that she will continue to be abbess until her death. And short of a scandal or an open rebellion . . . " he became thoughtful for a moment. "And then you saw for yourself," he went on after a pause, "the majority of the nuns want to keep her. Out of two hundred votes, scarcely forty went to anyone else."

"There have been fresh developments since that, Father," she said.

The monk gave a pout to show he was not convinced.

"New developments? The death of the Novice Mistress? Mother de Montfort died of consumption. Several members of her family have already died of the same disease. In addition to which she was favoured by very extraordinary graces which might have hastened the end. No, you see, the facts which should be the most conclusive are really very thin arguments. And it is only facts which count. Tendencies, impressions, sympathy . . . all these count for no more than wind, before an ecclesiastical tribunal. Note that I entirely agree with you, because I know how things really are. But that is not likely to bring about a canonical decision of such a revolutionary nature, so long as Mother Rouart does not agree to it."

The eyes of Sister John of the Cross grew sad.

"Well, then, Father, we shall never escape," she said. "It is no good even dreaming of Mother Rouart's agreement. She pursues a policy of prestige, of grandeur. In this place grandeur suits and satisfies the majority. Many of us have to do the best we can to put up with it."

There was silence for a few moments. "At Saint Benedict's the Fathers are in favour of our group," she added.

The monk gave an imperious gesture. "Do not involve the Fathers in this conflict," he said sharply. "That would be the way to muddle everything. I am here with a very clear mandate and full powers to implement it. You can be sure that the difficulties have been foreseen. We are going to make an attempt. I showed you the situation in the darkest possible light, because in fact that is the real position if one only judges by facts. And it is quite certain that the judges of the Congregation of Religious judge only by facts. Like all judges, for that matter! But, thank God, there are perhaps other arrangements in view. That is why I am here. Oh! I know quite well that you and a few others are waiting for the deposition pure and simple of Mother Rouart. As things are it is almost a joke. In your letter you speak of the Holy Office, of heresy, of condemnation, of I don't know what besides. You go on and on. It can scarcely be taken seriously. Fortunately Mother Stanislaus's letters are more subtle. It is a matter of age and character. Although I cannot understand how she could have envisaged for a moment leaving the abbey without an indult. Women are terrible! We are no longer living in the Middle Ages, my child. To say that Mother Rouart is a heretic is to use a very strong expression. To say that she has heretical tendencies and that her judgment is warped is to state an indisputable fact, and that is why a way has to be found to save the abbey from her. The way is my affair. I have in my pocket a paper which announces the decision of the Sacred Congregation of Religious that a co-adjutrix must be nominated. The name is still blank. It is for Mother Rouart to fill it in." Sister John of the Cross made a movement. ". . . Under my control, of course; and I may tell you that three of your Sisters are already on the list. It is only necessary to leave her with the impression that she is choosing. That will ask for a little tact, a little diplomacy. One thing is certain, and that is that I shall not leave here without there being a name written in black on the white space of that paper."

He spread out the first fold of a parchment.

"Or else. . . ." He made a gesture whose apparent vagueness strangely emphasized how inexorable and overwhelming the issue might prove.

The young nun's eyes had a piercing light in them, and as she spoke an authority which had gradually been establishing itself in her voice reached a high degree.

"The Mother Abbess will refuse," she said. "There is no possible doubt of that. She is fortified by too many things; were it only by the recent votes in the Chapter."

"In that case . . . I have told you that I have full authority," said the monk. "Don't ask me any more."

Suddenly the expression on the face of Sister John of the Cross changed. A sort of fear or dread was written on it— uncertain but deep.

"Oh, Father! What are you going to do?" she said. "I am very much frightened by all that may come about. You do not know Mother Rouart. She can be terrible."

"It is indeed a risk," said the monk, as he rose to his feet.

"But it has to be taken. Sister . . . I shall be seeing you again, whatever happens. Will you ask the Mother Portress to tell Mother de Neuville that I am waiting for her?" he added.

Sister John of the Cross had risen, but she still remained near the grille—motionless.

"At what time will you be seeing Mother Rouart?" she asked.

The monk gave an indulgent smile and pulled out his watch. "At five o'clock, I hope."

"Father . . . I am going to think so much about it. I am going to shiver so much," she said with a return of the childlike tone which was so charming.

The monk smiled again. And perhaps there was something a little unusual in his smile. The brown eyebrows of the young Sister drew together in perplexity. She bowed her head, then raised it and looked at the monk. She looked deeply into his eyes, and then something in her seemed to give a start. A picture from long ago, vague at first, then clearer and finally with perfectly firm outlines, came before her.

"But, Father . . ." she said. "You are. . . . You are Cardinal X.—the Chief Cardinal Penitentiary."

Almost unconsciously she knelt down, as though overwhelmed. The monk put his finger on his lips, then he traced a discreet cross in the air.

"So through this sad business I have had a privilege which would have been impossible to obtain in any other way," she said, with a look of inexpressible confidence.

"Hush!" he said. "I am before all things Father F. of the Order of Saint Benedict. Goodbye till we meet again. Keep your secret."

On the table there was a book illustrating some twelfth-century enamels.

With a mechanical gesture the monk turned some of the pages.

"What a pitiless blue!" he whispered to himself.

27

The clock in the courtyard was striking five as the Cardinal went up the narrow staircase of polished oak which led to the Abbess's parlour.

The oblate Sister opened the massive door with its bronze peephole and heavy bolt from the old prison.

"Please come in, Most Reverend Father," she said. "Our Most Reverend Mother is already waiting for you, I think."

The black curtain was, indeed, drawn aside behind the grille, and the Abbess was standing in front of the great sun-lit bay.

"I hope that your Eminence has had some refreshment," she said in a welcoming voice. "The train was a little late, I believe," she added, as the Cardinal nodded courteously.

"It was, indeed; nearly an hour, Madame. A plane would have been preferable. But there is no direct airline from Rome, and the change at Nice would have wasted too much time."

They sat down.

"I only received the telegram from his Eminence, the Cardinal Prefect, yesterday," continued the Abbess. "I am entirely at his disposal . . . and yours, Monsignor."

She was seated in a high Gothic seat, made comfortable with cushions and very majestic. Her expression was one of simplicity and peace. Her lively manner attracted sympathy.

"This woman is amazing," thought the Cardinal. "Where did I read that in order to bring to light certain mental disorders one has to lead the person who is suffering from them progressively to the sensitive points in his delirium? Otherwise he will appear the most sagacious man on earth. All this is very difficult."

"Mother, I have been thinking about this interview of ours for some days," he began. "It is an interview of a very official character, but I should like to make it as easy as possible, if you will help me."

"I likewise have been preparing for an official conversation for some time past, your Eminence. I know that some of my daughters criticize my government. They do so openly, with no regard for the dignity and powers vested in me. Others no doubt are affected by this evil influence without even knowing it. And yet I am doing my best."

"Madame . . . it is true that certain complaints have been made about you. It is true that the canonical report of Dom Hilary Lemaître is not favourable to you."

The Cardinal said no more.

"But it is equally true, your Eminence, that when they insulted me six months ago by trying to force a coadjutrix upon me, the vote of the Chapter was conclusively in my favour."

"Most of all, it proved the arrogance of the members of your community, as a whole, Madame," said the Cardinal quietly. "It is obvious that your nuns are not very accommodating. If the Sacred Congregation of Religious wanted to give you a coadjutrix, it had its reasons. And there was insolence in replying to it by an almost unanimous vote in your favour."

"One can twist the matter to suit oneself, Monsignor."

"Even admitting that the attitude of the community can have another aspect, this one at any rate is true, and there is no getting away from the fact whether you want to or not."

The Abbess thought for a moment. "You see, your Eminence, there is something which appears to have been overlooked," she said in an easy manner, almost smiling. "It is the fact that I am the canonically elected Abbess, and no one can do anything to change it."

"That will certainly be your best line of defence, Madame. But, for that matter, no one has ever dreamed of depriving you of this title. A coadjutrix is a coadjutrix and nothing more."

"Don't let us play upon words, your Eminence. A co-adjutrix always has plenary powers, and in that case, the abbess would no longer count for anything. She would still take precedence, but you must agree that that does not amount to very much. It would be better for her to retire."

The Cardinal made a gesture, indicating that at least on that last point they were in agreement.

"A coadjutrix is only suitable where the abbess is old or very . . . feeble. Two authorities are inconceivable where there are constitutions like ours. Moreover, a Benedictine abbess by virtue of these very constitutions is an abbess until her death."

The Cardinal was silent.

"It is not love which makes a marriage, your Eminence, but consent. Neither do good qualities or virtues make an abbess, but canonical election."

The Cardinal smiled.

"Without going so far as that—for, after all, canonical election is not a sacrament—I agree that your line of thought is fair enough. But let us stick to the point. You are the canonically elected Abbess of D——. That is a fact. You will continue to be that until your death, or until the day when you relinquish your office of your own free will. No one has any doubt about that and no one is opposing you. But there is this to take into consideration: a careful study of the Abbey as a whole, and a long and meticulous canonical visitation, have given our superiors serious reasons to think that your government is going astray. That it is no longer in line either with the intention or the tradition of our founder. I have thought long about this before God, I assure you, Madame, ever since the affair was confided to me. This is no reflection on your character or your virtues. You are a most exemplary nun. I might say irreproachable. But I do not think you are suitable for government. The two things are quite distinct. So a remedy must be found. A remedy which, it would appear, is urgently needed."

The Cardinal allowed a long moment of silence to elapse.

Outside, they must have been bringing the sheep in for milking. Their bells were sounding from all the neighbouring meadows.

"His Eminence the Cardinal Prefect thinks that it is suitable for you to name your own coadjutrix," he said at last. "May I ask you to do so?"

The face of the Abbess had grown very pale.

"You must tell the Cardinal that I refuse, your Eminence. My daughters have elected me. They did so for the first time twelve years ago. They did so again (and the second election was in defiance of our very constitutions) a few months ago. Nothing more is needed for the mark of the Holy Spirit to be recognised."

"Nothing more is needed to prove the ferment of pride which characterises all the proceedings of your community, Madame. That is the truth. Unfortunately," the Cardinal went on after a moment, "I am obliged to take back to his Eminence a positive decision. I therefore advise you to comply. Unless you want a scandal!"

"I have given you my reply, your Eminence. I am not going to change it."

"Shall I then be obliged to summon the Chapter myself and direct it to choose a nun to assist you?"

"I have very little taste for the irony of certain words, your Eminence."

"And I have very little for the arrogance with which you oppose me. You are totally lacking in humility, Madame."

"That is possible. Nevertheless I abide by what I have said. My government is my own affair. My daughters belong to me. I need not give an account to anyone as to the way I am leading them. Not to anyone but God."

"You must give an account to Rome, Madame."

"Not even to Rome, Monsignor. So long as I am faithful to our Rule."

"Fidelity is in the spirit not the letter, Madame. The letter is only the sign and servant of the spirit. And as I have just said to you, the best test and proof of it is humility."

The Abbess was the first to rise. "I will put up with whatever is necessary, your Eminence. I do not forget that your dignity opens the enclosure to you, and excuses you from everything. The Mother Portress will show you the way in. You will understand, I think, that it would not be becoming for me to appear in an assembly called for the sole purpose of deposing me. The Mother Prioress will receive you. Good evening, your Eminence."

She bowed and went out of the parlour.

The Cardinal had not moved.

"A woman of the seventeenth century," he murmured as he rose to his feet. "Awkward and noble."

28

It was the evening of the next day and October had come. At Saint Benedict's the monks had just finished singing Vespers. They were coming out of choir, in procession—a long black line, with their hands hidden and their faces pensive and recollected. Perhaps they were already preoccupied with the work to which they were returning.

Finally a novice brother closed the double oak door which led into the cloisters. As they walked, the Fathers were taking off their cloaks, exchanging a few rapid whispers concerning their work or special business. They still formed an animated mass of black tunics. There were hurried steps, long strides, brief pauses.

The parlour bell rang. A flight of crows cut through the sky. Their sonorous call floated down. The Father Abbot had stopped at the end of the cloister in front of a large jutting-out doorway. He had already gone up two of the steps. His eyes seemed to be searching for one of his monks. The Fathers were hurrying towards their various tasks. There was hardly anyone left now. At last Dom Gregory appeared, coming out of a side sacristy. The Abbot signed to him, just as he was turning off in the direction of the library.

"Come," said the Abbot. "I have to talk to you about something serious."

His tone was sharp; his keen expression was charged with irritation. The two monks did not speak as they passed along the corridors. Their steps rang out on the mosaic pavement. There was no sun. The weather was uncertain. The sky was of that chill, lifeless white which is the summit of sadness.

Perhaps it would change soon, since in the east there were breaks in the clouds with gleams of pearly transparency. But certainly the next few hours would be oppressive.

They entered a study on the first floor. It was full of books, and the table was littered with a confusion of letters and papers. But, as a matter of fact, this confusion was probably only apparent.

"You know what is going on at the nuns' abbey?" said the Abbot excitedly, his voice quivering.

They were both standing. The room was getting dark, but they had not troubled to switch on the light. They gazed intently into each other's eyes.

"Yes. Oh! It is only by chance. I do not think that anyone else here has heard. But, for my part, I know," repeated Dom Gregory with a certain despair.

A second passed.

"I hope that it is not I whom you have chosen for this business?" he added.

"Yes, it is! I shall go, of course, but you will come with me."

"Perhaps you could have spared me this? Given the fact. . . ."

"In the first place, I never spare those I love from anything where devotion to the general good is involved. Besides, it would not be a bad thing for your presence to allay . . . in short, I mean. . . . There are some people who count on you over there . . . on your support. Is that not so?"

"Which means that I am to make myself an accomplice. . . ."

The Abbot made a sharp gesture. "Please. . . . There is no complicity in obeying a legitimate order, and I am giving you such an order. Just as I have been given mine. We are merely the agents of a higher authority. You know that quite well."

He was walking up and down the room. On the wall there was an enamel of the Romanesque period. It represented Urban the Second consecrating the altar of Cluny. The touches of gold were all that remained visible of it in the half light.

All of a sudden there was a look in Dom Gregory's eyes which came sometimes when he was trying to keep vaguely in view the funny side of people and things—but now there were gleams of a disquieting brilliance.

"It will be something beyond imagining!" he said. "Have you spoken to the Abbess . . . since?"

"No. And I can assure you that I am not going to mince matters. Under the circumstances it is necessary to set to work in good earnest."

"But . . . I hope you don't approve?"

"Of course I don't. But still less do I approve of a resistance which is beginning to turn the whole business into a drama."

In a corner of the room there was a long table with a silk cover. On it were piles of brightly coloured magazines which Dom Gregory was turning over in a haphazard way.

"For my part," he said, "I think that under the circumstances Mother Hildegard's bearing is not without distinction. A passion which accepts annihilation in order to gain satisfaction has a certain grandeur!"

"My dear Father. . . . Let us leave literature out of it, and lyricism too, if you please! Mother Rouart is the shepherdess of a flock. She must sacrifice herself for the good of the community. God alone knows how it will all end."

"She has indeed come upon strange pastures."

"How far will it go? One wonders. . . ."

There was silence.

"You are proposing to do . . . what has to be done . . . this evening?" Dom Gregory said at last.

"Tomorrow. After High Mass."

"Who will sing the Mass?"

"I shall."

"And doubtless I shall be the deacon and Father Anthony the subdeacon?" Dom Gregory said sarcastically.

The Abbot gave a rather tired smile. "Nothing can be hidden from you," he said.

It was quite dark by now. Father Gregory lit the lamp on the writing-table.

"May I sit down?" he asked.

The Abbot made a gesture of assent and sat down himself on the other side of the table.

"You want to have a rough idea of what has happened, don't you? That is what you are waiting for?"

"Oh! You see . . . I know the essentials."

The Abbot nodded. He seemed to be thinking.

"Do you know how many votes Mother Hildegard collected?" Father Gregory continued after a moment.

"She only needed nineteen more to be unanimously elected. That is to say that she had gained another twenty since the last Chapter. It really doesn't make sense."

"Was it the Cardinal Penitentiary who presided over the Chapter?"

"It was he in person; and with an exhortation which should have been an order—an injunction delivered in the oratorical style which is his speciality. I can imagine the insinuating tone he must have taken, heavy with threats. Moreover his reputation is firmly established. He is a past master at dealing with delicate, complex situations. But none the less, the fact remains that these women are quite mad," added the Abbot. "It is a matter of rebellion, a real revolt. There is no other word for it."

The Two Nuns

A few minutes passed. Dom Gregory was thoughtful. "How do you explain it?" he said.

"I think, Father, that it is Royer-Collard who used to say: 'Democracy is by nature violent, warlike, contradictory.' Although our traditions as a whole are more feudal than popular, we join up with democracy by means of our universal suffrage. So you can draw your own conclusions. Now there is another aspect of the question. Take the Abbey Council. There you have ten nuns, carefully picked by the Abbess— ten nuns of whom at least four are powerful personalities and four others represent respect for tradition. Let us take Mother Teresa of Avila first, for example. A short time ago she was made Mother Vicar. She is a direct lineal descendant of the German Scholastics: fierce, totalitarian, and otherwise very austere and mortified. She has great intellectual honesty. She is supposed to be very close to Mother Hildegard, but that is not at all precise. For her, the Abbess, whoever she might be, is simply God's representative on earth. And no one has the right to set himself up in judgment on a government which exists by divine right. She will never abandon this point of view." He took a deep breath, filling his lungs. "Let us see: it is Mother Cecilia who comes next. Since she retired from the novitiate, she lives in a holy state of fear and trembling. She is seventy years old, or nearly. She is of the same school as the four great elders among the nuns who remain the pillars of the house, and whom Mother Hildegard has kept on the Council not—believe me—without reason. They are Mothers Odilon, Lupus, Barnabas and Saturninus. But Mother Cecilia has a timid, scrupulous temperament, which the others have not. For the rest, all these aged nuns have for some time looked with an indulgent and amused eye upon what they call the 'innovations of our young Fathers'. Mother Odilon is ninety-seven years old. She still has her head screwed on the right way, and a very good head it is, I can tell you. I hear her confessions, so I know what I am talking about.

"To continue. The new Novice Mistress, Mother Clement,

146

comes next. She is absolutely devoted to Mother Hildegard. That goes without saying. No, don't smile. Nothing is further removed from this particular nun's mind than self-interest. If there are any calculations, they are elsewhere. She is thirty-five. She has been trained for eight years with a view to giving her some responsible office. The soil is good. That is all. That is why she was chosen. Mother Hildegard's foresight is almost infallible. Now I am coming to the Mother Bursar, Mother Irenaeus. I will say nothing about her except that it is certain that she voted for the person who appointed her. She is the least interesting of them all—unless, perhaps, the word 'interested' were used in the pejorative sense. Oh, nothing very serious. Let's say that she plays the part of the Greek Chorus to perfection. So, out of the eight, we are left with only two. Of Mother Anselm, the Prioress, I will only say that she has most certainly given her vote elsewhere. But she has no following. She is a solitary soul. No one knows anything about her or her thoughts. She is gracious, and her society is very agreeable. Her virtue is of a very high order, but one does not notice anything remarkable about her at first." For an instant the Abbot paused. ". . . And to end the list we have Madame de Neuville. Your dearly beloved Mother Stanislaus. She remains as the only combatant in the Council—the only one who is fiercely independent. And she and Madame Anselm are the only ones who have managed to some extent to keep their heads. I am not singing you her praises, Dom Gregory. First, because you do not count for much in this affair, and for that matter neither do I, her confessor! And secondly, because there would be a great deal to say about Mother Stanislaus and her intelligence, which is very high. Everyone knows it. Well, all that leads to a conclusion and enables us to understand how the average opinion was directed. The imitative instinct in the masses is a force to be reckoned with. Mother Hildegard once said: 'Votes have no value in themselves. They are only useful for counting.' Here we have the proof."

A few minutes passed. Dom Gregory seemed to be thinking.

"The Council of the Ten[1] is indeed surprising," he said at last, with a smile. "I am well aware that the mere fact of belonging to a minority creates a situation which fosters neurosis. The Worthies of the Venetian Republic would have had no cause to envy these nuns. But all the same! There is nobility in the way they are acting, Father," he added gently. "There is a nobility in refusing to be forced (even by an injunction) to abandon a cause which one believes to be just."

"Nobility of soul is a luxury which one must sometimes manage to do without if one is to go on living, Dom Gregory. You are taking a literary line, you are a knight of chivalry, a romantic. All that is very moving, but you see what it leads to. And this is only the beginning. They will continue to the very end. Anything may happen. And even if Mother Hildegard were to give way . . . it would be all over with her now."

"She will not give way."

Although he did not care much for the Abbess, and was inclined to judge her with severity, Dom Gregory had a certain pride and perverse admiration on his face.

"No, she will not give way," he repeated. "She would prefer a freely chosen exile. And I approve of her in that. The Lord's Anointed is sacred. Our Constitutions and our Rule teach this, Dom Germain."

The Abbot shook his head, as much as to say that with regard to Mother Hildegard he had nothing more to learn. As for the Lord's Anointed. . . .

There was a long, tense silence, full of foreboding. Then someone knocked on the door, and Dom Gregory stood up.

"Well then, I am going to the abbey," he said.

The Abbot made an imperious gesture.

"Oh no! I beg of you. Don't go spreading more trouble over there." He controlled himself and went on in a gentler

[1]Secret tribunal of ten members in the Republic of Venice, 1310–1707.

tone. ". . . There are some whom you are protecting, and who are fond of you. And there are . . . the others. You ought to understand. These women must be in a state of stupefaction . . . impossible to imagine. They must be left in peace. From what I know of Mother Hildegard the whole community will spend the night in the choir, praying. So . . . it is better to leave them. Tomorrow . . . tomorrow will be soon enough," he added, his tone coming down a whole octave, all his anger gone. There was in his eyes that fundamental sorrow which sometimes strikes down the strongest of men and is then like the pain of a child.

A monk came in.

"Well, then . . . we will meet again later," said Dom Gregory.

"Tomorrow," said the Abbot.

29

The night passed, and it was now the second of October. The Feast of the Guardian Angels. It was a bluish morning—a delicate pale blue like watered silk. The woods were wet, the ferns and grasses fresh. On the pond, water-spiders with their long legs were coming out of the aquatic plants. From time to time a fish rose to the surface. In the fields there were lambs still sleeping, and wild flowers and autumn smells. The monks had left their abbey very early. They were following the forest paths. It might perhaps have been half-past seven.

The Father Abbot was walking beside Dom Gregory. They hardly spoke. Their faces were sad and anxious. Father Anthony had started still earlier. Perhaps he had to hear confessions? The High Mass would be at nine o'clock, as on any other day.

"I don't think that the order of things which is to be established today can last very long," said Dom Gregory.

"Neither do I."

As a protection from the drops of water falling from the trees the Abbot had pulled his black hood over his head. They were moving along the dew-drenched paths with long strides. The colours of the trees were extraordinarily rich, ranging from fawn to yellow and then through every gradation of gold.

"Will the course in Ecclesiastical History be interrupted?" asked Dom Gregory.

"I think that is highly probable, since we shall no longer have access to the convent," replied the Abbot. "It is very unfortunate for the student Sisters," he added.

Father Gregory's eyebrows drew together and his face took on an expression of lofty disapproval.

"No access to the convent . . . none at all?" he said.

"So it would appear. I shall have to go into it all with his Excellency, but to judge from the instructions which have already been communicated to me, that is how the matter stands."

"But you surely can't mean that we shall no longer be able to see our daughters?"

The Abbot stood still. "Father Gregory . . . I wonder whether you have quite realized the full scope of this measure . . . and all it will entail? *For the time being, the nuns will be deprived of the help of the monks who normally minister to them. They will also be deprived of the help of any other priest—even though he be a relation or family connection.* That is clear enough, I think?"

"But look, Father. I have novices among my daughters. I have young, newly-professed nuns, who are not yet members of the Chapter and have nothing to do with all this business."

"You have *one* daughter among the newly-professed nuns, Dom Gregory," said the Abbot, with an irony which came very near to a smile. "Sister John of the Cross is a daughter who could manage for some time without any help, I fancy. Don't you agree? Oh! I know that you have a very special place in your heart for her," he added; and he hesitated, between teasing and sadness.

"The question doesn't lie there, Dom Germain. Please don't let us shift it. I understand that for a time the sacraments will be refused to the nuns. Besides this, I understand that the Blessed Sacrament will be removed from the tabernacle. Surely such measures are drastic enough without having to add this ostracism to them."

The Abbot made a gesture meaning that it was obviously very distressing and sad, but in spite of all his sympathy he could do nothing to change it.

"No, indeed," said Dom Gregory. "I had not realized that the visits to the parlour and the lectures and studies would be stopped. If that is the situation, I don't know what we are heading for."

"Well, you see . . . once they adopt this line. . . . And then you must remember that the nuns would go to confession in the parlours or the lecture rooms. They could plead a case of absolute necessity. Had you not thought of that?"

"There is a meanness of soul in making things impossible to bear. Men and women should be left free to choose . . . whether to gain merit or to sin. What do you make of this essential indetermination, which constitutes our greatness or our wretchedness? We are nothing if we do not keep our power to choose, our power to respond to grace or refuse it. To have recourse to the emotional effects of certain actions and gestures in order to obtain, through our feelings, an acquiescence which our reason would have refused, constitutes the vilest abuse of power."

"In diplomacy, there is always a touch of meanness of soul," said the Abbot. "It is only the end that matters."

He smiled a little, with a certain resigned bitterness. But this dropped from him with the words he uttered, leaving him free, compensated, but probably in a profound solitude.

"One of the miseries of the human state," he added a little later, "is that we are always oscillating between these two poles: exaltation and baseness."

His voice betrayed intense tiredness combined with deep sorrow. For a few instants neither of the monks spoke.

"You see," said the Abbot, "I am not worrying about the individual nuns who will eventually come out of it all right, either through their energy, their patience . . . or through subversive decisions, whether temporary or definitive. Decisions which the nuns will now have the right to make. No, I am worried about the community as a whole . . . about the lay Sisters, for instance, who have had nothing to do with the business and who are now going to be deprived of their communion each morning—of their confession each week. Deprived, above all, of the presence of the Blessed Sacrament in their midst. Yes, it is them I am anxious about."

"I agree with you in that," said Father Gregory with great seriousness.

He was crushing a sprig of mint in his hand.

"Is there any limit to the time these measures are to be pursued?" he added.

"The order says 'for the time being'. This implies until there is submission. Unless in the meantime——"

"In the meantime?"

"—we witness the pure and simple deposition of Madame Rouart."

There was a pause.

"During the coming days, it might have been desirable that you should still be allowed to have access to her," said Dom Gregory.

"Oh! You know . . . as to any chance of her listening to me! I am to see her for a last time this morning. . . . Actually I have certain final arrangements to settle with her."

The Father Abbot was far more deeply affected than Father Gregory by circumstances which he considered painful, but above all unprecedented. For him their unprecedented nature was far more serious than the suffering and pain. He was a man of excellent judgment, energetic and warm-hearted. But his character lacked that aristocratic sense which is developed in early childhood and cannot be taught. It imparts the taste for a certain kind of risk, and the power to accept as natural and inevitable whatever tribulations may occur as a result of respect for a few jealously preserved, leading ideas. He therefore judged very severely all that did not follow the great monastic line, whose wisdom all down the centuries had been proved beyond a doubt. He judged Mother Rouart, but he also judged, and perhaps with more severity, an ecclesiastical tribunal which had been able to take such audacious measures.

He walked with his head down, absorbed in his thoughts.

"His Excellency preferred to pass on to you this task which might well be called an unpleasant and heavy one. It is true that you rank as a bishop. All the same! He might have been there."

The Abbot made a gesture. "Perhaps it is better not to make too much of a show in this affair."

"Perhaps," said Dom Gregory in an indifferent voice.

They reached the Abbey. The clock in the courtyard marked a quarter-past eight. There was no sign of life around the portress's lodge. At the entrance to the outer gardens, two oblate Sisters were talking in low voices. The flowers were strangely distinct and white in the morning light. The lawns had been freshly mown. The privet and box were glistening with rain-drops, and there was still humidity in the air. But the sky was the same pale blue, and soon the sun would come out.

The Sisters stood aside, without saying a word. They looked sad and embarrassed.

"Will you kindly call Mother Abbess for me, Sister?" said

the Most Reverend Father, addressing the older of the two.

She bowed, silently. Then she went off towards the house. A thrush began to sing.

"Do you want to see anyone, Father Gregory?" said the remaining Sister. She spoke in a serious, candid manner which was characteristic of her and very charming.

"I will see Mother Stanislaus and Sister John of the Cross," he said with the gentle, protective smile which he often gave the nuns, especially the very young ones, even when he was not their counsellor or their father confessor.

Left alone, the monks exchanged a few vague remarks. Then they went to their respective parlours.

Inside, the Abbey seemed deserted. The long cloisters were empty. Empty also were the workrooms—the illuminating and manuscript rooms—the libraries—the halls where linen was sorted and stored—and habits looked after. Quite bare and deserted was the workroom where the embroidery of altar vestments was usually done—with its great frames on which were stretched marvellous moirés, embroidered and re-embroidered with many-coloured silks. The whole life of the house seemed to have taken refuge in the choir. The nuns were praying, kneeling in their stalls or close to the grille. Some were prostrated with their faces to the ground. Others were sitting near the confessional, waiting their turn.

An hour passed. At last the Abbot came down from the parlour. His face was expressionless. He looked older, hard. This hardness in him was an adjustment to inextricable difficulties.

The oblate Sisters were waiting for him in the passage on the ground floor. They were very attentive—watching his face. But he seemed to be absorbed in the solitude of his own feelings and had no words. The Sisters withdrew, abashed.

There is a smell of solitude as there is a smell of death. It causes the crowd to make away.

The Abbot did not even turn his head; as the great bell was sounding the first stroke for High Mass, he went towards the sacristy.

The service proceeded as usual. The voice of Father Anthony, who was singing the Epistle, seemed strangely tense and shrill, and several times it broke. It was Father Gregory who sang the Gospel, in a clear, fervent voice. The Abbot gave out no notices, going on immediately to intone the Creed. The liturgical vestments were pearly white, embroidered with griffons in scarlet silk on a background of damasked gold. The sun was beginning to brighten everything with reflections of still delicate colours. It was Dom Gregory who gave communion to the Sisters of the novitiate at one of the side grilles. At the central grille the Abbot, assisted by Father Anthony, gave communion to the nuns.

There did not seem anything specially moving or solemn about this particular morning. The Abbess had her usual expression, except that a strange calm had descended on her. No doubt she was drawing her strength from the certitude she had that she held her office from God alone.

The nuns' faces were peaceful again. There was no joy in them, but no sadness either. They showed scarcely any sign of fatigue, though it was true that most of them had spent the night in prayer.

After the Last Gospel, the monks returned to the sacristy. Then they came back, and the Blessed Sacrament was exposed and the last Benediction given. After that the Abbot took away the ciborium.

He had himself put out the sanctuary lamp.

And the door of the empty Tabernacle remained open.

Then the abbey entered into a deep silence.

In the courtyard the big gilded hand of the clock seemed to traverse a dead, meaningless space.

Even the bells of the cattle at pasture in the neighbouring countryside were scarcely audible. The red-roofed houses, grouped here and there, whence a long trail of white smoke rose at dawn, seemed struck motionless as though by a spell. It was like the old stories in which a bad fairy, with one stroke of her wand, imprisons people and things in a web of silence. The whole village was plunged into a strange state of apprehension. It had begun with whisperings and clandestine meetings, where gossips gave free range to their imagination; first in sly, hesitant insinuations, and then openly and shamelessly attacking the Abbey. As for the rest of the village, without quite understanding the situation they inclined by instinct towards the side that seemed best armed and most likely to prevail. On market days the peasants formed groups in the square, talking in low voices and nudging each other rudely with their elbows whenever strangers appeared whom they suspected of coming to spy on what they were thinking, and to inform the authorities. One might have imagined oneself back in the days of Napoleon's Concordat, seeing the conversations suddenly stop when a policeman or even a postman came by.

At the Abbey, people had been coming to find out what was happening. To see with their own eyes. It was incredible. Old Sister Constance, who was the senior of the Oblates, had resumed her vigilant watch at the portress's lodge, answering the visitors' enquiries with the words of Saint Mary Magdalene before the empty tomb on Easter morning: "They have taken away the Lord." And she added no further information. Her face showed dull rancour. It was she who heard all the disagreeable comments and the unkind words. She who sometimes saw people smiling. These things made her suffer, but her anger dared not take any precise direction, and for the moment she was still loyal to the Abbess. She was sixty-five years old, and in her eyes the abbey had always stood for the rock, the citadel, the impregnable fortress; like one of those mediaeval castles isolated on an island which preferred extinction to surrender. And the Abbess, was she not the incontestable sovereign? Perhaps she felt that one would be wrong to rebel even against injustice if it was accepted and sanctioned by tradition.

The oblate Sisters, who were not confined to the enclosure, could have gone daily to Mass and communion at the parish church. They could also have gone to the Fathers' Abbey, Saint Benedict's; after all, they were not members of the Chapter . . . but they felt that they were inseparably bound to their community. Not one of them crossed the threshold of the little village church during all the months the schism lasted, nor did any make their way to Saint Benedict's.

From the very first day, the Abbess had said to them: "Of course you are free, *but* . . ." and her whole character was expressed in that little word, which she had uttered one morning and which seemed like the organ-point in a symphony. No one would have dared to infringe it, to override in any way or set aside this *but* . . . so naturally laid down after the assurance and declaration that they were free.

The chatelaines of the neighbourhood came to visit the Abbess, who received them with gratitude and the air of someone who is for the time being unjustly defrauded of what has always constituted her privilege and, indeed, gives all its meaning to her existence in this world. This last point was true. She was suffering—in her pride, of course, but also in her heart and her monastic habits.

One of the oldest among the lesser gentry of the district, a great friend and benefactor of the Abbey, who had one of his sons at the monastery, gently pointed out to her that the legitimate authority of the bishop is of immense value and was always respected in the primitive Church. He did so with all possible tact, but the Abbess refused to listen to any explanations, saying that she knew she was in the right, that she would bear with patience the arbitrary yoke laid upon her and all the punishments, and that she would do so for as long as was necessary. On that day the visit was cut short and the land-owner did not show himself again.

The parish priest of the village, who was under the same

order as all the diocesan priests, and who was even more afraid of the gossip in the corridors than of his archbishop, did not come.

For the first few Sundays after the schism, cars still came from the nearest town, and indeed from much greater distances. From within a radius of a hundred to a hundred and fifty miles numerous worshippers were in the habit of coming to the Abbey for the Sunday High Mass. Normally it was scarcely possible to park all the cars in the great courtyard. Then the news spread. People heard it and the traffic was doubled. Then, following on the excitement, a complete silence descended. Public opinion in the towns very quickly became hostile to the Abbess, who understood this from the first weeks, and only received a few very rare friends. Anyhow, the visits became less frequent and took on a character of curiosity which almost amounted to insolence.

Several postulants and even some novices left the Abbey at the request of their parents and on the advice of their directors. The Abbess made this a pretext for increased austerity, and encouraged the community to follow her in what she called "a renewal of fervour". For the most part they did so.

Inside the convent the regular life continued. During the hour allotted by the Rule to attendance at the first Mass, the Sisters read the proper for the day in their missals, and spent the rest of the time in mental prayer. During the usual time set aside for High Mass they were not bound to any particular exercise, so long as they stopped all manual work.

At first the nuns stayed in the choir. Later they retired to their cells, or visited each other. The first austerity soon relaxed. The Abbess appeared not to notice. During the first weeks the Prioress wrote to her brother, the bishop, who as a matter of fact had heard rumours of what was going on, although he lived more than three hundred miles away. He came to the abbey, did not ask to see the Abbess and talked for long hours with his sister.

The next day at the communal recreation the Abbess smiled at Mother Anselm with the graciousness which she always put into her relations with her assistant.

"Monsignor Denoix preferred not to see us," she said. "I understand. His Excellency is obeying orders." Her tone was almost playful—as though she were a party to what had been going on. Mother Anselm was imperturbable and, as always, full of tact and moderation.

"All this is very difficult, your Grace," she said, almost with a smile.

Meanwhile, in the group formed by the nuns of the Council they talked about other things.

The old Mothers pressed around the Abbess. It might have been said that they wanted to protect her.

The four ancients—all over ninety, though this did not prevent them from getting up every night for Matins—said very loudly that the Archbishop had been imposed upon, that the Cardinals had been tricked, that they were surrounded with young priests who in the old days would never have dared to cause such a scandal.

In other words, they were quite brazen. They added, learnedly, that "Madame ought to hold her own". The Abbess listened with an indulgent smile. But she did not tell them to be quiet, which she could have done with instantaneous success, even by a gesture.

The community as a whole had a deep respect for the four veterans. It was due not only to their age but to the quality of their virtue—a manifest virtue which assumed every form, and had never flagged during seventy years or more.

Mother Odilon, who was ninety-seven, had entered the novitiate when she was twenty. At that time there were no temporary vows. The novices took the final vows at the end of the canonical year of probation. Mother Odilon had therefore been wearing the large-sleeved *coulle* for seventy-six years. She had celebrated her ruby wedding anniversary at the grape harvest, and the nuns murmured their admiration when she passed.

Every evening after the singing of Compline, when she went in her turn to kneel in front of the Abbess to receive her blessing for the night, the ever-renewed emotion of the young sisters was at its height. The Abbess always tried to restrain her at the first movement, but, strong-willed and peremptory, the old nun would push her superior's arm away, and would kiss the ring of office only from a kneeling position. The Abbess then helped her to get up and she accepted this help, but without the slightest relaxation in her features. Her face remained austere and grave because they were in the choir, and the terrible majesty of the Lord was watching over His sanctuary, as formerly the Spirit of God moved upon the waters, and for her austere, insatiable virtue the slightest weakness was a sin.

Apart from this, during the times of recreation she was as merry as a lark and amused everyone with her witty comments and her sly humour.

To go back to the first day: it was the feast of the Guardian Angels, and ever since the morning the nuns seemed to be stupefied, wandering in the great house which would henceforward be lonely, emptied of all they cherished.

It struck five o'clock.

Sister John of the Cross knocked at Mother Stanislaus's door. They remained a long time shut in together. When they came out, their faces had an air of fierce decision. It was well known that Mother Stanislaus thirsted for violent sensations. No doubt she was waiting to act until the days needed for her to use up her reserves had passed? Those nuns whose activities brought them into contact with her at that time knew, all the same, that the time which was to pass before she took some definitive action was limited.

It was now half-past six.

A wind was whistling among the leaves. Suddenly the rain came beating down hard. Mother Stanislaus went to the portress's lodge. She asked for an urgent call to the Fathers.

After a moment's hesitation and an imperious gesture from the Mother Councillor, Mother Peter of Verona obeyed. Mother Stanislaus shut herself into the telephone box and went on speaking for a long time.

Later on, when the community bell was sounding, and she went to the refectory, she seemed more enveloped than ever in her obscure and ardent silence.

30

The great bell was silent. Only the bell for the community exercises was to be heard now, and also the silvery and almost aerial bell which called the nuns to the parlour.

A week had passed. It was a mild, dull morning. In the woods there were red partridges and guinea-fowl. Beside the lake ducks were hiding in the rushes and disappearing into the copper-coloured ferns and heather with a dry sound like rustling paper. The surface of the water reflected a whitish light. For several days now the quails had been in flight, escaping from the probable rigours of winter. The wagtails were coming from the north with the cool winds. Benedict, the gardener, was lighting bonfires with twigs. It was Saturday.

In the choir a great many lay Sisters were engaged in the weekly cleaning, helped by some of the novices who happened to be free that morning. The sacristy doors and those that gave on to the atrium were wide open. Open, too, were the large stained-glass windows beyond which the coppery beeches were visible.

The Sisters were taking out the strips of carpet from the stalls. The square clips in chased metal were carefully cleaned. With chamois leathers dipped in furniture paste, the cleaners set to work with methodical application to polish the carving and elbow rests of the stalls. They energetically brushed everything that could be brushed. They ran their vacuum cleaners and electric polishers wherever it was possible.

The chief Sacristan was a young Mother who had only recently taken her final vows. She was called Mother Scholastica. Given the importance of ritual and ceremonies in Benedictine abbeys, as well as their great complexity and variety, her responsibilities were heavy. A discriminating taste was needed, skill and rapidity of movement, and the ability to make quick decisions. Mother Scholastica, who had been trained in the disciplines of the arts, was admirably suited to her task.

At this time, when the morning was at its height, Mother Scholastica, vigilant and industrious, was washing the leaves of the potted ferns. She performed this rite with an air of serious concentration, using a piece of cotton-wool dipped in warm water. And she did it as though there were nothing in the world more conducive to her happiness. She had donned a long overall of white linen which entirely covered her habit. She was tall, slim and agile. Her smooth, amber-tinted face had a serene beauty. From time to time she glanced at her improvised workers with the tranquil authority of a queen bee, her eyes full of kindly solicitude. Then she would go and lend a hand either to fasten a carpet, to hold a stool or to move a statue. No one spoke unless it was absolutely necessary and then only in whispers. In the choir-loft Mother Francis de Sales was practising a Bach fugue on the organ.

The young Mother went into the sacristies. They were part of her domain, these three immense communicating halls reserved for the storing of ornaments, chasubles, dalmatics, marvellously embroidered linen, candle-sticks, reliquaries of silver or enamel, fine wax candles and sacred vessels. The whole circumference must have measured several leagues, and it was well known that the contents were worth a fortune.

The leaded stained-glass windows threw velvety shadows on the beautiful red-brown of the parquet floor. The light was shot through with delicate tints, like gems. As she entered, the second and third Sacristan Mothers looked at each other as though hesitating about what they should do. Then they seemed to make up their minds, and a few sentences were exchanged in low voices. As though by instinct they had all three gone to a long, raised table where the altar linen was laid out. Mother Scholastica carefully examined the linen and batiste edged with precious lace. Then, without another word, she left the sacristy.

Outside the enclosure, beyond the grilles, the oblate Sisters were arranging flowers on the altars.

In the nuns' choir the cleaning was finished. Only a few lay Sisters had remained to put the finishing touches. One of them was carefully arranging the Abbess's stall. There was devoted affection in the way she touched the breviaries, the missal, the Rule and books for personal use, also the little ivory hammer and the one made of polished wood with which the Abbess controlled the movements of the community. With infinite care she wiped the bulb of the electric lamp, and polished the copper switch. All her gestures were slow and respectful. There was something suggestive of the High Priest in the Holy of Holies, putting in place the Ark of the Covenant and the Loaves of Proposition. Finally she put back in its place the red cushion whose velvet cover she had just brushed up. She glanced around to make sure that all was correct, and unfastened her blue linen apron. Then she bowed towards the Altar and went quietly out.

Mother Scholastica crossed the atrium. She had taken off her linen overall and was now dressed as for choir. She quickened her step. She looked preoccupied. Her thoughts seemed to be engaged on strange, unknown paths. But, when observed with closer attention, she was seen to have an unwonted, transfigured expression in her dark eyes and her radiant smile. The sunshine had now reached the cloisters, warm and golden. The Mother's form was bathed in it. Then she disappeared in the direction of the Abbess's apartments.

31

From Madame Stanislaus de Neuville, O.S.B.

To The Reverend Father Gregory de Carennac, O.S.B.

Dear Father Gregory,

A few days ago I had a visit from some of my relations. I know that my last two letters are being talked about in Rome. One was addressed to His Eminence the Cardinal Prefect, the other to our Most Reverend Father Abbot General. I enclose copies of both. I will not say anything further about them now. Their meaning is clear for anyone, and for you most of all.

I am awaiting decisions which have now become inevitable. I cannot accustom myself to the spectacle of the incessant degradation of people, ideas, feelings and language. I long for this decadence to be halted.

Apart from that, my actual position suits me. I do not want to change it in any way. I am resigning myself to the daily difficulties, and, believe me, I am doing so without any regrets. Life is going marvellously in our little group; with a great deal of affection and sweetness, much patience and much common sense. And I have confidence in one thing: as we are nearing the bottom, there must be a very good chance for us to rebound. We shall soon know whether I am condemned to lose that confidence also.

You know that in the depths of my soul I am not at all patient. But the methods of the impatient have always struck me as calamitous. And more often than not it is I who moderate the impatience of our circle—above all among the young, newly-professed nuns who would put everything in a blaze.

I should have loved to tell you some of the little trifles

which amuse people less critical than I am about amusements, but my letter is long enough already and the bell is sounding for Vespers.

Benedict will bring you this with a few messages from those of us who are your children. I prefer to make as little use as possible of our oblate Sisters, so as not to upset consciences which may still be undecided.

Mother Stanislaus de Neuville, O.S.B.

P.S. A discovery which will be a valuable lesson for everyone has just been communicated to us and has obliged me to re-open my letter.

Given the very exceptional seriousness of the circumstances, I beg of you to break the rule about visiting us, and to come to the abbey tomorrow.

There is nothing to fear. Sister Peter of Verona is on our side. If she is not one of your daughters, it is only because she has another confessor. At any rate she is sensible, upright and courageous. As to the oblates, they would be too frightened to speak. If the thing becomes known, half the abbey will think and say that I have gone to negotiate about the deposition of the Abbess.

It matters little to me and it does not matter much in itself. It is enough if ten or a dozen people know what is really happening. They will know; and I have acquired the right not to sacrifice the liberty of my conduct to the vanity of outward appearances. Please say this for me to all our friends at your abbey. I imagine we are gaining more of them every day.

Sister John of the Cross, who has also reopened her letter in my room, is waiting for me to close mine up again before she takes all the correspondence to Benedict.

Goodbye, then, till tomorrow, Father.

32

"It is a real revolution, Father," said Mother Stanislaus quietly. "One might imagine that we were back in the blackest days of the Terror. The Blessed Sacrament is now clandestinely exposed in the inner choir. You must note, Father, that we are very glad about it. But, all the same, it is a curious state of affairs."

It was quite warm in the parlour, and a pleasant smell came through from the wood fires which were still kept burning in the adjacent rooms where visitors had their meals.

It was Sunday afternoon, during the calm period of leisure before Vespers. The light was still golden—perhaps copper-coloured would be more exact—like the light in certain paintings by Jordaens.

Dom Gregory de Carennac was listening with visible interest.

"Yes, they tell me that Mother Scholastica found some fragments of the consecrated Host on a corporal. The Abbess took this to be a clear sign from God in her favour. We were told about it yesterday before Vespers. After the Office she herself exposed the Blessed Sacrament."

The monk seemed to be more and more interested, but not at all worried. Perhaps Mother Stanislaus thought he should have been.

"The thing was done according to the correct forms," she went on. "The fragments of the Host were detached by means of the paten and put in the ciborium. It was then covered with a chalice veil and placed on a little table in front of the grille. The sanctuary lamp is now burning again, and it is as though nothing had happened."

Dom Gregory's eyes had a light in them suggestive of admiration. "So now we don't know quite where we are," said Mother Stanislaus. "Apparently two and two no longer make four, and parallel lines all meet in the end. Moreover, I don't think it will be long before it all comes out."

The monk was perplexed, but with a smiling perplexity which, for an instant, irritated the Mother Councillor.

"But look, Dom Gregory," she said in a tone of friendly familiarity, "I asked you to come to enlighten me with your judgment, so that I might know a little what line we ought now to take. Many weeks may still pass before Madame Hildegard is deposed, and . . ."

Father de Carennac made a gesture in which surprise mingled with a discreet rebuke.

"My dear Mother, I do not in the least believe in such important resolutions," he said at last, with a perfect calm. "We have not seen each other for a week, but I have been thinking a great deal. Would you like to know what my feeling is today?"

Mother Stanislaus made a movement to show that that was obvious.

"Well then, they wanted to proceed by intimidation. They did not take into account the energy of her whom we must still continue to call your Abbess . . . since that is what she is."

The Mother looked at the monk fixedly with eyes that defied him.

"Yes, Mother, that is what she is. And you can trust my experience, and the experience of the wisest of our Fathers, that is what she will remain. They wanted to take some action. They thought that Madame Hildegard would choose an assistant for the moment. They thought she would give in, for fear of something worse. That would have pacified people here and outside; people who are upset about little Sister Andrew—about Mother Mechtild. Then there are the Dominicans in Rome. What more can I say? Do you want me to be more explicit? Three names were in the Cardinal Penitentiary's notebook. Three. And do you know which? There was the name of Mother Teresa of Avila, and that of the young Mother Helena. Both entirely devoted to Mother

Rouart. Trained in the seraglio, if I may say so. The pick of the Abbey stud!"

"It isn't possible!"

"Yes, Mother, yes, it is. After all, I know what I am talking about. We have had a few visitors since these recent happenings. We now have a very good idea of all the stages of the plan. Don't you want to know the third name?"

The Mother made a gesture which implied that she knew quite well what was coming and was ready for anything.

"The third name was that of Mother Dominic de Chabot."

"It is incredible!"

"The Mother Secretary is a nun whose virtue and breeding justify the highest hopes. Madame Hildegard snubs her, of course, but she is in all the secrets. She is definitely the *grey eminence*[1] of the house. Her employment gives her access to the Council without exposing her either to the outward criticisms or to the responsibilities and burdens of a councillor."

"I know that, of course. But that does not mean . . . Never should I have dreamt of such a thing."

"Exactly . . . not even you . . . you whose eye is so keen. You realise now what hidden forces she has at her disposal. 'Always beware of the one you forget', says the proverb."

"This has taken my breath away, Dom Gregory. I simply can't get over it."

"Ah! Mother Stanislaus, you would have made a very poor diplomat. You spend all your days on the roads of Judaea or Cappadocia, at the time of Saint Basil and Eusebius. . . . By the way, your article is remarkable! The resistance of Eusebius faced with the decisions of the Council of Nicaea. It is 'seen' with such pertinence! But surely you make a diabolical attack on Saint Athanasius in this affair?"

They exchanged a smile in which their former friendly complicity was restored.

---

[1] Reference to discreet and diplomatic Père Joseph, confidant of Cardinal Richelieu, known as *l'Eminence Grise*.

The Two Nuns

"Diabolical is the word, Father. There are aspects of the life of the Bishop of Alexandria which deserve such an attack. And then, you know quite well that I always attack the 'saints' in favour of those who have not succeeded in being raised to our altars after their death," she added ironically.

"Not always, Mother. You are forgetting Tertullian."

"That is quite another story," she said in a voice once more serious and sad. "It is an old story. A good deal more could be added. But I don't take back anything I have written. Let's return to the matter in hand, though," she said after a moment of silence. "I know that I am ignorant of many facts and many elements. That is why I asked you to come, Dom Gregory."

"Well! I have something even better to tell you, Mother. Do you know that Mother Teresa of Avila is actually on the list for the Abbey of V., where they will probably be electing a new abbess in a few months?"

There was an incredulous light in Mother Stanislaus's eyes and also an unconscious hint of secret amusement.

"Now, I have told you," continued Dom Gregory; "and I have told you this because I know. Within six months Mother Teresa will be Abbess of V. You see how well things manage to arrange themselves. Some action had to be taken. . . . It has been taken. I don't know what will come of it, but I am certain that, whatever it is, it will not be so bad for Mother Hildegard. . . . And when all is said and done, she is a very great lady," he added with that quiet nobility of tone which he always preserved.

The room was bathed in warm light which brought out the soft loveliness of fragile green plants and the beautiful deep red of the heavy Flemish cloth, edged with long silver tassels, on the table close to the Father. Mother Stanislaus was silent for a while.

"Father," she said at last. "You cannot see the question from the same angle as we do."

"But indeed I can; I can and I do. . . . I follow you in all

169

the main lines of your thought. Please don't think I am abandoning your group. It is the group of reason. And as far as feelings go I am with you too. I am not an outsider. I am a monk. I also have difficulties with my superiors: and, in the first place, with Dom Germain. We often come up against each other, you know."

Mother Stanislaus's eyes were smiling, but very soon she became serious again, with a certain hardness in her expression.

"*In vain does Nero prosper!*"[1] she murmured.

"Really, Mother, I think that what you lack . . . you, also . . . is moderation. When one comes to think about it, Mother Rouart is perhaps innocent with regard to a certain state of affairs which does undeniably exist, and is extremely unfortunate, but whose deeply embedded foundations were laid long before her time. You only have to look at some of your most excellent aged nuns!"

"Admitting that to be true, there has been plenty of time for her to take steps to remedy it. She lacks neither the power nor the audacity. But no. It is part of her nature to tighten everything—to make everything harder. That is the very opposite of what is needed for the opening out and blossoming of the spiritual life of this Abbey. And may I beg you, Dom Gregory," she added vehemently, "not to confuse purity with innocence."

The monk thought for a while.

"Yes, Mother Stanislaus, more moderation, please! I was right about that. Forgive me if I have strayed into a field which does not belong to me. Lively and constant as our relationship is, it is only intellectual. I do not want to trespass on Dom Germain's preserves. But our friendship is of long standing and affectionate, and I am speaking to you as a brother to his sister."

"Oh! you know . . . discussion is often very difficult with Father Abbot. He is also the director of Mother Hildegard."

[1] "*C'est en vain que Néron prospère!*"—Chateaubriand.

The Two Nuns

There was a gentle knock on the door from the enclosure side, and without waiting for a reply, Sister John of the Cross came in. Her face was illuminated. This is no exaggeration, for the sun fell straight into her steely grey-blue eyes which, in her happiness, or maybe just her satisfaction, had regained all their childlike lustre.

"As usual, I arrive after the Gospel," she said. "Good afternoon, Father. Today it is not only sad news we have for you. Mother Stanislaus must have told you."

She sat down. Father Gregory smiled and there was gravity and tenderness in those eyes of his which penetrated to the depths of her twenty happy years.

"I know, and I am glad that you should have this temporary consolation. Because, you see, I have no very great confidence either in the present or in the immediate future. You probably still have some hard times in store."

"What do you mean by temporary, Father?" said the young Sister, her eyes solemn again. "I do indeed hope that we shall be able to keep . . . Our Lord."

She said "Our Lord" just as Mary of Bethany must have said it, with the same deeply moving inflections of tranquil confidence.

"After all, it was He who wanted to stay," she added, in the peremptory accents of the very young.

"There is still so much youthful ingenuousness in this child," thought Father Gregory, as he rather sadly shook his head.

"You think that everything is going to be made known," he said. "Tomorrow, or even today, perhaps. No doubt certain measures will be taken? Unless . . ." He rose to his feet. "I would rather not stay too long today," he added. "I am disobeying orders in coming here, and if I want to return . . . Mother Stanislaus will tell you the essentials of what I think about it all. Have confidence. Goodbye! We will meet again soon. The way you have found for correspondence through Benedict is perfect," he added, with a smile of indulgent connivance. "What imagination! It must have been my little Sister John of the Cross who thought of that?"

She was standing planted in front of him. The protection of the grille was between them, but she was giving herself entirely; and there was a certain half-feigned indignation in her expression.

"Yes, indeed, it was I," she said, pronouncing the words with audacious clarity, her eyes looking at those of the Father. "It was I. If we had to depend on you for practical ideas!"

And all of a sudden a sense of aching bitterness invaded her as she remembered the days spent in waiting for him—with no classes, no letters, no visits.

Then Dom Gregory laughed aloud, but with happiness in his eyes.

"Good gracious! A little more and you would be making a scene for me. I'm off. Goodbye for the present," he added. "And make the most of this free time by working on our history course. Tell all the others. Don't let these weeks be wasted. Go over the Council of Basle again. This is more than ever the time to meditate on the objections there are to giving the Council pre-eminence over the Roman Pontiff."

The young nun's eyes were happy again with lights that suggested the colours of flowers and sky. Mother Stanislaus smiled pointedly.

"All that does not tell me whether I ought to make up my mind at last to go to Rome," she said. "Ought I to wait? I am perplexed. It is all very difficult."

"Wait, my dear Mother; you ought to wait. Rome has not replied. Rome is doubtless allowing time for things to be restored to some semblance of calm. Watching events . . . seeking a solution. In all probability you will soon be hearing what is Rome's good pleasure."

"Father is right, Mother. You must wait," said the young nun. "Besides, if you don't, what shall I do here all by myself?" she added in a half-serious, half-joking tone. "Whatever should I do?" she repeated.

Dom Gregory went out, with a farewell gesture. The two nuns walked down the cloisters silently, busy with their thoughts.

33

It was the fifteenth of October, the feast of Saint Teresa of Avila. The midday recreation had been prolonged so that all the nuns, lay Sisters and novices could go together to pay their respects to the new Mother Vicar and to offer her their good wishes and proofs of their affection.

The two large common rooms on the ground floor were divided by a partition which could be pushed back, if occasion required, to form one immense hall where the whole community could move about freely.

Today a beautiful autumn sun was shining. It was still mild for the time of year. The Sisters had decorated the whole place with garlands of dark-red carnations, lilies and roses. Benefactors and relations had sent a profusion of flowers, either bunched together or arranged in bouquets. The nuns were dispersed in little groups of four or five, talking in friendly fashion. They stood or sat, according to their age and character, and also to the difficulty or ease with which they managed to find their friends, in this assembly of three hundred people which, depending on one's point of view, could be compared to an immense charity bazaar or to a university reunion at the end of a convention.

There was an atmosphere of great gaiety among the groups. Since the abbey once more had its Lord within its walls, or to be more exact, since the community had discovered that the

Real Presence had never ceased to be there, living in their midst, the whole feeling of the house had changed and the tension had relaxed.

The news must have already become known outside the abbey, because the faithful were coming back to pray in the church and to make brief acts of adoration before the Blessed Sacrament. Yet no one had dared to ask the slightest question. For that matter the oblate Sisters seldom showed themselves and scarcely spoke to anyone. The Abbess had not had a visit from the Bishop. It was clear that the authorities were shutting their eyes to whatever was going on.

Mother Teresa was surrounded by other nuns. The group composed of the Abbess and Councillors were admiring the illuminated cards and parchments which had been given to her. Among other marvels there was a miniature of the Saint of Avila. It was a line drawing in sepia with no colouring—only graded shades of brown, and it was very austere in feeling and interpretation. There was sternness and emaciation, and those glowing eyes which seemed to consume the face. The style was so severe that one would have taken it for an engraving or etching. The Abbess congratulated the novice who had painted it.

Mother Vicar seemed particularly pleased with this present. There were also some elaborate gothic illuminations on fine parchment of greyish-yellow or mother-of-pearl shades. They were enriched with old gold, and surrounded Mother Teresa's favourite biblical or sacred texts.

Soon two o'clock struck. At the same instant the bell rang, marking the end of recreation, and silence descended upon the great hall. Sentences were left unfinished. The happy laughter faded out. There was nothing but silence—an enormous silence, made more enormous by the numbers—more vast because of the presence of this great muted crowd moving without noise, careful of every gesture as though in a sanctuary.

Everyone was now standing. Every face was serious again.

Already the Abbess was pronouncing the ritual sentence of the obedience: "Have your Reverences anything to say?" She waited for a moment, but on feast days or days of special leave like this, no one ever wanted to speak.

There was no need even to announce the Office for the day. All necessary notices had been given out in the refectory by the Reader.

"You may go then, your Reverences . . . Go in peace!" said the Abbess.

Thereupon the multitude began to flow out of the great hall, moving along the cloisters, making their way to the libraries, the work-rooms, or wherever their diverse occupations took them. Only a few nuns remained, waiting their turn to speak to the Abbess. She was standing in front of her chair, ready to go herself, like anyone else. They must each have had something urgent to say, maybe a special permission to ask for, or a piece of advice needed that very day. The last was Sister John of the Cross. She knelt and kissed the ring. It was with some astonishment that she felt the Abbess's hand resting on her shoulder, gently but firmly.

"Mother, I am tired," she said. "May I be excused from Matins tonight? It will be the first time since . . ."

"Yes, of course. It is enough if you tell me you are tired." The tone was kind—almost maternal.

"Well now, since you are here, will you come back to Our office?" she added. "I was just on the point of sending for you." Then, turning to her secretary who was waiting a few steps away, she said, "You can go on ahead, Mother Dominic. Today sister John of the Cross will accompany Us."

According to monastic ritual the Abbess cannot go about alone in the Abbey.

They crossed the hall. There were some bouquets still lying on the tables. The chairs had not been put back into line. It made one appreciate the work of the lay Sisters, who were already opening the windows and arming themselves with brooms.

The Abbess and her companion went out. As they passed along the cloisters they did not speak. Yet the Abbess, wherever she goes, is dispensed from the rule of silence. Even in the choir and the most strictly silent places, this rule gives way, automatically, if she sees fit. But doubtless at this particular time she may have been thinking that there is something fervent about certain silences? Sister John of the Cross could not have said what was the quality of this fervour. There are fervours of hatred.

A young Mother passed. She had turned back the bottom of her habit over her tunic and had tied an embroidered apron of heavy linen round her waist. She was carrying a large empty basket and a pair of gardening scissors.

"Don't cut all our chrysanthemums, Mother Jerome," said the Abbess with a smile.

"Oh, Mother, there will always be plenty. There are magnificent beds of them this year."

She had a serious and rather moving voice, full of a certain hidden hopefulness. She was the second sacristan. Her form was already disappearing down one of the garden paths.

Sister John of the Cross made a movement as though to draw back, as they entered the large study. She came there very seldom, always unwillingly, and generally with a certain fear which she could not explain.

"Sit down, Sister," said the Abbess.

She folded her strong hands on the table.

"This is what I want to tell you," she said. "I have been thinking of you for some time. You are not very busy, apart from your course of studies, and for the moment, alas! we have no Fathers."

Sister John of the Cross thought: "Whose fault is that?" but her face showed nothing.

"I should like to have you with me," continued the Abbess. "I have been thinking about it for some time. In two years you would be able to replace Mother Dominic, for whom I have something else in store."

She stopped. Sister John of the Cross sat very still.

"Until your final vows, you would help Mother Dominic, who would train you. It would take about two hours each day, I should say, and your studies in philosophy would scarcely suffer at all."

Sister John of the Cross still said nothing. She already felt as if a bitter flood were rising in her heart—it was rising—it would stifle her. She was doubtless praying that the Mother would not notice anything.

"Oh! I know that the history of the Church interests you more than my correspondence. I have no illusions as to that. But . . . for a whole year you have had no fixed employment. That is rather unusual."

"I work for Mother Stanislaus, your Grace."

She would have liked to say that divine truth sometimes comes to us when we are at leisure—when we are perfectly open to it and completely at the disposal of grace. . . .

"I know you work for her. I know that quite well; but I have other ambitions for you than to see you take her place one day in what I suppose we must call her work, since she has no other."

The heart of the young nun almost stopped beating, her breath was quite taken away.

"Oh! Your Grace! Mother Stanislaus's books are among the most important contribution of French scholarship to the history of the Church."

She was speaking almost feverishly.

"Of course! To be sure they are. But after all, there is the Abbey. There is the participation of all its members in the common task. You are before all else a Benedictine nun, Sister John of the Cross. Before all else. And an Abbey is: 'Jerusalem, all of whose stones are joined together, to form but one body.' An Abbey is a unity embracing many means of grace. There is a practical thought upon which it is necessary to meditate. Surely I do not have to tell you how much

our attachment to a tradition so much greater than ourselves
adds to our nobility."

There was a silence.

"I had begun to learn Hebrew."

"I know that you have a great gift for languages," said the
Abbess calmly. "You are very gifted for everything, as a
matter of fact."

Sister John of the Cross no longer thought of answering, or
of defending her position. She seemed to have no strength.
She was suddenly overwhelmed, disarmed by this solidity—
this immense calm. The Abbess automatically opened the
large red morocco diary which had been placed on the table,
to see what appointments had been entered for that afternoon.
The silence became oppressive, motionless, intolerable.

"No, your Grace! Oh no! I implore you. I could never
do it, never!"

Her face was that of a child in tears. Her distress was confused—with no way out. Like an inward vibration which was
gathering momentum and would certainly pass out of control.

"It is impossible, Mother," she went on, in an entreaty
which, without her knowing it, expressed a certain tenderness.
"To type? To fetch the letters? When there are the Early
Fathers and the Church and the Holy Scriptures. Oh no,
your Grace. No."

To leave all that constituted the salt of her life—the joy—
the flame which consumed her, and made her live and begin
again each day to live, and be renewed. No. That she could
not do. It was impossible. The answer must be no.

Her voice plunged into childhood, with the notes of desolation and loneliness. Oh, what long years of her life she
would have given to find someone to lean on now—some
protection. An arm to hug her very hard. Not these cold eyes
which weighed on her—going right through her—disdain-
fully—almost pityingly. What a child she was still! And
what a mixture of affection and hardness—of obstinacy and
surrender! She blew her nose and wiped her eyes.

The Abbess was marking a register. She was checking an immense flat book which must have been one of the house-keeping or estate account books.

A long time passed. Finally she shut the book and raised her eyes. "You will come tomorrow morning," she said in a neutral voice. "After Terce. Don't go to Matins for a week. Get some rest. It seems that you are in considerable need of it. Oh, and please don't cry like that," she added irritably. "I thought you had a courageous heart and a proud spirit."

The blue-and-red patterns of the carpet swam before the young Sister. She bowed silently.

Her hand trembled on the door handle and the catch slipped noisily. The Abbess picked up the telephone receiver.

"You can come in now," she said to Mother Dominic.

34

She was running now on the path that led to the farm, the path on which she knew she would meet Benedict. It was three o'clock. The head gardener should be there now, giving out work to the other men before going off himself to some autumnal task.

First she had been to knock at Mother Stanislaus's door. She wanted to calm her troubled spirit; to cry her heart out at the knees of "her little mother", the only one who had always understood her, who always guessed what was in her mind—who foresaw everything. But Mother Stanislaus's cell was empty, and on the door the ivory marker hung uselessly on its cord, giving no indication as to her whereabouts. The young Sister glanced into the first library—the one where Mother Stanislaus sometimes worked—but she was not there;

nor was she in the manuscript room. Should she get the bell rung for her? A newly-professed nun does not ring for a Mother Councillor in this way. Mother Peter of Verona would not understand if she asked her to sound the bell—or else she would understand too much.

Perhaps she should look in the parlours? But that would waste too much time. And it would be useless. She would see Mother Stanislaus later. She must—she absolutely must—get into touch with Benedict, and she must do so before he went back to the Fathers! She ran along the path. Her eyes were dry now. She was wrapped in her great white woollen shawl which came down below her waist.

Goodness! To think of all her joys—and now—they were trying to tear them away from her. Alas, we appreciate only our past.

At last she reached the poultry yard. The head gardener was there at the entrance to the outhouses. He was talking with a lay brother. Some of the brothers from Saint Benedict's and a few gardeners had obtained the indult necessary for entering the enclosure, and were thus able to come every day to work for the nuns. Benedict wore boots of dark brown leather and an olive-green corduroy jacket. As he talked he was filling the deep bowl of his short pipe. He must have been about sixty years old, and was sturdy and well set-up. He was attentively listening to some explanations and his face was in profile.

The brother was the first to see the young nun. But already Benedict was turning and taking off his cloth beret as he came to meet her.

"Good evening, Sister!" he said, bowing.

He had a perfect knowledge of each and every distinction in the hierarchy of monks and nuns and never used a word that was out of place. He knew exactly the shade of deference or respect required.

He saw the upset face of the young nun, but his eyes showed no expression.

"Sister," he said, in his usual controlled voice, "can I do anything for you?"

The brother had disappeared. Beyond the high fence of wire-netting they could see hundreds of hens. The cackling was interminable. They moved a little away.

"Benedict," she said in a faint voice, quite out of breath, "you must please take this to Dom Gregory—immediately."

She showed him a folded envelope, concealed in the sleeve of her habit.

He coughed. "Immediately? Father de Carennac is at T., Sister. He has gone for the day. I took him there this morning after his Mass. He will not be coming back till this evening, by the seven-twenty bus."

Such acute disappointment showed on her already sad face that Benedict was touched.

He seemed to be thinking. Then he made a gesture to show how distressed he was at his powerlessness.

"There is nothing to be done about it, I am afraid," he said. "But I will give it to him this evening."

"No, Benedict, no! I can't wait till tomorrow to see him."

She hesitated for a second, then made up her mind. "You must help me, Benedict. You must."

She went up to him—within touching distance. For a long moment she spoke in a low tone. The face of the old gardener became grave. At her very first words he had gone pale—not very pale, but the rings round his eyes were accentuated.

He had the disinterested attitude which, combined with the experience of age, confers dignity and wisdom on a character. And if he only dared. . . . But her tone would brook no denial or discussion, and he did not take the risk. Now she had spoken, she had regained all her calm. Her eyes were still tinged with melancholy, but her mouth was almost smiling, with a little pout that was rather charming and childlike.

He kept twisting his cloth beret between his fingers. "Sister, what you are asking me to do is very serious," was all that he said.

She put a finger to her lips. "Don't say a word, Benedict. Not to anyone. It is a secret between us. I take all the responsibility. Just tell Dom Gregory that he is wanted when he comes in. But don't say who wants him, whatever you do! And . . . we will meet this evening. I am counting on you."

Already she was taking the field path back to the convent. The head gardener stood still, lost in thought. His eyes followed the thin white-and-black figure outlined against the almost colourless sky. A gentle breeze was blowing.

She was walking quickly. The rain had stopped. A slight mist was coming down. The clock struck four.

"Now, Lord, You are going to help me. You will, won't You? You must."

35

It was eight o'clock in the evening. Already the nuns were spreading into the cloisters and staircases on their way to their cells. The blessing which follows the Office of Compline had been given.

At last the Abbess left the choir. Three hundred times she had traced the sign of salvation with her thumb on the forehead of her daughters. Three hundred times she had given her ring for them to kiss.

It was now the time of the great silence. The Abbess went back to her apartments. The cloisters were white in the moonlight. Soon there would be no one about. The first period of rest enveloped the abbey until Matins.

Sister John of the Cross put out the last light in the cloakroom. She had muffled herself in a long black woollen shawl. The top of her white veil was scarcely visible. She waited for a moment. There was no sound anywhere. The last lay Sisters must have gone up to bed by their stairs in the direction of the cloister of Our Lady. As on every other night, she had smiled at Mother Stanislaus, who had caressed her cheek. They parted in silence and without kissing each other as they sometimes did.

She knew that the cloister door had been shut as usual. She had heard Mother Stanislaus taking the keys back to the sacristy. Only the door of the atrium which opened on to the lime avenue was never locked.

Noiselessly, and with infinite precautions, she went back the way she had come. The doors of the choir were wide open. She crossed the atrium. The boards creaked. She gave a start. Her heart was in her mouth and her hands were trembling.

A few seconds passed.

She walked quickly under the trees which would soon be without leaves, laid bare, as though dead. In spite of the cool night air she was hot inside the shawl, which covered her completely. Now she was following the dahlia path. At the Calvary under the cedars, the shadow of the three crosses seemed to her gigantic. At that second the moonlight fell on the face of Christ, who was speaking to the good thief: "With me in Paradise. Soon, almost at once. Today." She was overcome by it. Never before had she noticed the serenity of these faces—serenity in agonizing pain. She passed the grottoes. The pond was glistening. The shadows of the elms seemed like souls in torment, imploring Lazarus for a drop of water to cool their tongues. Echoing from the rocks, the ten sonorous strokes of the curfew made her jump. She took out her watch. It was indeed eight-thirty.

She hastened her steps. She still had a mile to cover before reaching the little wooden door in the enclosure wall which no one ever opened, where Benedict would be waiting for her. There was no fear of anybody being in the gardens at this time. No one ever came out before Matins. Not even in summer. Yet she preferred to keep in the shade of the wood.

It was hardly any further: and she would feel safer hidden from the full moon, which frightened her.

Not for an instant did the idea occur to her that she was taking an exceptionally serious step. A step which in itself entailed excommunication. It was not until later that she understood that this step had been hidden in the back of her mind for many months—that a blind force was driving her on. That the most insignificant pretext was therefore enough to make her start on this road which was already irremediably marked out for her.

As she walked, however, trampling on the brittle little twigs, her feet sinking into the thick carpet of leaves, her heart thumping in quick, sharp beats, she saw nothing. She was thinking only of Dom Gregory.

How was he going to take this thing? This unheard-of thing she was doing? It was so extraordinary, so unimaginable, that surely nothing like it could ever have been seen in the memory of monks or nuns. She did not even know whether he loved her. That is to say . . . whether he loved her differently from the others—from his other spiritual daughters. There were several of whom, without saying so, she was jealous—madly jealous. Those two novices whom she detested now, forgetting that it was she herself who took them to Dom Gregory a year ago. But a year ago? How far away all that seemed. There were also two young Mothers with serious faces and gentle eyes. She did not know much about them: and she did not want to.

It was about herself she wanted to know. Did he love her more than the others? Did he love her in the way that made her own heart beat as though it would break, and her throat contract, and her hands burn with fever? Then there was that desolation when he let several days pass without coming. And that joy when he sang High Mass, or when, at Low Mass, he gave her communion.

Did he love her in that way? Was he really, she hardly dared say it, in love with her?

The Two Nuns

There certainly was great affection between them—always. And there were those quarrels, affectionate, teasing. But the Father never gave in in those quarrels, with all that calm he brought to bear on her. And then those moods when he was sulking and sometimes never asked for her in the parlour for a whole week—when he would not ask her anything in the history classes, and scarcely seemed to see her. She remembered the famous day when no one answered a difficult question, when she could have done so, and the Father knew she could. And then Sister Patricia had complicated everything by saying: "Sister John of the Cross knows that, surely." She had blushed, and replied in the affirmative with her eyes. But the Father had seemed not to notice her; after a few minutes of waiting vainly for the answer, he had himself explained about the condemnation of the Three Chapters (at the second Council of Constantinople), where errors favouring the Nestorian heresy had been detected.

Then there had been those reconciliations, those times of return. The warm affection in his letters. Those notes which began: "Dear little daughter" or "Dear Odile" in memory of the old days. But never had he written: "My dearest." Did he write like that to the others? There had been all those things and so many others besides: allusions, the affectionately watchful expression in his eyes. But when all was taken into account, the Father had never said anything which the most minute examination could have interpreted to mean a departure, even for an instant, from the rôle of professor and priest. And how was he going to react now? This evening, over there? How was he going to take her amazing action? And Benedict? And the scandal that was going to bind and mark them, all three? Not that Benedict was not to be trusted. . . . But . . . Oh, dear!

She crossed a field. She could see the wall. The great wall that still separated her from her sin. She could turn back even now, back to her cell. But no. She knew quite well that it was too late. The devil was already there, laughing at her from the undergrowth, following her step by step, surrounding her with compelling shadows. The moon showed his outlines on the ground. Nine o'clock struck. A key grated softly. The door was slowly pulled open. How difficult it was to move it! And she could not tell whether that was because of the weeds or because the hand was trembling over on the other side. Or because of her own hesitation on the brink of this chasm.

Benedict was there. His head was uncovered, and his face so tense and serious that she was afraid.

"Sister," he began. He hesitated, stumbling over what he would have liked to say. Then he held his tongue. For, after all, he was only the gardener, and despite his age and all the confidence with which he was surrounded, there are certain limits which cannot be crossed.

"Sister," and his eyes said, "There is still time." His hand was stretched out to her, but it was as though he sought to keep her back from the precipice—this false step which would change everything—this act which would mark her with a dark shadow and take all the untroubled purity from her brow.

He, standing on the threshold, was still outside, while she was still enclosed in her peace. He did not even think about her innocence. No; that was not the question. It was her peace; the tranquillity of her days; the calm of her nights. As yet there was nothing to touch its surface or to disturb it. He saw only this enclosure which she had vowed never to break.

Perhaps, he thought, if everything were taken into account, it would have been better that Dom Gregory. . . .

But no! Never would she have allowed her enclosure—this walled-in garden with its clear water-springs set apart and sealed—this enclosure of hers which was also her sisters'—never would she allow the enclosure which belonged to them all to be violated. She would prefer to assume the whole burden of her guilt.

She also held out her hand—a hand that was supple and feverishly hot. It was as though she was asking him to help her to cross over the tall weeds, with her long habit. "And you see, Benedict, I did not even have time to turn it up."

But, for his part, he did not touch her hand, as though leaving her free and responsible for her step—this descent which was beginning.

"Good evening, Benedict," she said in a soft voice, which was nevertheless very distinct. It was a voice which dispersed the hovering shadows. "Good evening. Has everything gone all right?"

He looked terribly sad as he stood there in the moonlight. Suddenly he was like an old man, worn out and withered.

"Father de Carennac came back at six; by car, with some people from T.," he said in his ordinary voice. "I told him that tonight at nine o'clock someone would be waiting for him in the cloister of the outer Church."

"You said *someone*, Benedict?"

"Isn't that what your Reverence wished me to say?"

He said "your Reverence" with a certain respectful affection, which placed her very high—inaccessible, still pure—always pure. Even if ... but no, that question could never arise.

He said it just as a few months earlier he would have said: "Isn't that what Mademoiselle Odile wished?" when she came down from X—— for retreats or visits, before she made her decision. How far away it all seemed!

She placed her hand on the old man's arm: "Yes, Benedict, that was just what I wished you to say."

With what fluid rapidity she spoke. Her voice was like a bird's wing in the wind. She was already completely given over to this joy which was surging up in her and acting like an overwhelming power, or a charm which could not be withstood.

They were now crossing the clearing, where the moon threw livid little patches of light everywhere. They were not talking any more. He understood how frightened she must be. He understood that it was now of Father Gregory that she was afraid. He made a gesture as though to dispel a certain train of thought which was going to become painful and for which he would perhaps reproach himself, so delicate was the feeling of reverence he had for her.

She misinterpreted this gesture and took an oblique turn towards the fields.

"No, this is the way, Sister. This is shorter," he said. "In fact, it is a short cut we have taken. You will see; we are arriving."

The wind had freshened. The screech owls could be heard bumping against the trees. And then, suddenly, shadowy and feudal, the abbey rose before them, its lines picked out as in an engraving by the light of the moon. It was majestic. It was unexpected. She recognized the path leading to the farm, the garage and storage sheds for implements and tools. When, as an aspirant, she had come to see Dom Gregory, she must have taken this path. Yes, of course, she remembered. . . . She used to come from T. by the main road and leave her car at the hostel. And how she used to love this walk between the apple trees, with a frosty blue sky overhead.

She shook off all these sweet visions which were floating around her. There, straight in front, dark, massive and patterned with moonbeams, stood the Carolingian apse of the Abbey, flanked by its two spires. She went round the church and along the gallery with its little arcades and its two semicircular bays leading to the monumental porch.

All at once she was alone. Alone beneath the moon, with moving shadows which seemed to be walking. Her heart stood still. She ran over the wet moss, but soon she was in the light again with a view stretching away across the plain and the little hillocks over to the east.

She entered the cloister. The tall form of Dom Gregory was just visible. He was moving slowly, his hood pulled down over his forehead. She could see the side of his spectacles. He was looking towards the horizon. Then she ran to him, her heart on fire, her eyes dim with tears. At first she did not say a word. She clung to his shoulders, to the strong arms which did not give way or fail her. They were strong as a rock. She pressed her head against his chest. She felt its warmth and its strength. She hid herself there, sobbing and murmuring her devotion. Her forehead scarcely reached up to the monk's chin. With the gentlest of movements he pressed her to him. He did this very firmly, and she felt all the tranquil protection which would envelope her for the future and for ever . . . which would defend her and keep her safe from everything.

As soon as she was a little calmer, he drew her under an archway. He made her sit down beside him on the granite seat, bathed in moonlight. He held her in his arms and let her talk with all her fury, all her indignation, which had found an outlet at last after being kept back too long. He replied with softly murmured words. He rocked her as though she was a sick child. For a long time he caressed and soothed her.

She told him everything. How terrified she had been. Above all, how she wanted to go away, but that now she would never go. He pressed her more closely, but there was no smile in his eyes.

At last he put her away from him. He took her face, still wet with tears, between his hands. His gestures were slow, as at the altar. She read in his grey eyes a trace of acute suffering, and she saw also the ardent light of a love so immense that it shares in all our sorrows.

It was not her nature to draw back. She held his gaze for a long time with her blue eyes, now free from tears

"You must never abandon me," she said. "Never."

Midnight struck. And from the steeples of the two abbeys the first bell for Matins rang out across the countryside.

He rose to his feet.

"We must go now," he said. "Benedict will take you back. Tomorrow morning I shall be celebrating Mass in the parish church. I will return by your abbey. I will see you at eight o'clock."

She smiled. "You will never scold me for ... this evening?" she said in a voice which had become gay again—her eyes full of tender affection.

He put his hand against her face, the childish quality of which showed still more in her happiness. He caressed it gently. He had firm, wise hands and they were also tender.

"We shall see all about that tomorrow," he said.

Benedict came out of the shadows. He had been keeping faithful watch, but he was uneasy.

"Take the shortest way back," said the monk, "and do not leave her before you get to the farm. Even within the enclosure I don't much like those woods after dark."

The second bell for Matins sounded over the plain.

Twice she turned to look at him. He was walking towards the inner cloister. He was moving slowly.

"Dear Lord! I could close my hands on all this happiness. How long, O Lord, will my hands remain open?"

36

She opened the door of the manuscript room. It was raining. Near the windows there were bushy pale-green ferns in stone-coloured flower-stands. It was quite early in the morning, perhaps about nine o'clock, but they had already turned on one light down at the far end. Just one, which left the rest of the room in a grey half-light.

For a moment she stood at the door, hesitating. She had pulled out her watch. Then she appeared to make up her mind in spite of various difficulties known only to herself, which probably had to do with the limited time at her disposal.

Three days had passed since the night at Saint Benedict's.

At the far end of the room a nun was standing consulting a card-index. She must have been the Mother-in-charge, for she was wearing the long double veil of silk gauze which reaches almost to the knees.

Sister John of the Cross came towards her, but she seemed not to notice anything and to be completely absorbed in her researches. Having come right up to her, within touching distance, the young Sister stopped for a moment. She looked worried and embarrassed. She was twisting the end of her leather belt with her fingers.

Mother Stanislaus looked round. She had an expression which was serious and at the same time mocking. Only slightly so, however: there was just an amused, almost frivolous, gleam in her eyes.

"So then, it is over . . . hothead?" she said in a low voice, looking her over with a peaceful glance.

She put her long engraved-silver pencil down on the table.

There was no one else in the room. Now she was not looking at the Sister any longer, but had sat down and was opening an old volume with very much-worn parchment pages. The minutes were slipping by, marked by the sand of an invisible hour-glass.

"Mother . . . something has happened to me . . . it is something terrible."

Mother Stanislaus did not raise her head.

"But, listen, Mother! Please listen to me. It is wearing me out. Listen . . . I think, I think that I am in love . . . well, it is just this; I love Dom Gregory in the way one must love a man in ordinary normal life."

She took a step back. The trees in the park outside looked black and extraordinarily big, as though they had suddenly been enlarged.

"So that is your great piece of news?" said the Mother Councillor.

"But, Mother . . . after all!"

Her hand was trembling on the edge of the table. The sand went on falling in the hour-glass. Mother Stanislaus was writing on sheets of pale-green paper.

Then the young nun dropped on to her knees and pressed herself against the long black veil.

"I have known that for a very long time," said the Mother, going on writing. "It is not exactly a new discovery."

"And you let me love him? You left me to this misery . . . this cross which has become rooted inside me?"

The Mother smiled, but there was a certain melancholy in her expression. "Misery? A cross? Don't let us exaggerate. And besides, my dearest, is it really possible . . .? Come, look at me and tell me honestly; is it possible to prevent you from doing anything?"

"And now . . . what is to become of me?"

"Why, you are going to continue to live—just as you have been doing all these months. Nothing has changed. This affair did not start only yesterday. Really now! Is it possible that you are completely lacking in what Bergson calls intuition, and Pascal heart?"

The young Sister looked so disconsolate. But it was above all the anxiety lest he did not love her which was tormenting her.

"Do you think that he loves me too . . . on his side?" she asked very humbly.

The Mother let a moment of silence elapse.

"How should I know?" she said at last. "Have you seen a white doe in your dreams? Have the angels of the secret valley smiled to you?"

Then with sudden violence, but in a voice breaking with tears, the young nun cried out: "Oh! I've had enough of your teasing, quite enough. I want to go away. Do you understand? I can't go on with this deception. Soon it would become a hell on earth . . . a continued, never-ending madness."

The notes on the green paper became longer.

"Go away?" said the Mother calmly. "Where to?"

The young Sister made a gesture implying: *Where to? As though that mattered!*

"Yes," she said, "I want to go away. No matter where, but with him. I want to go very far away. To leave the Order —and this habit. With him, it would mean purification for me. I should touch land at last. Regain strength and courage."

In the Mother's eyes there was all the surprise in the world. And really it seemed as though it was sincere.

"With him? But, my dearest, you must surely be joking?"

"You mean, don't you, that he does not love me enough?"

"No indeed . . . not that. It is of you that I am thinking— of you who do not love him enough. What would you find when you had gone through this door? When you had passed beyond this mirage? You do not love him in that form."

Then Sister John of the Cross became attentive, all of a sudden, and watchful.

"Tell me what is at the bottom of your mind? Come on, tell me."

"Well look: it is Dom Gregory that you love. Father Gregory of the Order of Saint Benedict. What would you make of Marquis Pierre de Carrenac? My poor darling, he would not weigh very much on your scales if he were no longer a Benedictine monk or even a priest."

The little Sister was listening with her eyes opened wide. She was pensive and suddenly very calm. Her arms hanging down limply.

"What things you say! First of all: a priest. He would always be that."

A nun crossed the room, placed some typed copies and a folded apron on the table and went off to the libraries.

"You should stop tormenting yourself," said the Mother, "and live your life religiously. Your daily life. Live it here, in all tranquillity: seeing Dom Gregory as often as possible, until this passes."

"And if it never passes?"

The Mother made a gesture of weariness and experience. "No more of this, please," she said, her nerves on edge. "Besides," she added, "there is always God."

"Pray don't involve God in this. What a mania you all have for referring to God all the time! God has nothing to do with this."

She was abashed. Her eyelids were tired and tears were ready to flow if she gave way for an instant. Then, at last, she made up her mind, as though there could be no secrets between them.

"I went to Saint Benedict's three days ago. At night."

The Mother went on writing on her pale-green paper. "Was it Benedict who did you . . . this service?"

She nodded like an unhappy child.

Some bells were ringing in the distance. They sounded muffled, as though in snow. In the room below some novices were practising on harmoniums. Heavens! How they got on one's nerves! Surely Mother Francis de Sales could not approve of what they were doing—at that time of day!

"Well, Mother? Have you nothing to say? I went out. I left the enclosure; at night. Do you understand? Yes or no?"

"You are hoping to dazzle me with this daring exploit? It does not seem very important to me."

What an art she sometimes had for expressing the most startling ideas in the most measured tones! What a balance between scepticism and fervour.

"Oh, Mother! There you are again, ready to damp enthusiasm. All this joy. How little liking I have for your eyes at this moment; and for your irony, which never believes in what is pure and sincere. Your masters are the sceptics. You follow them alone."

"Don't talk nonsense. There are sceptics among the philosophers. There are none among the moralists and the teachers of wisdom. And now it is my wisdom that is speaking, and it is for your good. Scepticism has a meaning in things which are outside our experience. It has none in all the problems which are concerned with that experience."

She no longer knew . . . whether it was heaven . . . or hell.

"In fact," she said, "you think what I did was natural? You scarcely disapprove of it?"

"I don't go as far as that. But it was logical. You have been working up for a climax. You have attained it. Now, after scaling the summit, you must face the repose of the plain below."

"Repose?"

"Yes. . . . Well, I mean a certain kind of repose. You would like to unite love and tranquillity, perhaps? That is very ambitious, to say the least of it."

"There is nothing to laugh about," she said.

And that was true; there was indeed nothing to laugh about.

"So now, when I see him, it must be in the parlour, only in the parlour? With that grille between us? After all. . . ."

"Yes, after all. . . . You can't keep on running through the woods at night. . . . That is obvious." She made a gesture implying that after all a medal has its reverse side, that after all there must be an after-taste with its little mortifications— implying also the nervous irritation born of all this pettiness. . . . All this. . . . Oh, how unimportant it was!

"And besides . . . now that our classes are stopped," the little Sister went on, "and everything is so difficult, or as good as impossible . . . these complications for meeting. The complicity involving Mother Peter of Verona . . . our oblate Sisters. . . . Don't you understand?"

No. She did not understand.

"And then the work that I have been doing for the past few days with her Grace. This work. . . ."

The Mother was apparently interested at last. It was as though they were now touching on more serious matters. Getting away from futility.

"Oh yes! By the way, how is it going? Do you get on with Mother Dominic?"

Surprised, her eyes grew softer, with the hint of a smile. "Yes. Not too badly. It doesn't make any difference whether I work with her or somebody else."

There was a light in the Mother's eyes. But could she reach anything in the young Sister apart from this love? Could she get away from it?

Well then, she must hit hard, without sparing her, in order to safeguard the future.

"Come now! We have had enough of this," she said severely. "Enough of your reveries! I beg of you to carry out your task as well as you possibly can and to show an interest in it. I have good reasons for asking you to do so. And you will!"

The young nun seemed to wake from a dream. The tone was suddenly so cold, almost icy. She drew away and then, as though unwillingly, she stood up. What, after all, was the good of staying on her knees beside this Mother who made no gesture and was taking up her long pencil again from the manuscript on which it had been lying.

"And how about the Father?" she asked timidly.

"The Father? Oh yes! That, of course, has to be settled. Well! Carry on with this adventure as best you can. It is not so very serious . . . and if you are prudent . . ."

"So you sanction it. . . . You think it possible. . . ."

The Mother made a gesture of weariness. "Naturally. See Dom Gregory as much as you like. You will soon have had enough of him. There is nothing we so soon lose our taste for as the easy, familiar things. One would have to be totally lacking in experience, and bent on your ruin, to shut that door for you."

Then, altering her tone, she added with icy coldness: "But with her Grace, watch your step. You have enough courage and nobility of heart to rise above all pettiness in this adventure, which is far more important than the other. You can take it from me. Go on your way, without forgetting that Christ praised the wisdom of the 'mammon of iniquity'. That is a text, Sister. And it is clear."

Goodness! How she said "Sister" in that freezing voice.

"And now, goodbye for the present. Let me get on with my work."

She felt utterly desolate. Such solitude encompassed her; she felt she was sinking.

"Mother Stanislaus! Why do you talk to me like this? If only you knew how frightened I am. Yes, I am frightened. Don't you realize that in this house everything is always known? For the last three days I hardly dare look at the Abbess. It is as though what I have done were written on me. And then, Mother Dominic, with her strange eyes. Her smile that never changes and the sadness that weighs on her. Her placidity! It is as though I stood naked before her."

The Mother laughed and her laugh was clear and resonant, without a break.

"Under Phillip Augustus they were afraid of John Lackland of England, and above all of Innocent the Third. Under Louis the Eleventh they were afraid of Burgundy and of *Tristan l'Hermite*. Under Louis the Thirteenth it was *Père Joseph*[1], the taxes and possibly England. Under Louis the Fourteenth they were afraid of the king, La Brinvilliers[2] and the Papal Bull *Unigenitus*. Under Louis the Fifteenth, the Jesuits. It is Mother Dominic de Chabot who is to be feared today."

"Oh please stop, Mother. You may laugh and make a joke of it, but that does not prevent my antennae from warning me of danger, and my antennae are never wrong."

"I believe it was Hugo who said that a sense of danger such as you are suffering from is due to a guilty conscience. At the moment no one knows anything of your moonlight exploit. I can assure you of that. I knew nothing of it myself and I should have been one of the first to hear as a member of the Council."

Then the Mother seemed to depart from the severe line she

---

[1] The confidant of Richelieu.
[2] Marquise de Brinvilliers, famous poisoner.

197

had been taking. For an instant her clear eyes lit up with that marvellous smile she had.

"Come, dearest one . . . let us try to see things with more serenity. God is in heaven and we . . . on earth. Goodbye for the moment."

A little gesture of the hand—a gesture of tender affection at last! And this same irony making her words pointed as a stiletto.

The radiators under her fingers were still hot. Steam made the high grey windows look like cotton-wool.

Some Sisters were coming in, with books, papers and rolls of parchment.

"I have compared my text with that of Victor Cousin."

"For the dialogue of Socrates and Crito?"

"Yes. It fits in marvellously. I assure you it does. I will let you see it."

"Why, here is Mother Stanislaus! What a piece of luck."

She still heard their steps on the parquet floor. A desk banged. And then there was that Sister Thomas Aquinas who was a spiritual daughter of Dom Gregory and whom she detested! And who was already joining the ring round Mother Stanislaus! That Sister Thomas Aquinas who swore only by Aristotle and her patron saint! She sometimes said silly things, but her mind was brilliant.

Goodness! How sad that staircase seemed, and those long cloisters! And then the expression of her Grace, which for that matter was kindly enough—even affectionate . . . and all those letters to open . . . and the eyes of Mother Dominic.

Those deep green eyes, so calm, which were almost black!

37

The long black car glided into the abbey courtyard and stopped before the main entrance. Rain had been falling on the languid autumn gardens. The sky was a milky white with streaks of gold and turquoise. Under the trees there was a great carpet of yellow leaves.

It was four o'clock in the afternoon, and a fresh little breeze was coming from the east as the Archbishop stepped out of his car. In spite of his height he looked shrunken and gave the impression of a very old man. It was being said that since his niece's death he had changed so much that he was scarcely recognizable.

The oblate Sisters rushed to meet him, the gravel crunching under their feet.

"My dear daughters," he said. "I have come to see whether her Grace, the Abbess, can receive me." He spoke with the calm courtesy of those who are set apart from the ordinary run of mankind as a natural result of their birth rather than of the dignity of their office.

The long car was already drawing up against the wall of the north wing, just where the Virginia creeper formed a magnificent red tapestry.

The Sisters were leading him towards the stairway at the end of the corridor.

"Would your Excellency like to have a cup of tea first?" they asked.

He made a gesture to refuse, but at the same time to thank them for their offer.

"I have not much time, but I particularly want to see her Grace."

They bowed. His steps were heavy and the wooden stairs creaked as he went up.

When he entered the parlour he saw the Abbess behind the grille. She was wrapped in a certain cold dignity, and a shade of sadness lined her face—but nothing excessive.

"You see, I have come," he said. "I had to come in the end; because, after all, things can't go on like this. You must surely understand . . . and think about it sometimes."

He had not even sat down. His tone was uncertain, as though he did not know exactly where the present events were leading, and as though he were feeling his way.

"My visit is not official. You need have no fear."

She made a gesture, implying that whatever happened she was not afraid.

"Oh yes! I know. You have reached a point where you have no more to fear. That's what you mean, isn't it?"

He settled himself in the huge armchair and put his hat on the table.

"Monsignor, I believe too firmly in the priesthood of our Lord to be able to accept that a soul chosen and marked with his seal, as a symbol of Christ, should be so grievously injured."

He shook his head. "Come, come! I know what you think. But after all! Where is it all going to lead you? Don't you agree that it is time to compromise . . . to . . .?"

She made a movement.

"I have to use certain words. Do not attach too much importance to them."

A moment elapsed.

"Our Lord has granted us a great grace at this time," she said at last, in an attempt to relieve the uneasiness. And from her manner it was so obvious that she considered Our Lord's action to have been entirely due to His desire to make up for the insufficiency of His ministers, that the Archbishop's breath was taken away for an instant.

"You have a very personal way of interpreting events," he said courteously, and with his usual gentleness—but this afternoon there was a great weariness in his voice.

"At any rate, whatever anyone can say, is it not a clear sign of the love God bears us?" she asked.

The Archbishop sighed.

"I know that your community is exploiting in its own way what has come about by chance . . . or I should say rather, perhaps, by carelessness or inattention?"

"There is no such thing as chance, Monsignor," she observed calmly.

He began to lose patience. "It is all part of your ridiculous naïveté to think that the whole monastic world is holding its breath as it witnesses the marvels in progress at this abbey. I know that. You admit it, don't you? As far as that goes, you have seen that I am shutting my eyes to what is happening. . . . Rome may possibly have heard about it. But not through me, I promise you. No: you see, Mother," he went on, "this afternoon I have come to you as a friend. I have come to tell you, and indeed to beg you, to make an effort. Rome may not be so much against you as all that—in spite of appearances. A gesture from you, and possibly things would be restored to their normal course. Do you realize, Mother, that for the best part of a month three hundred members of your community have been deprived of their daily communion? And all because of you? Of your obstinacy?"

"But they are putting up with it very well, your Excellency. In souls of noble stock, tribulation only serves to increase courage and faith. That is a recognized fact."

Then her expression became distant; she seemed suddenly to withdraw—to isolate herself in the heart of a mysterious solitude.

"A month," she answered. "That is long enough to change everything in a life—and in a heart."

The Archbishop had let his hands drop on to the ledge of the grille. They made a dull thud. All at once he became very red. He mopped his face with a handkerchief.

"Of course . . . of course. Looking at the matter from your point of view, I must admit that your virtue is of a rare quality.

What a pity it is so badly directed! To preserve peace and happiness under such conditions can be no more than a feat of endurance—a wager."

"Happiness consists in always saying 'yes' to God, Monsignor . . . and, often enough, 'no' to men."

An infinite sadness came over him. It submerged him. He smoothed his forehead with the hand on which his ring was shining. His hand was trembling slightly. A hand corded with purple veins but still shapely, with very light-coloured nails.

"Couldn't you lead your community by less unusual paths? Paths which are less desolate, I mean? Because you must find a way out," he added resolutely, "even if you consider yourself to be in the right. I implore you to come to some decision . . . for the common good . . . so that order can once more be established."

"Do you not think, Monsignor, that we might trust in God?" she said. "I know that humanly speaking the future is dark."

"But, Mother, let us speak humanly, please. We are concerned with a very human situation. A whole abbey, with all its monastic life, is completely disorganized so that what you consider to be your dignity should not be offended—so that nothing should interfere with what you declare to be your powers. Nothing could be more human, I think? Nothing calls for more of the fraternal charity which Christ teaches. Surely all that is worthy of consideration. . . . I think," he continued, "that it was Sainte-Beuve who said of Louis the Fourteenth: 'He had nothing but common sense, but he had a great deal of it.' Well, then—common sense is a very valuable gift, Mother. It is very useful to have an accurate and timely perception of when to act, of what gesture to make, of what direction to take and what orders to give. Good government does not require great virtues, but it does need common sense."

He said this so simply that his familiarity with the gift was obvious. It was clear that he possessed it and enjoyed exercising it.

The Abbess was silent.

"Come! Think it well over, my daughter," he went on after a moment. "You must end this deadlock. You really must. You have here among your daughters several novices who have reached the time of their first vows. You have a young nun who should be making her final vows in a few weeks. Are you going to put off all these ceremonies?"

"Monastic profession is a step which can be taken in the community, and the rite can quite well be carried out under the direction of the Abbess, your Excellency," she said calmly. "The outward ceremonies are side-issues and are often very worldly. Our Father Saint Benedict was not a priest. The essence of the monastic state does not lie in the priesthood."

He gave a gesture of disappointment: "Evidently you have an answer for everything," he said. "What is so sad in all this business is that your daughters follow you and that you bear the responsibility for all this rebellion."

It struck five.

"Monsignor, you have always been very good to our abbey and to me myself. I should like your Excellency to understand how much it pains me to disappoint you. But what can I do about it? I cannot go against what has been for centuries the fundamental idea of canonical election."

She always came back to the question of her election, her rights and her powers. It was impossible to get away from it.

"You could always make a gesture of humility, which Rome would certainly know how to appreciate—with clemency. I ask you to think it over. Two more postulants have left you, I believe. After all, I don't want the whole novitiate to break up—this novitiate which is so fervent and interesting from every point of view. Surely you understand."

The Archbishop rose to his feet. He seemed very old and broken.

"I must go. I hope to have a letter from you soon, Mother. A letter. . . ."

He said no more. He was stricken with a sense of powerlessness. He made a farewell gesture, very controlled and full of tact.

"Goodbye, Monsignor," she said.

The long black car slid away, down the avenues of the park.

38

Then came the Feast of All Saints. It was a bright sunny day but very cold. On the vigil, the Abbess had called her Council together to discuss the question of the novices' clothing.

As Monsignor had said, two postulants would very soon be finishing their six months' probation. It was time for them to be given the habit, and a decision was imperative. When they were questioned, one had resolutely chosen to wait. She would wait as long as need be. The habit does not make the nun, and so long as she was living the monastic life, so long as she was at the Abbey. . . . The Abbess was grateful to her, and from that moment inscribed her name in the golden book of her loyal daughters.

The other postulant, who was over twenty-five, was seriously thinking of leaving. She hoped that anyhow the time spent as a postulant would count in another abbey. When Mother Stanislaus expressed doubts about this, she decided to remain until Christmas. After that she would have to see. Her director, a Jesuit Father, was leaving her without letters or advice. She was suffering a great deal about it.

Sister John of the Cross was still working for her Grace. She did so for two hours every morning. The Abbess did not take advantage of her. It was enough that she had mastered this wild young creature who only spoke of councils, heresies or conclaves, and who would say quite naturally: "You understand, Clement the Sixth . . . perhaps . . . but at the same time one must not forget . . ." or: "If Innocent the Tenth had not protested against the Peace of Westphalia, favourable as it was to the Protestants . . . you can form some idea of what would have come about," and she would quote Gerson and Saint Bonaventure and had an answer for everything. The Abbess smiled at her now, in a friendly way, and sometimes even joked with her.

"I know that Dom Gregory has never completely stopped coming to the parlour," she said to her one morning. "Oh, no one told me any tales. You can restrain your fulminations, my daughter, and leave poor Mother Peter of Verona in peace. But there is a rumour—a secret? Come along! It's an open secret. But so long as it is he who takes it upon himself. . . . To tell the truth, the prohibition concerns the Fathers, not us. So go to the parlour, my dear child. You can go as often as you like."

Sister John of the Cross expressed her thanks with a look in which there was a certain sweetness. She did not like people to talk about Dom Gregory. This was her secret. Her great preoccupation. The object of her existence. She did not want anything to change between them. After having found him, the only new thing that could happen would be to lose him. She scarcely breathed his name even to Mother Stanislaus, who replied to any confidence on this subject with a smile which the young Sister considered quite unseemly. Yes, unseemly, that was the word.

Her relations with Mother Dominic were strictly limited to their work. The Mother Secretary was naturally reserved. It was obvious that she did not miss anything, but she scarcely spoke at all.

So it was All Saints' Day! The high, stained-glass windows of the common room were dazzling with rose-coloured sunshine. It was a winter sunshine, with patches of fine mist here and there.

At recreation the Abbess gave out that Sister Martial had a chill. She had had to stay in bed since the day before, with a high temperature. There was also cause for anxiety about her heart, which had always been her weak spot. Sister Martial was a lay Sister—the little Sister who was employed in the personal service of the Abbess. In her case the term "little Sister" was no mere figure of speech, because that is what she was. She was already over sixty—tiny, nimble, lively, always on the alert, with eyes like black olives. She was full of ideas, apt suggestions and unexpected talents. She was entirely devoted, body and soul, to her Grace, who was fond of her in her own way, often snubbing her, but unable to do without her.

This was momentous news. Sister Martial was never ill. She would never have taken to her bed except in the direst necessity. Of peasant stock, thin and wiry, she was very hard on herself, she slept little and, in addition to her work for the Abbess, she did a thousand useful services which were asked of her as favours in all directions. She rarely spoke, and her cross manner scared the postulants and novices. To gain a smile from her, or even a glance, had been the object of intrigues still remembered after five years.

The apartments, and particularly the bedroom of the Abbess, constituted her fief of which she jealously guarded the entrance. Even Mother Dominic was not always well received. She had made her profession at K——, and when Mother Hildegard, already Prioress at D——, was elected Abbess, Sister Martial had asked to be allowed to join and serve her. Rome probably thought this request to be in order —or, at any rate, they saw no drawbacks and granted it.

Now Mother Martial was ill. The Mothers of the Council commented gravely on the event. Each one of them had a lay Sister appointed to her service, and a certain friendship always established itself between the nun and her attendant. Then the Abbess told the Mother Councillors of the recent visit of Monsignor. In the groups near her seat there was some raising of eyebrows, but they waited in vain: her Grace gave them no further information about it.

Meanwhile Sister John of the Cross came into the hall where they were gathered. After bowing before the Abbess, who gave her a smile—quite by chance—she took up her position in a corner not far from the Mother Councillors. The white woollen veil which she still wore did not permit her to go up into the higher rows, but she usually sat in one of the recesses formed by the french windows, and always, when she arrived soon enough at recreation and these places were still free, she chose one on a level with the Abbess. Sometimes she found herself in the company of old nuns who had not attained to any special office, or else among very young Mothers who had only recently made their final vows. These places were rather to the side, but anyhow they were fairly near the "sanctuary" or "the Holy of Holies", as the nuns would say with a smile.

The others who were waiting to take their final vows (there were only a dozen of them all told) remained at the far end of the hall. This was their normal and officially recognized place, in view of the order of their profession. In the centre of the hall, however, the rows were hard to distinguish, because the nuns moved their chairs about to form ever-changing conversational groups.

Sister John of the Cross had taken her seat. With silent, cat-like curiosity, she turned her gaze in the direction of the Abbess's group. Near her, two aged Mothers were talking of the day's feast and of the ritual ceremonies still carried out in certain German abbeys. They were recalling memories. It was a holiday of obligation, so nobody had brought any sewing. The groups were engaged in animated conversation. The recreation was at its peak. The Abbess was talking with Mother Stanislaus now. The atmosphere seemed more relaxed between them. Mother Stanislaus was smiling and her face was peaceful.

Sister John of the Cross thought of the "celebrated change

around of alliances" of which Louis the Fourteenth had already conceived the usefulness in his instructions to the Comte du Luc and of which Louis the Fifteenth reaped the benefit. She knew better than anyone that this truce could only be an apparent one. The Mother Prioress was exchanging mysterious confidences with Mother Odilon. The face of the old nun showed obstinacy and joy over some good joke she had just made. Mother Anselm was laughing quietly.

There was nothing at all to show that the abbey was being subjected to a severe ostracism. Each day was isolated in a context where lurking thunder rumbled. And the succession of days passed in this way, without the storm breaking.

This All Saints' Day was going to call the nuns to order, and would record a steeply descending curve in the graph of their resistance, which was approaching its end. The conversations in the hall were at their height, when suddenly one of the doors opened. It was at the Abbess's end. The head infirmarian came in. She was a young nun and was dressed for work. Her sleeves and the lower part of her habit were turned back, and she wore a large white apron. It was obvious that she was coming, not to join in the recreation, but to warn and call for someone, and that this someone was the Abbess. Immediately, she knelt in front of her and whispered a few words. Instinctively in the group at the upper end of the hall voices were lowered. The Abbess rose to her feet. She made a gesture, indicating that everyone should remain seated and carry on with recreation. Then she went out.

A few minutes elapsed, during which conversation died down. The Prioress tried hard to bring a little life into it again, but no one had the heart for it any longer.

Sister John of the Cross gave a sign to Mother Stanislaus. Shortly afterwards they both bowed to Mother Anselm and left the hall by their respective doors. It was in the veranda above the Cloister of Our Lady that they met.

"Sister Martial must be very ill," said the Mother in a low voice.

Both of them were thinking about the thing which made the situation so serious. They could think only of that. Sister John of the Cross had an expression of the utmost perplexity.

"Someone must telephone to Saint Benedict's," she said, "to call in the Fathers."

"The Fathers won't come. This is not the first time that I have envisaged such a situation. The Fathers won't come," the Mother repeated. "At least not officially. Dom Gregory is the only one who might, and then we shall have to wait for her Grace to ask him. And in that case, she would have to do so before Dom Germain can veto it, as he certainly would. I know him."

"Then we must call Monsignor."

Her whole body, her every movement, proclaimed her anxiety, with such acute eagerness, such petulance. They were walking up and down under the white arches, drawing their shawls more tightly around them. Outside the wind was whistling. Dazzling sunlight fell on the grey stones.

"Listen; for the moment we don't know anything. We must wait. It is her Grace who has to make a decision. She will make it," she added gently. "It is not for us to act. Besides, it may not be so serious after all. So long as the Council has not been summoned."

At that very instant the infirmary bell rang, with its ten dull strokes, repeated two by two—that chiming which was unlike any other. The two nuns looked at each other. They were face to face. Sister John of the Cross had put her hands on the arm of Mother Stanislaus. Her face had become very pale.

"I am going to ring up Saint Benedict's," she said in a dull voice.

The Mother held her back.

"I am going to get the news. I will only stay an instant. I beg of you to wait for me here," she added in an imperious voice, "and not to do anything on your own initiative."

A few minutes passed. The young Sister had pressed her

forehead against the window. She was looking out over the gardens stretched beneath her: those gardens which would soon be dying. The last leaves of the beeches, the poplars and the aspens were falling. In spite of the sun, the ground felt the coming of winter. Suddenly she heard hurried steps, hushed voices. Taking a deep breath, she ran towards the oak staircase (the secondary staircase). The first-floor landing was almost opposite the infirmary. She went along a dark passage.

They must have put Sister Martial in a little room over there, at the end of the passage. There was a half-open door and people coming and going. She suddenly bumped into Mother Lupus, who was muttering strange words. She apologised humbly, but already the old nun was calling out very loud: "Oh! It's you, Sister Angel."

For Mother Lupus, Sister John of the Cross had never been anything but Sister Angel—even when she was a postulant and was Sister Odile to everyone else. Sister John of the Cross loved the old nuns very much, and they returned her affection.

"So then, Sister Angel, we are soon to go into mourning again. The doctor was not very proud of himself when he came today."

She said it so naturally and then went on: "You have come to see, have you? Curious, are you? The poor dear child. . . . She will not last through the night."

From the height of her ninety-six years, they were evidently only children, all of them, for Mother Lupus; and Mother Martial, who was in her sixty-fifth year, was no exception.

"Well, Sister Angel, I am going back to my armchair and my embroidery—to my skeins of silk. They have rung for us and they will ring for us again."

There was all the confidence in the world in her face. What, after all, was death? A simple passing over. So what was the use of worrying? And she went on her way, trotting over the parquet floor.

Sister John of the Cross went forward cautiously and anxiously, wrapped tightly in her shawl. Mother Irenaeus was coming out of the room. She made a little bow to the Mother Bursar, but the latter did not spare her a glance. As there was no further movement, she went nearer. The door of the room had been shut again. Through a rectangular window she saw the infirmary Mothers. In a corner near the bed she saw Mother Teresa of Avila and Mother Anselm, who were talking to each other in low voices. The passage smelt like a chemist's shop—with medicated lozenges and iodine.

But where was her Grace? And where was Mother Stanislaus? She waited a moment and then, suddenly, she felt her heart in her mouth. There, in front of her, with nothing but the pane of glass between them, she saw the face of the Abbess. She gave a jump. Then she ran to hide behind a great walnut cupboard in this passage where little by little things began to sort themselves out.

The Abbess opened the door. Someone whispered, "Shall I take your Grace back?"

"No, no thank you. There is someone who will accompany Us."

And suddenly, without knowing how it happened, she found herself kneeling at the feet of the Abbess. In the half-light. And how sweet this security was. She felt in her hand and against her cheek the great golden ring. It was cold—so cold! And the hand that was offered to her, which was given so completely to her that she could easily distinguish under her fingers the Abbess's ring of office, with its hard stone, from the more slender ring of her profession. In her confusion she dared to mark the difference with her slender little fingers. And the Abbess made no movement—she did not draw her hand back.

Then the young Sister pressed herself against her. She was still kneeling. She felt the caress of the long black gauze veil, which fell forward a little with the Abbess's gesture—as though to envelop and protect her.

"Mother Stanislaus is telephoning to the Fathers," she

whispered. "Dom Germain will send someone. Will you accompany Us to Our office?"

The Most Reverend Mother drew herself up, but the slender fingers held her back. Those self-willed, headstrong, self-opiniated fingers! She never knew how she dared to say: "I want to stay here, like this. . . . Always."

The Abbess leaned forward once more, without showing any astonishment in her eyes. She took the face in her hands —the face still so clearly marked with childhood. She wiped the tears away from the corners of her eyes, and from her cheeks. The Mother's brown eyes were alight with an unusual sweetness.

And Sister John of the Cross stayed there, kneeling, with her eyelids closed. Why was she there, she wondered? In this passage? Near this medicine cupboard? Was it because of Sister Martial? or Mother Stanislaus? or Dom Germain? or Monsignor, whom the Abbess said they were to call? Whom they had already called? But did all that matter now? Were there not centuries since all that happened?

She said words which did not follow, and the Abbess replied gently, speaking quite low, as though to a child. The door of the sickroom opened several times, without anyone noticing the group they formed. And her Grace no longer spoke of going back to her office. Was it really true that Mother Stanislaus was running all over the house in search of the Mother Abbess? Was Mother Martial really there a few steps away? Stretched out in the white room? And at the point of death?

She went on crying gently. She said such strange things. Things which surprised her herself.

"You must never give in. Never. God's chosen one. Until death. The Lord's anointed. . . . Like David. . . . His mark is upon you. . . . It can never be effaced."

How did she dare?

And then there was the great bell! It sounded one stroke— just one. Thereupon she jumped up, with a single springy movement, as though waking from a dream.

"The great bell," she said. "Good gracious! They must have been looking everywhere for you."

She was still talking familiarly. It was certainly a dream!

"And they must have sounded the little bell first. But we never heard it. Goodness me!"

The Abbess had not moved. She was gently stroking the cheek where there were still some tears.

Mother Stanislaus ran up. "I have been searching for your Grace," she said. "Dom Germain refuses to send anyone. Monsignor is not at the Archbishop's Palace. His secretary has no power to revoke the orders. What are we to do?"

She caught sight of Sister John of the Cross. Her eyes sped from the eyes of the young nun to those of the Abbess.

"Your Grace? What are we to do?" she asked a little roughly, as though to break the spell.

The urgency of the moment made equivocation impossible and simplified everything.

"I am going to telephone to Rome," said the Abbess.

They were going along the wide corridor, bright with sunshine. The eyes of the young Sister were fixed on her own. They were imperious and ardent. The Abbess smiled without slackening her pace.

"We are going to telephone to Rome," she repeated. "They will communicate with the Archbishop's Palace. Someone will come. It will not take more than an hour."

At the doors Mothers appeared. Their eyes were full of anxiety. She made a reassuring gesture. Someone would be coming. They must calm themselves. They could ring for the community to assemble? Yes. Of course they could. As soon as the Viaticum was brought.

The doors shut again. Mother Stanislaus's face registered a silent interrogation. The Abbess held her shawl out to Sister John of the Cross in a friendly way, as though it were habitual. Mother Dominic was asking for Rome. No one spoke any more. The waiting began; it was nervous and punctuated with sighs.

The young nun could not stay still. With her back turned, Mother Stanislaus looked out of the window—pensively.

The Abbess tore the wrappers off newly-arrived newspapers which had been laid ready for her. She glanced at them cursorily.

Then the door opened. No one had heard the knock. Her Grace raised her eyes. Mother Anselm was on the threshold.

"Mother Abbess . . . Your Grace must come," she said.

The Abbess rose to her feet. Sister John of the Cross found her hands were trembling. Over in the cloisters the bell had begun to toll slowly the innumerable strokes of the death agony. The strokes which are suggestive of a certain terrible fearfulness. The strokes that would not cease before the end came.

At three o'clock, as usual, they sang Vespers. The Abbess's stall and those of the Mothers of the Council were empty.

As the first Cantor began to sing the *Magnificat* the Mothers entered the choir. The Office continued. After the *Sacro Sanctae* there was a long silence. No doubt her Grace had forgotten to give the sign with her little ivory hammer?

No one moved. In front of the grille the Blessed Sacrament lay beneath its silken veil.

"*De profundis clamavi* . . . " the Abbess said at last.

39

There followed a series of days when everything seemed to stand still.

Sister Martial was buried in the Abbey cemetery on the second day after her death. The cemetery is over behind the cedars in the shadow of the gigantic Calvary. It was raining.

For the last rites, Father Abbot and Dom Gregory had entered the enclosure. The whole community filed past the coffin in a slow, black procession. They sang the High Mass, and when Dom Gregory left the altar he did not remove the ciborium containing the Blessed Sacrament.

Following the usual custom, there were no recreations between the time of death and the day of burial. The nuns wore their *coulles* in the refectory as a sign of penance.

There was silence everywhere, and the rain fell continuously. It had not stopped since the morning of All Souls' Day.

It had not been possible to get through to Rome till late in the evening of All Saints'. By that time Sister Martial was dead. The Abbot sent Dom Gregory immediately, but he was only able to give conditional absolution and a last blessing. Next day the Abbot came early in the morning. He spent a long time talking with the Abbess.

Now, at last, a pale sun was shining. Saint Martin's Summer was setting in. It was almost warm. There were bonfires of enormous heaps of dead leaves on the garden paths. Benedict had the melancholy air natural to country people at the approach of winter.

The Abbess's face showed signs of insomnia and grief. She scarcely spoke. During the recreations, which had been re-sumed the day before, no one dared to make any allusion to Sister Martial.

It was four o'clock in the afternoon. Mother Stanislaus was coming out of the cloakrooms. As she passed along the cloister the Abbess stopped her.

"Come," she said. "Do come and have a breath of fresh air before going up to your cell."

Her tone was calm and restful, but there was a far-off veiled sadness in it.

The Mother Councillor threw over her shoulders the shawl she had been holding. They left the cloister garden. The fountains looked like showers of iridescent jewels which one guessed to be very cold. There were no flowers left. The two nuns walked in silence along the main central avenue with its bare borders.

"You are wondering what I am going to do?" said the Abbess suddenly, in a rather flat voice.

"No, indeed. I am not wondering. I know."

Again there was silence.

"I suppose you approve," the Abbess said next.

"How should I approve? Or blame? I know the main lines of your telephone conversation with Rome the other day. That is all. And, as you may imagine, without anyone telling me. But, after all, there is a certain logic in everything: and, you see, we have known one another too long for me not to have guessed. But as for approving or blaming, I don't think I could. For the last few days such calm has come. . . . I don't know how to explain. . . ."

The gentle call of a bird floated away on the breeze.

"You can only know the main lines, it is true. Certain experiences cannot be communicated to anyone, so hidden are our underlying motives. I made this decision suddenly. Just like that! No one had any idea of it."

"No one, I am ready to grant you—no one except me. That is probably because I should have made up my mind to act as you did. We are enough alike from certain aspects, I mean above a certain level. The boundaries between the ordinary and the exceptional are perhaps narrower in my case than in yours—I cross them more nimbly and light-heartedly or, I might say, with less difficulty, than you do. That is all. And then . . ."

The Abbess was silent.

"And then, could there have been any other solution now? Any other noble solution?"

"Do you think then that I could only have chosen a noble solution?"

Her eyes lit up in what for a moment was almost a smile.

"Why, of course," said Mother Stanislaus.

They went on with their walk. From the side of the pond

a thin translucent mist was rising and enveloping the trees. It was really very mild. One hardly needed a shawl.

"So now you feel more at rest," said the Abbess. "Now that everything is coming to an end, your hatred is pacified."

"It is not on that account, Mother Hildegard. No, don't think that. I believe that a great many things have changed between us during the last few weeks—I might almost say the last few days. That is all. There are certain complete reversals which can come about in an instant. A gesture, a word is enough, and then everything is transformed."

"To rise above oneself. There is no other triumph," said the Abbess with infinite gentleness. "Self-conquest. That is the only victory which is worth anything, because through it we gain access to something which is far greater. To conquer the self is to widen out," she said again in a softer voice, "to cast off one's limitations."

There was a long silence. It was very sweet and soft, like the silky feathers of a bird which one strokes.

"There are few souls strong enough to stand success," she added, in a voice which had sunk to a whisper.

They were coming to the wing of the novitiate. Over the doorway the monogram of the Order caught the rays of the afternoon sun, so that the bronze lettering stood out in relief.

"Does anyone know your plans?" asked the Mother Councillor. "Can anyone have guessed them already?"

"Sister John of the Cross, in all probability! I have not said anything about them to her. But she is like you. She guesses everything. At least, I mean, everything important, serious things, sorrows—all that counts."

"Yes, when she loves. That is true. For some time now I have marvelled at her."

"I have discovered her too late. I found her like a pearl of great price. Sweet and gentle to the touch. And as for the heart—what rest she brings! What light! And she has such clear judgment, such lucidity joined with such a childlike quality."

"Don't say: Too late. Perhaps she will follow you? For our ruin or our salvation, the thing we long for with a great enough longing is always given us."

"I shall not suggest that she should follow me. Better still: I do not want her to do so." Her face lit up with affection. "I shall call a meeting of the Chapter tomorrow," she said. "A special Chapter."

"Your farewell Chapter."

"Yes."

In her eyes there was a kind of inflexibility. She was loyal and chaste, as though utterly detached.

"While we are on this subject," she went on, "you should try to get Mother Dominic elected. She has all the qualities needed to bring calm back to the Abbey."

"I guessed as much, as I saw her at work day by day during this difficult period. It is good that for once we can agree about something."

"Oh! If you were not so taken up with your ancient documents . . . I should surely have thought of putting you up for election."

The Mother Councillor made a gesture of refusal, and it was so obviously sincere that the Abbess smiled at it.

"Not that, please! You must be fair to me and admit that I have never aspired to rise from the ranks. As you say, my ancient manuscripts keep me in my place. And they have never ceased to enchant me," she added fervently.

They had reached the Oratory of the Angels. They stopped and their eyes met. They looked deeply and searchingly into each other's souls. Perhaps for an instant they had a vision of their eternity? Of the eternity which would be theirs in so short a time. Then, simultaneously, they turned away—without a word.

For a few moments they walked on in silence.

"It is not very likely that I shall be present at the conclave," Mother Stanislaus said with feigned lightness, as though to break this silence which was getting heavy and threatened to envelope them. "I shall be in Rome."

"And after that?" said the Abbess in a quiet voice.

"Afterwards?" For a second she hesitated with a kind of modest shyness. "After that? It is still very new and a close secret in my heart," she said.

They had been all round by the fields. They were coming back now, towards the Calvary.

"You are going . . . soon?" asked the Mother Councillor, with a slight tremble in her voice.

"In a fortnight. That will just give time to hand over temporary powers to Mother Anselm. After all, it may be definitive powers. Just the power," she added in a tired voice. "Who knows?"

"You could have waited for the spring. I don't suppose Rome will want to hurry you. Now you have made your decision. And in November . . ."

A few seconds passed in which even the sound of their steps seemed to be silenced in the dead leaves.

"I had a letter from Rome this morning which was certainly very ready to restore the peace between us. The Cardinal Prefect also spoke of waiting. He spoke of the spring, and better weather. Just as you have done. Really your gift for divination is miraculous."

"No. But I have been so much disturbed by you for so long that there is not much in which you could surprise me. And besides, I think so much about you—about both of us. In the depth of my heart I have always loved you. What are you going to do with your life now?" she added.

There was a wonderful serenity in the Abbess's whole bearing—that true serenity which does not come from the absence of passion but from passion which has been mastered.

"Oh! My life. . . . Well, you see as I stand here before you today, it seems as though I had just awoken—as though this were the dawn."

"Yes, the dawn. The dawn which is bringing in a new day after twenty years of combat. Perhaps one day I shall go back to K——? It is good if one can go back to die where one was born. How peaceful it was, that first springtime of the soul! Do you remember it all? Our enchantment? Our ardour? Those days of illumination. A vocation is the hallowing of a noble passion."

They were walking over rust-coloured heather. There were still leaves on the trees. Tomorrow there would be nothing but bare white trunks—wood—nothing but dead wood!

The parlour bell rang a complicated series of strokes which were intended to summon one of the Sisters of the novitiate.

Their feet sank into the dead leaves.

"*There is a time to get,*" said the Abbess, "*and a time to lose. A time to keep and a time to cast away.*"[1]

A little black cat ran between their legs, and with one jump fastened its claws into the bark of a walnut tree and began to climb.

"*All is vanity,*" said the Mother Councillor. "Nothing but an attempt to capture the wind. Nothing but ashes."

The night was falling. Five o'clock struck. A novice passed without seeing them. She was almost running. She crossed the garden. Her white veil brought a note of carefree joy into the darkness.

The large electric bulbs which hung all down the length of the cloisters suddenly lit up.

"*A time to rend,*" the Abbess went on murmuring in a low voice, "*and a time to sew.*"

On the threshold of the atrium Mother Stanislaus knelt before parting.

Then the Abbess went up the three steps and entered the choir. Perhaps there were some nuns there praying? Perhaps there was no one? Everything was dark. Only the orange flame of the sanctuary lamp was keeping watch far away in the distance—perpetually burning before the Blessed Sacrament.

[1] *Ecclesiastes* III.

Then gently and with great precaution, taking care not to think, not to remember, not to awaken any of her dreaded monsters, the Abbess knelt down. Dark waves started to break over her spirit, like a rising tide. She covered her face with her hands and remained motionless—no longer hearing, no longer feeling, no longer knowing.

She had doubtless entered that present where there is no more time? Perhaps the meaning of "*In manus Tuas Domine, animam meam*" was gently taking possession of her, while the echo murmured the Virgilian farewell: *Manibus date lilia plenis?*

Much later she wiped her cheeks and her eyes and silently, surrounded with a sort of aura of suffering, she left the choir, carrying her adversity with her. It was a blessed adversity rooted in the commandment she had received and accepted: "Thou shalt not say of anything: this belongs to me. For there is nothing thou canst possess as thine own: not even peace."